Winter's Harbor

"*Winter's Harbor* is a charming story.
with just enough angst to keep you turning the pages. ...I adore
Rey's characters and the picture she paints of Provincetown was
lovely."—*The Lesbian Review*

Summer's Cove

"As expected in a small-town romance, *Summer's Cove* evokes a
sunny, light-hearted atmosphere that matches its beach setting."
—*RT Book Reviews*

"From the moment the characters met I was gripped and couldn't
wait for the moment that it all made sense to them both and they
would finally go for it. Once again, Aurora Rey writes some of
the steamiest sex scenes I have read whilst being able to keeping
the romance going. I really think this could be one of my favorite
series and can't wait to see what comes next. Keep 'em coming,
Aurora."—*Les Rêveur*

By the Author

Cape End Romances

Winter's Harbor

Summer's Cove

Spring's Wake

Built to Last

Crescent City Confidential

SPRING'S WAKE

by

Aurora Rey

2018

ISBN 13: 978-1-63555-035-1

THIS TRADE PAPERBACK ORIGINAL IS PUBLISHED BY
BOLD STROKES BOOKS, INC.
P.O. BOX 249
VALLEY FALLS, NY 12185

FIRST EDITION: MARCH 2018

CREDITS
EDITOR: ASHLEY TILLMAN
PRODUCTION DESIGN: SUSAN RAMUNDO
COVER DESIGN BY JEANINE HENNING

Acknowledgments

I'm so grateful to everyone at Bold Strokes. You are my people and I love you. Particular thanks to Radclyffe and Sandy Lowe, who run a business I'm proud to be a part of. Also, to Ruth and Carsen for wrangling all the important details, not to mention the writers. And, Ash—I adore you for more reasons than I could count.

Thank you to Tracy for being my writing buddy and beta reader extraordinaire and to Jen for helping me reclaim the library and the lunch hour. I write more and better because of you both.

There's having your heart broken and there's being in a relationship that breaks your heart. This book touches on the latter. I know I stayed too long in relationships—of all kinds—that were bad for my soul. I want to thank the people that rallied around me and helped pull me through, who saw what I couldn't and loved and encouraged me anyway. I also want to thank everyone who has ever trusted me with their own hard story. I'm a better person for knowing you.

Dedication

For Crystal, my femme sister
I'm so glad we found each other.

CHAPTER ONE

Will stood on the lower deck of the Dolphin IX, listening to the brief lecture going on above her. Sunshine reflected off the water and, as the boat gained speed, the wind whipped her hair and cut through her Dolphin Fleet windbreaker. They rounded the narrow tip of Long Point and skirted the coast along Herring Cove before heading for open water. It was one of the last whale watches of the season.

Summer had been warm. Even now, in the middle of October, the real chill of fall had yet to arrive. Will wasn't in any hurry for it. As much as she enjoyed the changing leaves and drop in temperature, it meant winter was fast approaching. She'd yet to spend a winter on Cape Cod, but she'd heard enough stories that she dreaded it already. Of course, weather was only part of the dread. No steady income and no one around didn't help matters.

But real winter was still a couple of months away. For now, life was good. Will breathed in the sea air and closed her eyes. As she'd taken to doing each time she went out as part of the Dolphin Fleet crew, she offered up a moment of gratitude.

"Where are the restrooms?"

The question pulled her back to the present. Rather than resenting the interruption, she smiled and pointed to the narrow metal door. "Right behind you."

"Thanks." The woman led a little boy who looked to be about five into the bathroom.

Will tuned back in to the lecture. She liked Graham's delivery the most. Although she was still a graduate student, and only part of the crew as an intern, her knowledge base was solid and her enthusiasm for marine life infectious. Of course, Will had a bit of a soft spot for her. They'd started with the fleet at the same time. And while Will was merely a customer service member of the crew, they hit it off. Graham was sweet, funny, and profoundly optimistic. She'd only been entrusted with giving the lecture a few weeks prior and killed it. Will was proud of her, in a big sister sort of way.

She dashed up the stairs to the top deck to say as much, but Graham was surrounded by little kids oohing and aahing over a whale tooth or some other artifact from the talk. Since she was on service duty today, Will didn't linger. She returned to the main deck and headed to the canteen. Since the weather had turned colder, they sold a lot more coffee than bottles of water and soda. She sidled up behind the counter next to Liz and jumped in.

It didn't take long for whale sightings to begin and the interior room quickly emptied. Over the speaker, she listened to Graham and Charles, the more senior naturalist, talk about breeding behaviors and the tail patterns used to identify and track the whales. In her five months working on the boat, she'd learned a great deal about whales and marine life in general. She enjoyed it more than she expected, feeling an unusually strong affinity for the wildlife and geography of the waters surrounding New England.

She'd also found her sea legs. When she first started, choppy water would have her bracing her legs and grabbing onto the closest available surface. Now, she'd adopted a slightly wider stance, swaying with the rocking of the boat instead of fighting it. It made serving coffee a hell of a lot easier. At this point, she could serve customers and still steal glances out the window, even catching a glimpse of a whale from time to time between the people huddled along the side of the boat.

The boat stayed out for a couple of hours before heading back to shore. The line at the canteen picked up with people in search of a quick snack or late lunch. She served up clam chowder and chili, hot dogs and pizza. The crowds were smaller now that school had started, but still sizable and always enthusiastic.

Before she knew it, they were back in the harbor and pulling up to the dock at MacMillan Pier. Because she'd arrived early to do set up, Will was off the hook for cleanup. She grabbed her things and headed for the ramp to the dock just as Graham came down the stairs. "Are you done for the day?" she asked.

Will smiled. "I am."

"Want to grab a beer?"

"Yes. Yes, I do." They strolled down the pier together. Will stole a glance at Graham, whose eyes were shaded by sunglasses. She had this happy, bouncy energy that Will found infectious. It reminded Will of her own youth. She chuckled. When had she started referring to her youth in the past tense?

"What's so funny?"

Will shook her head. "Nothing."

Graham stopped walking and gave her an exasperated look. "Come on. Tell me."

"I was merely appreciating your *joie de vivre*."

Graham raised a brow.

"Really. You've worked all day, but you're still soaking up the sun, looking thrilled to be alive."

They continued walking. "I am thrilled to be alive."

"Exactly. And I love that about you."

They meandered down Commercial Street. Much like the crowds on the boat, the throngs of people in town had thinned. Will considered it the sweet spot—just busy enough to keep things interesting. They peeked in the window at the Squealing Pig, happy to discover only about half the stools at the bar occupied. Will held the door for Graham, who smiled at her then led them to a spot near the back.

Within seconds, they had matching glasses of cold Cape Cod Blonde. Will lifted her glass. "Here's to a great season."

Graham clinked her glass. "And to enjoying every minute of it."

They drank in silence for a moment. Will found her thoughts turning to what would happen next. She had two more weeks with the Fleet, helping to clean and winterize the boats for storage. That would get her almost to Thanksgiving. After that, though, her options were slim. She knew finding a full-time job in the off-season would be unlikely. But she hoped to piece together some part-time work and maybe do odd jobs here and there. For never having owned a house, she was pretty handy. Years working at one of the big box home improvement stores had taught her quite a bit.

"I don't think I'm ready for the season to end," Graham said.

"I feel you. Are you heading back to school?"

Graham shrugged. "I'm not sure. I didn't sublet my room, but I don't have classes or anything. I need to work on my thesis, but I could do that from here."

"I'm clearly biased, but I think you should stay."

Graham smiled. "Thanks. I'll think about it. I'm not sure my aunt bargained on giving up one of her rooms through December. Speaking of which, why don't you come home with me tonight?"

Will raised a brow at the suggestive phrase. "Are you propositioning me?"

Graham's cheeks turned crimson and Will almost regretted teasing her. "I mean, come to my house for dinner. My aunt has a full house for a wedding and is doing a clam bake for the rehearsal dinner."

That sounded far more delicious than the frozen burrito waiting for her at home. Still. "I'm sure the last thing she wants is an extra person to deal with and another mouth to feed."

Graham was unswayed. "She'll have an obscene amount of food. She always does. What if I said you could earn your dinner by helping me with cleanup?"

Will smiled. "Now the truth comes out. You're looking for labor."

"So you'll come?"

Will didn't mind helping out. She liked feeling useful. "I'll come."

"Excellent."

Will looked down at her jacket. Underneath, she wore a faded thermal shirt. "I should probably go home and change."

"Relax. I won't change, either. We'll stay behind the scenes."

"All right." It was a relief, really. This made it seem like she was coming to pitch in more than be fed a nice meal. Besides, she wasn't sure she had any nice shirts clean.

Graham glanced at her watch. "We should go. I think it starts in about an hour."

They left the bar and started walking toward the East End. The sun had set and dusk was quickly giving way to dark. "Shouldn't you let her know I'm coming?"

Graham shrugged. "She won't be looking at her phone anyway. Don't worry. It'll be fine."

"Okay." Will matched her pace to Graham's. If Graham didn't think it was a big deal, she wouldn't worry about it, either. She was looking forward to meeting Aunt Nora. From the way Graham described her, she sounded like quite the force. And Will had walked by Failte Inn enough times to be curious about the inside.

She tucked her hands in her pockets and soaked up the last of the day's warmth. The breeze carried the smell of the ocean and aromas wafting from the restaurants they passed. She'd been in P-town for six months and the reality of it still made her smile. She thought of Graham's earlier statement. Maybe there was something to be said for being thrilled to be alive.

❖

Nora crossed her arms and surveyed her back garden. Even without the lush flowers of summer, the space was her favorite. More than the perfectly decorated guest rooms or her meticulously appointed kitchen, the garden soothed her soul. It had been an overrun mess when she bought the place, used as little more than an extra parking spot and smoking area. Now, it was one of the features that drew guests to Failte, and had them returning again and again.

Had it been summer, she would have served dinner outside. But since the temperature would dip into the upper thirties by nightfall, her guests would have to settle for a small fire to cap off the evening. Still, she'd strung extra fairy lights, and half a dozen vintage hurricane lanterns hung from shepherd's hooks. Even with the chill, the space emitted a warm and welcoming glow. If she didn't have a thousand things to do, she could stand there and enjoy it for hours. But today she did have a thousand things to do and she wanted everything to be just right.

She turned on her heel and headed back to the kitchen. Tisha, her summer manager, was inspecting clams and loading them into steamer baskets. Corn and potatoes were already prepped, along with mussels and a bowl full of lemons, onions, and garlic. "How's everything in here?"

Tisha nodded. "Right on track. I'll have the drinks set out before everyone arrives, then be ready to go with hors d'oeuvres."

"Excellent. Do you need a hand with anything?"

"Not until we start steaming."

"Great. I'm going to change into something presentable. I'll be back in a few minutes."

Nora headed to her room at the back of the house. Although smaller than the guest rooms, it had the perfect blend of coziness and natural light. The southern-facing window helped, as did the mix of antique furniture and pastel walls. She took a moment, as she always did, to appreciate it before hustling over to her closet. She surveyed her options, wanting something nice enough for playing hostess and forgiving enough to allow her to work during the party. She settled on a dress with a floral print. It had such a nice cut, she felt feminine even after slapping an apron over it.

She put on flats that looked nice but wouldn't kill her feet, earrings, and just a little makeup. It was a party after all. She brushed her hair and studied her reflection, grateful the light color belied just how many grays had appeared in the last couple of years. Nora shook her head, refusing to fret about it. She pulled the front half back with a clip so it would be out of the way and stepped back from the mirror. Satisfied with her appearance, she returned to the kitchen.

Tisha greeted her with a whistle. "Don't you clean up pretty."

Nora gave her an exasperated look, then smiled. In addition to running things with the same efficiency and attention to detail that she did, Tisha managed to maintain a playfulness in her personality. As someone prone to seriousness, Nora appreciated the balance. Nora gave a little twirl, more for Tisha's benefit than her own. "Someone's got to do it."

Tisha laughed. "Better you than me. I like getting pretty, but charming a bunch of strangers is not my idea of a good time."

"You say that, but you're better at it than me."

"I'm good at scrubbing toilets, too. Don't mean that's how I want to spend my time."

"You make a good point." When she'd hired Tisha seven years ago, it had been for just that. Well, toilets and cleaning and other housekeeping. She'd returned the following summer and the summer after that, returning to Jamaica each winter to be with her family and work the high season there. Each year, she'd taken on more and more responsibility, becoming almost a partner for the high season as well as a friend. She'd be leaving in a couple of weeks and Nora already missed her.

Tisha finished plating a tray of bruschetta. "So maybe there will be a smooth-talking and handsome butch who comes tonight and sweeps you off your feet."

Nora rolled her eyes. "Not likely. The couple getting married is a pair of gay men in their fifties."

"They have friends."

This was true. Still, she didn't have the time or inclination to think about being swept off her feet. But she knew better than to say that to Tisha, who was constantly telling her she needed to loosen up, have a little fun, have an affair. "I'll be sure to keep you posted."

CHAPTER TWO

Graham led them down a narrow path to the front porch. In addition to the lights on either side of the door, thick white candles burned in decorative lanterns set on small tables and a welcoming glow poured from the windows. "This place is gorgeous."

Graham smiled. "Wait until you see the inside."

They went in the front door and Will did her best not to gape. The entryway boasted a gleaming wooden staircase and wide openings to the adjacent rooms. It wasn't over-the-top fancy, but it was beautiful, and nicer than any place she'd ever stayed.

"Graham, is that you?"

Will looked in the direction of the voice, but didn't see anyone. "Yes, and I brought a friend. She'll work for food."

Will chuckled at the assessment, in part because it made her feel about fifteen and in part because it was true.

"You know you can bring people over without putting them to work."

The owner of the voice came into view and Will blinked in surprise. She'd imagined sort of a Martha Stewart type. This woman was no Martha Stewart. Nor was she like any of Will's aunts—women on the far side of middle age who either clung to their youth or gave themselves over to their role as grandparents. Nora was something in the middle, older but with a kind of refined beauty and poise. Her hair was a sandy blond, perhaps with a hint of gray running through it, that fell in waves to her shoulders. She wore a floral dress that accentuated an hourglass figure. Over it, a dark green apron. She was stunning. Will swallowed.

"Aunt Nora, this is my friend, Will Lange. Will, Nora Calhoun."

Nora extended her hand. "Nice to meet you."

Will shook her hand and tried to find her vocabulary. "Likewise."

"You have an interesting name, Will. Is it short for something?"

Will smiled. "Willa. My dad had a literary streak."

"And her sister is Emerson," Graham said.

Nora smiled and Will's heart rate kicked up an extra notch. "How nice. I always wanted a name with a little more flair."

"I like it now, but as a kid, all I wanted was one that was more normal."

Graham laughed. "There was a kid who called me Golden Grahams for the entirety of second grade."

Will laughed, too, then realized they were likely keeping Nora from her preparations. "I don't intend to crash your party, but I really am happy to help."

Nora looked at Graham and shook her head. The girl had a huge heart and, as a result, was always bringing home strays. Usually, they were kids around her age—college students, seasonal workers, an artist here or there. This Will seemed different, older. At least Nora hoped she was older. Nora didn't want to think about finding a twenty-three-year-old attractive. And she definitely found Will attractive. "Everything out here is set. I'm sure Tisha wouldn't mind some help in the kitchen."

"We're on it." Graham took Will's hand and led her toward the kitchen.

Nora remained in the hall and watched them. Even in the same uniform jacket as Graham wore, Will stood out. She had a posture, a certain energy. Add to that blue eyes, a mop of short brown curls, and high cheekbones. She reminded Nora of Jordyn—physically, but also in the magnetism Nora felt in her presence. Nora shook her head again. She needed a trip down memory lane like she needed a hole in the head.

When Will glanced back and caught her staring, Nora quickly turned away. She took a deep breath and refocused her attention on the dining room. Neither the time nor the inclination. Understatement of the century.

She spent a minute fussing over the table in the dining room, then glanced at her watch. Her guests were due in a few minutes. Nora took the lighter from her apron pocket and made her way around the room, lighting candles.

The wedding party arrived with some of their guests. The grooms, a pair of teachers from Rhode Island, had been so easy to work with. They'd not even planned on a rehearsal dinner, but with so many of their family and friends coming in the day before, they begged Nora to throw something together. And she was happy to oblige. Nora greeted them, then headed to the kitchen to bring out hors d'oeuvres. She spent the next two hours moving in and out of the kitchen, checking the chafing dishes she'd set up on her buffet and making sure everyone was happy.

She didn't see Will, but knowing she was around put Nora on edge. Not angry or nervous, just aware. Different from the kind of awareness she felt with guests or Tisha or Graham. Not unfamiliar, but something she hadn't felt in a long time.

Trying to shake it off, Nora went to the back yard to light the fire and set out a tray of ingredients for s'mores. It wouldn't have quite the charm of a beach fire, but the grooms had requested it. The guests moved outside and Nora returned to the house to grab the basket of throw blankets and pashminas she'd put together for guests who wanted them. On her way back to the yard, she caught a glimpse of Graham and Will in the now empty dining room, eating. She nodded her approval and passed through the kitchen. "I'm going to deliver these and check on things, then I'll be back to start cleaning up."

Tisha waved a hand. "Take your time and tend your guests. I'm fine in here."

She didn't intend to take her time, but Nora found herself pulled into several conversations. She didn't mind the chatting. And although she didn't want to saddle Tisha with all the cleanup, playing hostess was as much a part of the job as cooking meals and making beds. As she went about the familiar routine, she wondered if Will had left for the night. She shouldn't be disappointed by the possibility, but she was.

When she finally made it back inside, she found Graham and Will at the sink, laughing and washing dishes. Seeing Will the second time gave her the same jolt as the first. Just like the feeling that had stayed with her most of the evening, it felt uncomfortably familiar. Annoyed, she stepped the rest of the way into the kitchen. "I meant what I said. You don't have to earn your dinner."

They turned to look at her in unison. "I'm happy to help," Will said. "The dinner was exceptional."

Graham tipped her head toward Will. "What she said."

She glanced at Tisha, who simply shrugged. "They take good direction."

Nora decided to let it go. They were young and had the boundless energy to match. She returned to the back yard just as the last guests were trickling in. Some had already set up camp in the sitting room to drink wine and laugh and play games. A few had gone to bed, including her grooms. She loved the vibe of a wedding party in the house. She always considered her home, her inn, a happy place, but weddings brought an extra level of joy.

She picked up the yard, blowing out candles and poking at the remains of the fire. It should go out on its own, but she hated to take chances, so she filled a bucket and doused the embers. Satisfied everything was in order, she returned to the house.

❖

When they'd finished the dishes, Will dried her hands and turned to Graham. "Do I get the tour?"

Graham grinned. "I can't show you the guest rooms, since there are guests in them, but everything else, sure."

"I'll take it."

Graham gestured to the space around them. "This is the kitchen."

"So I gathered." It was a beautiful space, a mishmash of professional-grade appliances and French country decor that somehow worked. It reminded her of those insane home kitchens on cooking shows, the ones that were too perfect for any normal person to have. But this one had a lived-in feel.

They exited through a swinging door to the dining room, where they'd had their dinner. The French country feel continued. A massive farmhouse table had seating for twelve. The sideboard had been cleared of chafing dishes and set up as a coffee bar. Black and white toile curtains stood in contrast to deep red walls and complemented the black metal scroll work of the chandelier. "I love this room."

Graham nodded. "Aunt Nora handled all of the design herself. She bought the place when I was still a kid and it was in terrible shape."

"I love that the style is a mix of traditional and eclectic."

"Wait till you see the library and sitting room." They left the dining room and entered a hallway. Graham gestured up the stairs. "There are three guest rooms upstairs, including a suite. One more down the hall on this floor, along with my aunt's room and the one I'm staying in."

"Nice."

They crossed into a large room with tall windows that faced the front garden. A sofa, love seat, and two chairs flanked a fireplace. Some of the guests from dinner sat, drinking wine and talking. Another pair of chairs were tucked into a corner with a small table. It felt homey. Like the fantasy version of homey that had never actually been home for her, but homey nonetheless.

Will imagined sitting by the fire with a book. She could see Nora in jeans and a baggy sweater, curled up at the opposite end of the sofa, their socked feet entwined.

Where did that come from? The image was so vivid, she had to shake her head to chase it away.

"This room is great, but the library is still my favorite."

Graham's voice yanked Will back to the present. "There's more?"

Graham led the way to a door at the back of the room. A moment later, Will found herself in a space probably a third the size of the sitting room. It felt even smaller thanks to towering bookshelves that lined three of the walls. "Wow."

"I know, right?"

A much smaller sofa, that appeared to be an antique, sat opposite two leather wing chairs. Even without a fireplace, the room felt even more inviting than the sitting room. "I'd spend all my time in here."

"When no one else is in here, I do." Graham grinned. "I think that makes us nerds."

Will smiled. That word had generally been reserved for her sister. She liked the idea that someone might think of her that way. "I'm okay with that."

Graham led them out of the library and down a short hall past the kitchen. "Aunt Nora's room is there and I'm..." She opened a door. "Here."

Will stepped inside. The room was cozy—full bed, narrow dresser, and a small chair in the corner. Smaller than her room, but with nicer decor. "This is very cute."

Graham bumped her shoulder. "Thanks. It's an add-on room people can book with the adjoining one if they have kids. The regular guest rooms are much nicer."

Will shrugged. "I think this one is plenty nice."

"And best of all, it's free. I tried to pay Aunt Nora rent, but she refused."

"I'm sure she loves having you around."

It was Graham's turn to shrug. "I hope so. This was the best summer of my life."

The fact that Graham would be leaving soon made Will a little sad. Other than Emerson, there was no one in P-town she'd spent more time with. She hated the idea of becoming friends who texted and saw each other once a year. "It's been pretty great. And to think I applied to the Dolphin Fleet on a whim."

"Did you?"

Will nodded. "When I decided I wanted to stay in town, I needed a job. And I wanted something that wasn't retail or bar tending."

"So, you joined a whale watch. So random."

"But if I hadn't, we'd never have met."

Graham's face grew serious. "I don't even want to think about it."

Not wanting to tread into overly sentimental territory, Will smiled. "Shall we go see if your aunt needs any more help?"

"Sure."

They found Nora in the dining room, putting dishes and glasses into the buffet. "Thank you again for the help," she said.

"Happy to do it." Will offered a warm smile. "I'm still pretty sure I got the better end of the deal."

"It's nice of you to say so. You two have any other plans for the night?"

Graham looked at Will expectantly. Will shrugged. "I hate to admit it, but it's already past my bedtime."

Nora returned the smile. "There's nothing wrong with that."

Graham rolled her eyes. "The two of you."

"Are you a morning person at heart or is it the line of work?" Will asked.

"I always have been." Nora shook her head. "Much to the consternation of my sister, with whom I shared a room for fifteen years."

Will laughed. "My sister is exactly the same. She got up early when we were kids because she's an overachiever, but she hated it. These days, she keeps the craziest hours."

"One more reason to be glad I'm an only child," Graham said.

Will raised a brow at her. "And to think you turned out not the least bit spoiled or difficult."

Graham pouted dramatically, but then grinned. "Funny. So, I'll see you tomorrow?"

Will turned to Nora, who seemed to be watching them with mild amusement. "Now I think she's trying to get rid of me."

"Am not."

"I'm just kidding. But it is late. I should get going."

Graham walked with her to the door. Will stole a final glance at Nora as she left, hoping to share a smile or some other moment of connection. Her attention was back on the dishes, though, and she never looked up.

By the time Will got home, she was exhausted. She peeled off her clothes and threw on her robe. As she was walking to the bathroom for a shower, Kaylee emerged from her room. "Wow, you look fancy. Hot date?"

"Very." Kaylee grinned. "Hopefully, I won't see you later."

"Since I'll probably be sound asleep in under an hour, I would hope not."

Kaylee gave her an exasperated look, but laughed. "You're too young to be such an old fart."

"I'm way older than you and I worked all day. I can be as much of a fart as I want."

"Just know I'm going to drag your ass out before the season completely ends."

"Deal."

Kaylee picked up her wallet and keys and opened the front door. "Have a good night."

"You, too. And Kaylee?" Kaylee turned. "I hope you get laid."

She quirked a brow. "Me, too."

Kaylee left and Will headed to the bathroom. After her shower, she padded back to her room. Since it was quarter after eleven—well past her usual bedtime—she stripped off her robe and crawled into bed naked. She picked up her book, but instead of opening it, let her mind wander back over her day. No, that wasn't accurate. Will let her mind wander over her interactions with Nora.

From the moment she saw Nora standing in her beautiful inn wearing that perfect dress, Will was taken. She always had a soft spot for that slightly older, polished kind of beauty, but her reaction to Nora went beyond that. Will was more attracted to her than she'd been to a woman in a long time. Her voice, her mannerisms—everything about her only intensified that attraction.

And now Graham was about to leave and she'd likely have no occasion to cross paths with Nora again. Even in such a small town, it was hard to imagine they moved in the same circles. Or that a chance second meeting would amount to anything.

Will opened her book and attempted to read.

It didn't help that she'd shown up in her work uniform, traded some help in the kitchen for dinner. The whole thing reminded her of high school when she'd go home with one of her teammates after a soccer match or basketball practice. Her friends' parents would serve them dinner, then shoo them off to study. Of course, some of those study sessions had turned into her first explorations of being attracted to girls. Only in this scenario, she wanted to make out with the mom and not the best friend. Will sighed. It wouldn't be the first time she'd had a mom crush.

Only Nora wasn't Graham's mom. Even as an aunt, she pegged Nora as no more than twenty or so years older than Graham. Which made her only about ten years Will's senior. And there was nothing weird about that at all.

Not enough age difference to be creepy. Will set her book back on the nightstand and scratched her temple. Probably not a compelling case to get Nora's attention. Of course, she had caught Nora looking at her twice over the course of the evening. Technically, that could mean anything, but Will liked to think at least a hint of the attraction might be mutual.

Will switched off her light and stared into the near dark of her room. Even if she didn't get the opportunity to pursue Nora, she was glad to know that part of her brain—and her body—still worked. Although she'd confided her general longing for a relationship to Emerson, she hadn't felt a real spark since ending things with Kai. And since that time had included an entire summer in P-town, she'd actually started to worry. So she might be attracted to the wrong women, but at least her ability to feel attraction in the first place wasn't broken.

Will chuckled to herself. Compared to the train wreck of her relationship with Kai, maybe being attracted to Nora wasn't such a bad thing.

Chapter Three

The rehearsal dinner was Tisha's last event of the season. As she did every fall, she packed up and Nora drove her to the airport in Boston. And, as she had since opening the inn ten years ago, Nora would handle the off-season solo. The bookings had already begun to thin and, with the exception of holidays, she already had stretches during the week of no guests at all. Nora was curled up on the sofa in the sitting room, sipping tea and trying not to feel blue about it, when Graham came in.

"Are you alone?" she asked. Her tone was incredulous.

Nora smiled. "I am."

"Don't move. I'm going to make some tea and I'll join you." Graham started toward the kitchen, then turned back. "Do you need a fresh cup?"

"I'm good, thanks. I just sat down."

Graham returned a few minutes later with a steaming mug. She'd swapped her shoes for slippers, but she took even those off to curl her feet under her. "I love it when there's no one here."

Nora chuckled. "I can't say I agree entirely, but I know what you mean."

"Does it make you sad when everything slows down? Or do you like the break?"

"A little of both." Nora thought about the cold, dark days ahead. "It's nice for the first few weeks. And I usually have people over the holidays. It's mostly January that feels a bit grim."

Graham nodded soberly. "Yeah."

"What about you? Are you looking forward to getting back to your life in Maryland?"

Graham sighed.

"Is that a no?"

"How would you feel if I stayed the rest of fall?" Graham set down her tea and looked at Nora with anticipation.

"What do you mean?"

Graham shrugged. "Since I'm not doing classes this term, I'm in no hurry to get back to school. I don't want to take up one of your rooms, but I'd love to stay. I could help out."

Nora sighed. Under most circumstances, she'd be thrilled to keep Graham around for a couple of months. With her busy season winding down, they'd actually get to spend quality time together. But something told Nora that time with her favorite aunt wasn't Graham's primary motivation. "Is that the only reason you're looking to stick around?"

"I love spending time with you. And even now, P-town has way more charm than Baltimore."

Nora nodded. "Does it have anything to do with that girl you brought home the other night? Will?"

Graham sat up straight. "I invited her for dinner. You make it sound like more than it was. We're friends."

The speed and vehemence of the reply made Nora think there was perhaps more to it than Graham wanted to share. But harping on it wouldn't help. And truth be told, Nora didn't really want to know. She got a funny vibe from Will and would be happy if Graham's interest in her didn't go any further than friendship. "All right. You don't need to convince me."

"Does that mean I can stay?"

Nora smiled. Graham had been born while she was still in college. And while they'd always been close, Nora most treasured the last few years when Graham could stay with her for long stretches of time. It felt like her chance to play the role of older sister, rather than the younger one she'd been in reality. "Of course you can stay. You are welcome here anytime."

Graham beamed and threw her arms around Nora and squeezed. When she pulled away, though, her face was serious. "I can pay rent, you know. I feel bad that I'm taking up space you could be using."

The room she'd given Graham was technically a bedroom she could use for guests, but it was small and she never booked it as a standalone reservation. It had been easy enough to take it offline when Graham arrived for the summer. With the high season over, she doubted she'd have need for it even if it was available. "You'll do no such thing. You're family."

"Well then, you'll have to let me pitch in around here."

Nora nodded. She had a few winter projects in mind, on top of her usual deep cleaning, and having an extra pair of hands would make them go more quickly. "I think that could be arranged."

"Thank you." Graham beamed. "Oh, I'm so excited. We're going to have fun."

"I'm going to remind you that you said that when we're waxing floors."

❖

Will looked at her phone and smiled. Graham had been moping about the end of her fieldwork for the better part of a week, but suddenly seemed to be in better spirits, including orchestrating a happy hour to celebrate the final sail of the season. Since they weren't on the same schedule, Will promised she'd be there.

Although Will had another week of work lined up, she had her own touch of melancholy over the end of whale watching season. When she'd applied for the job shortly after arriving in Provincetown, she never would have expected it would turn into something she loved so much. Nor could she have predicted the friends she'd make. Graham was her closest friend by a long shot, but she'd hung out with half a dozen other members of the crew at one point or another.

Part of that fun, free-spirited vibe stemmed from the fact that the crew was young and mostly unattached. And if a few of her previous jobs had that, Kai never let her join in. She still couldn't believe just how isolated she'd let herself become. Will sighed. One more reason to appreciate her freedom.

By the time she got to Nor'East, the Dolphin Fleet crew had taken over nearly half of the outdoor seating area. She stopped at the bar to grab a beer, then went out to join them. Graham spotted her almost immediately and came over, a huge smile on her face. "Guess who's sticking around until Christmas?"

Will didn't figure it was a trick question. "Yeah?"

"Aunt Nora insisted she didn't mind and I found someone to sublet my room."

"Really? That's awesome." Graham had hinted at wanting to stick around, but Will didn't think she was serious.

"One of my roommate's friends broke up with her girlfriend, so she needed something quick."

"Sounds like a win-win." Will smiled. The idea of Graham sticking around for a couple of months made the impending slow season less daunting.

"I'll work on my thesis, we can hang out. It's going to be great."

Hanging out with Graham would be great. So would having more occasion to see Nora. Will didn't say as much to Graham, but the prospect of spending more time at the inn and in Nora's company made Will's stomach leap with anticipation.

"I'm going to help her with some projects. Maybe I'll rope you in." Graham took a sip of her beer. Her eyes lit up. "Hey, that's actually a great idea. Do you have work lined up for the rest of the fall?"

She had a couple of leads, but nothing solid yet. "I'm working on it."

"Maybe Aunt Nora will hire you. I think she wants to paint and redecorate some of the rooms and she does a crazy deep clean when there aren't any guests."

Will nodded. Part of her wanted to jump at the chance. Part of her hesitated. She didn't want Nora to think she couldn't support herself. Then again, she was pretty good at around-the-house sort of projects. It might be a way to impress Nora. Not to mention spend a lot of time with her. "Well, if she's looking for someone, I'd definitely be interested."

"I'll mention it to her. It would be so much fun to work together."

Will wondered what Nora was like when she wasn't in full-on hostess mode. Low-key and relaxed? Or did she maintain that controlled poise that Will found both sexy and a little intimidating? She realized how badly she wanted to find out. "I have some relevant experience from when I worked at a home improvement store."

Graham gave her a quizzical look. "When did you do that?"

"A few years ago. I started as a cashier, but ended up rotating through most of the departments. I learned a ton. I can paint, build basic stuff. I stay away from plumbing and electric."

Graham shrugged. "That seems reasonable."

Will grinned. "And safer."

"I'm pretty sure it's painting and stuff she has in mind. I'd love the company. And I'm sure she'd pay you. I just don't know how much."

Would working for Nora help Will's cause or hurt it? If she never saw Nora, she didn't even have a cause to worry about. And, even if she didn't want to admit it, she could use the cash. She'd saved up enough to mostly make rent, but she'd need to bring in some money if she planned to eat all winter. "I'm sure she's reasonable and fair. So, yes. Please include me if she's open to it."

Happy hour concluded with lots of hugs and well-wishes, hopes to meet again the following year. After, Will walked to the store to get things to make dinner for herself and Emerson. She'd seen so much less of Emerson since she'd practically moved in with Darcy and Liam. And now that they were about to close on a house in Wellfleet, Emerson made a point of scheduling time to hang out. Will appreciated the gesture as well as the promise of sister time. Both of her roommates were working late, so she had the apartment to herself. She changed into sweats, put on some music, and got to work.

A couple of hours later, Emerson sat cross-legged on the sofa, shoveling pasta into her mouth. "This is really good."

"Thanks." Since moving to Provincetown, Will had been spending more time in the kitchen. She'd come to find cooking both relaxing and adventurous. Not having to worry about Kai, who shunned both messes and carbs, made a huge difference. Her roommates had even taken to giving her money for groceries in exchange for dinner a couple nights a week. Tonight's concoction was Bolognese and, for her first attempt, she was pleased.

"So you're done with the Dolphin Fleet?"

Will nodded. "They're closed for the season. I'll stay on a couple of weeks more to help with the winterizing, but I'll need to find something to tide me over until spring."

"Alex might have something at the café. All her seasonal staff is long gone. I think she usually has just Darcy and Jeff for the winter, but she might take someone else on part time."

"I'll stop by tomorrow and talk with her. Thanks."

"And you know I can float you a little if you need it."

Will shook her head. "No way. You put me up when I came to town and now you have a house and a family to take care of."

"Speaking of the house, I think there might be some projects there. I'm not sure if it's stuff we can do or if I'll have to hire a contractor, but I'd love your thoughts."

Will had seen the house before Emerson and Darcy put in an offer. She hadn't looked closely, but she had a feeling it was more cosmetic work than anything structural. "I bet we could do a lot of it ourselves. When do you close?"

"Next week. We're both a little terrified, although I'm not sure if it's buying a house or the prospect of moving."

"The house is great and the moving will be a snap. You've got me to help and we don't even have to deal with appliances."

"Right." Emerson offered a nod of determination, then smiled. "You always know what to say to make me feel better."

Will leaned over and nudged Emerson's shoulder with her own. "The feeling is mutual, Em."

When Emerson left, Will indulged in an extra long shower. She put on clean pajamas and climbed into bed. She wondered if Graham would convince Nora to hire her for the projects at the inn. Based on what she saw her one time at Failte, everything looked perfect and professionally maintained. Still. She probably had more experience than Graham.

As it had a hundred other times since they met, the image of Nora filled her mind. The way her hair curled around her shoulders and the cool, reserved way she looked at Will. It made absolutely no sense to pursue Nora romantically, if for no other reason than she seemed utterly disinterested. Will sighed. She had such a penchant for wanting what she couldn't have. And now Nora—beautiful, elegant, reserved Nora—sat squarely at the top of that list.

CHAPTER FOUR

S o, I've been thinking," Graham said over breakfast.
"Why does that worry me?" Nora was kidding. Mostly.
Graham folded her arms and pouted. Or, more accurately, she pretended to pout. Nora knew better than to think she'd throw an actual tantrum. "Kidding. What have you been thinking?"

"I can clean with the best of them. And although I haven't except for once when I was fifteen, I can probably paint a room."

"Okay. Haven't we already discussed this?"

"Yes. I've been thinking how great it would be to do more."

"More what?"

"More whatever. Painting, building stuff."

Nora studied her niece. Clearly, the girl had something on her mind. But she'd be damned if she knew what it was. "Building stuff?"

"You know my friend Will? The one I brought over the night you did that rehearsal dinner."

Oh, she knew. "I remember her."

"Well, she's pretty handy and she doesn't have a lot planned for the off season and I thought it would be cool if you hired her and we could get so much more done."

Nora blinked a few times, trying to process Graham's train of thought. Red flags flashed. "Is this your idea? Or hers?"

Graham sat up straight. "Oh, it's totally mine. I thought it would be fun to do stuff with her now that we aren't working together. And then I thought she might not have a job lined up for winter, which she doesn't. And it turns out she worked at a home improvement store and knows how to do all sorts of things. Not plumbing. Or electric, she said. But more than me."

Nora pressed a finger to her temple. She had so many problems with Graham's proposition, she didn't even know where to start. "You didn't promise her anything, did you?"

Graham shook her head. "No. I was thinking out loud and mentioned it. She said that if it turned out you did want some things done, she'd be interested. We left it at that."

At least that was an appropriate response. That meant Will likely wasn't trying to insinuate herself into a job. Or other places, like Graham's bed. Nora sighed. "I don't know."

"You've talked about painting all the upstairs guest rooms. If I had help, we could do that and more. She knows what she's doing."

Nora wasn't opposed to hiring someone to help with the work, especially someone trying to make a go of living in town year-round. She might not be crazy about Will and Graham spending lots of time together, but if Will knew what she was doing, Nora would be happy to have her services. And if it meant spending more time with Will herself, well, she'd just have to keep a professional distance. "Okay."

"Okay, you'll hire her?"

"Okay, I'll talk to her."

"Excellent." Without waiting for another word, Graham picked up her phone. "I'll text her right now."

Nora sipped her coffee and wondered how quickly she would regret this. Maybe Will knew less than Graham implied and she could get out of it. Almost as quickly as Graham stopped typing, her phone chirped. "Did she answer you already?"

Graham nodded. "She's free this afternoon or tomorrow morning, whichever is more convenient for you."

She could interpret Will's promptness a dozen different ways. Not ready to give her the benefit of the doubt, Nora filed the detail away. "I've got a doctor's appointment tomorrow, so this afternoon would be better." Graham started typing again, so she added quickly, "Only if she really is free."

❖

By the time Will stood in her front hall a few hours later, Nora had thought through the projects she'd like done and planned out the questions she intended to ask. Hopefully, she'd figure out quickly enough whether Will could actually do the work. And what her intentions were.

"Thank you so much for the opportunity to talk with you." Will extended her hand. Nora shook it. She seemed nervous, but in a good way. The way that meant she was treating this like a job interview. She'd dressed nicely, too. Nora told herself she appreciated that Will took the conversation seriously. It had nothing to do with the fact that Will, in gray pants and nicely pressed oxford, could drive Nora to distraction.

"Thank you for making the time to do it on such short notice. Shall we sit?" She gestured toward the dining room.

"That would be great." Will walked in ahead of her, took a seat, and sat up straight with her hands folded neatly on the table.

Nora realized she was frowning and plastered a smile on her face. "Graham tells me you have some DIY experience?"

"More training than experience, to be honest, but the training was good. I worked at both a small hardware store and a larger home improvement center. I learned basic carpentry and hand tools, painting, and wood finishing."

Nora nodded. "Impressive."

"I didn't want to be presumptuous, but I did bring a copy of my résumé." Will leaned over and pulled a sheet of paper out of her messenger bag.

Nora accepted it and skimmed the contents. On one hand, it was a smattering of experience that told her Will seemed to lack professional focus or ambition. On the other, there were no gaps and she spent an average of three to five years in each position she held. And she seemed to possess the skills Graham had promised. "Not at all. You seem to have picked up a lot over the course of your jobs."

Will swallowed and told herself to relax. "I like to learn new things. I never could bear the idea of a desk job, but I wanted more than basic retail."

Nora made a face and Will instantly regretted saying what she said. But then her features softened and the expression that remained was kind. "I could definitely use another pair of hands. The pay will be fair, but it won't include benefits."

Will nodded. Being around Nora every day would be benefit enough. Getting to use her hands, and getting paid, felt almost too good to be true. "I don't know anything about plumbing or electric, but I'm willing to do just about anything else."

"Painting mostly. Moving furniture and doing a deep clean. The hours won't be regular, I'm afraid. We'll have to schedule everything around my guests. It does mean, at least, you won't have to work weekends."

Will smiled. Was it as easy at that? "I'm used to irregular hours. I don't mind. And I really appreciate the opportunity."

Graham, who must have been hovering just around the corner, popped her head in. "When do we start?"

Nora laughed, so Will let herself chuckle as well. "I'm helping my sister move later this week. Otherwise, my schedule is completely open."

"Let me get my reservation book." Nora stood and disappeared into the kitchen.

Will looked at Graham, who waved her arms around in a silent happy dance. It was cute, but Will was still trying to make a good impression. "Would you be cool?"

Graham rolled her eyes, but gave Will two thumbs up as Nora returned. "I've got guests this weekend, but Tuesday through Thursday of next week looks clear."

Will smiled. "Works for me. Do you know where you'd like to start?"

"One of the rooms upstairs has sadly dated wallpaper. I'd like to remove it and paint. Can that be done in three days?"

"Absolutely. Especially if Graham is helping."

Graham offered a salute. "At your service."

Will stood and extended her hand again. It was the professional thing to do, but part of her simply wanted to touch Nora again. When their hands touched, she felt the crackle of a static shock. Nora jerked her hand away. "Sorry," Will said.

"No, no. I think it was me." Nora reached out and took Will's hand.

No shock this time, but Will experienced an entirely different kind of spark. She wondered if Nora did, too. "I'll see you next Tuesday. Is eight o'clock too early?"

Graham groaned. "How's nine?"

"Either works for me," Nora said.

Will looked at Graham, who gave her a playfully pleading look. "Let's say eight-thirty."

Graham gave Will a quick hug. "I'll take it."

Nora said goodbye and Graham walked her to the door. "Thanks for hooking me up."

"I'm glad it worked out. I'm so excited we're going to still be working together."

"Me, too."

Will left the inn and headed toward Emerson's condo, stopping at Wired Puppy for coffees. The wind had picked up and rain seemed imminent. She hunched her shoulders against it and wondered how long she had before it turned to snow. Probably better not to think about it.

She knocked on Emerson's door. When it opened, she found a bedraggled version of her sister on the other side. "Hi."

Emerson's gaze went from Will's face to the cups in her hands and back. "Oh, my God. How did you know I was on the verge of giving up?"

Will smiled. "I didn't, but I'm glad I'm here."

Emerson accepted one of the coffees and stepped back so Will could enter. It took only a second to understand the source and extent of Emerson's state. Her place was a disaster. Emerson offered a sheepish smile. "It's going slower than I thought."

"Slower? Have you actually packed anything?"

"Yes." Emerson's answer was emphatic, but when Will gave her a stern look, she recanted. "Some. A little."

She pointed to a pile of exactly three boxes in the corner. Will shook her head. "You're terrible at this."

"I thought I should sort through things, get rid of some stuff."

"It's a noble idea. And when you start a month before you're moving, totally reasonable. When you're moving in two days, not so much."

"Oh." Emerson frowned.

"The closing came together faster than you expected, so it's not entirely your fault." It really had. Within a month of putting her place on the market, Emerson had a buyer. And she and Darcy had found an adorable little Cape Cod-style house off Long Pond Road.

"Thanks. Does that mean you're here to help?"

Will pretended to consider, even though she'd shown up with the intention of helping. "I could be persuaded. Especially since I got a job today."

"You did? Where?"

"Not full-time or anything. I told you about my friend Graham from work?"

Emerson angled her head. "I think so. Grad student, right?"

"Yeah. She's staying in town through Christmas. Her aunt owns Failte Inn and hired us both to paint a couple rooms and do some other projects."

"That's cool. Are you two..." Emerson trailed off in a way that invited Will to finish the sentence.

"Good friends. Nothing more."

Emerson looked at her with concern. "Are you still feeling gun shy?"

There were a million different, yet completely honest, ways she could answer that. "No. I mean, maybe a little. I don't want to make another terrible mistake, but I'd be lying if I said I wasn't lonely. I don't think a celibate life is for me."

Emerson smiled. "That's good. You deserve to find someone, or to have some fun if you want to. I know you feel like you stayed with Kai longer than you should have, but she was still the fuck-up in your relationship."

"I know." She did know. And Emerson had helped to drive home the point when Will confessed the extent of Kai's abusive behavior. But that didn't mean she'd entirely finished beating herself up about it, or questioning her judgment.

"Are you interested?"

Will blinked at her, confused. "Huh?"

"Graham. Are you interested in her?"

Will shook her head. "Oh, no. It's not like that. She's very pretty. Smart and funny, too. It's," Will paused, "she feels like a kid still. Kind of innocent."

Emerson smirked. "And you're so jaded and world-weary?"

Will rolled her eyes. "In relative terms, maybe."

"Why do I feel like you aren't telling me the whole story?"

Will sighed. One thing hadn't changed through the years, even when they hadn't seen much of each other. Emerson could still read her like a book. It was kind of annoying, considering she was the younger of them. Annoying, but also nice. "I met her aunt."

Emerson raised a brow. "And?"

"And she's gorgeous. Like, movie star gorgeous."

Emerson made a face. "How old is she?"

"Not old." Will straightened her posture. "Early forties, maybe? I think she's Graham's dad's younger sister. Or maybe her mom's. I can't remember."

"And you have the hots for her?"

On a most basic level, the answer was yes. She did have the hots for Nora. But even though they'd only spent maybe twenty minutes total in one another's company, Will felt like it went deeper than that. Not that she could articulate exactly what that meant, but it was definitely more than a passing infatuation. "I'm attracted to her. She has this poise, an elegance to her. I appreciate it and want to muss it up at the same time." Emerson studied the box in front of her. The lack of response, paired with her refusal to make eye contact, told Will that she didn't approve. "What?"

Emerson looked up. "What? I didn't say anything."

Will shook her head. "You didn't have to. I can tell."

Emerson crossed her arms. "What can you tell?"

Will mirrored the gesture. It was how they'd faced off for as long as she could remember. "That you don't think she's someone I should be attracted to."

"You can't help who you're attracted to. It just happens. Acting on it is another matter."

"Okay, fine. You don't think I should act on my attraction to her." She was being defensive, but she couldn't help it. Probably because part of her knew that pursuing Nora would be a terrible idea.

Emerson shrugged slowly, like she was weighing whether or not to say anything. "It's not that she's older, but she seems to be in a very different place in her life than you. And if you're friends with her niece..."

She trailed off again, leaving Will to fill in the rest. Will sighed, irritated with Emerson, but more so with herself. "I haven't asked her out. And I probably won't. For all the reasons you mentioned. And then some."

"You know I'm not telling you what to do."

Will sighed. "I know."

"I just worry about you."

"I know that, too."

"And I want you to be happy."

"Yeah." Will knew Emerson cared about her. And, despite being younger, had a tendency to be protective of her. It wasn't that she resented it. She resented the idea that she needed protecting, especially from her own bad choices.

"I didn't mean to be a killjoy. What can I do to make you feel better?"

Will squared her shoulders and smiled. "Nothing. I'm here to help you, remember? I'm perfectly happy with my life right now. And you're right. I will find someone and I'll probably do better if she's someone even remotely in my league."

Emerson pointed a finger at Will. "Hey, I never said she was out of your league. You're a great catch in any league."

At the compliment, Will's irritation melted. How could she hold a grudge against her biggest champion? "Thanks. That's not exactly what I meant, but thanks all the same."

"I mean it, though. You're going to make some woman very happy someday. And she's going to know how lucky she is to have you and treat you the way you deserve to be treated."

Will cringed. "Okay, we're venturing into pep talk territory here. You know how I feel about pep talks."

"All right. No more pep. I promise." Emerson laughed. "I still find it ironic that someone who was on more sports teams than I could even name hates pep talks."

Will raised a finger. "There's a difference between getting pumped up for a big game and coming to terms with my poor choices in the romance department. I hate pep talks about my love life."

"Point taken. I'm done."

Will took a deep breath. "Great. How about we get to work?"

Emerson looked around, seeming surprised that the chaos hadn't worked itself out when she wasn't looking. "Right."

They spent two hours packing. Now that Emerson had let go of the need to purge, things moved quickly. She did manage to toss some old art supplies and at least a dozen paint-splattered shirts, so there was that. By the time they called it a night, Will guessed more than half the condo was packed.

Emerson surveyed the space with a pleased look on her face. "You're a life saver."

"You needed a nudge more than anything, and I'm always happy to give you a kick in the ass. Gently, of course."

"Of course. Well, it did the trick. I'm no longer terrified Darcy will come over and see how little I've done."

Will arranged several boxes into a neat stack. "How are things at her place?"

Emerson shook her head. "She and Liam are packing and organizing machines. Other than the things strategically left out to use this week, they finished days ago."

Will smiled. "I love that."

"Me, too. Except that it's made me feel like a total slacker."

"Eh, it'll pass."

"Thanks. I'm heading over for dinner soon. Do you want to come?"

"No, you go do the family thing. I'm good." Will tossed her now-empty coffee cup in the trash and went to the door.

"Okay. I'll see you Friday?"

Will nodded. "I'll pick you up to go get the truck at seven."

Emerson followed. "God, that's early."

"I know. See you then."

Emerson put her hand on the knob, but stopped. "You know I support you, right? And you can date whoever you want. Well, except Kai."

Will took a deep breath. "I know."

"I just don't want you to get hurt."

"I know that, too. And I know my track record lately hasn't been all that great. I appreciate you looking out for me." Even when it irritated her.

"You certainly did it enough times for me." Emerson pulled Will into a hug and then sent her on her way.

CHAPTER FIVE

Nora pulled into Martha and Heidi's narrow driveway and cut the engine. She'd been happy that Will couldn't start for a few days, since she had plans of her own. What had started as a bridge group some ten or twelve years ago had morphed into friendship. Two of those friends had become a second family, sharing birthdays and illnesses, holidays and hard times. It also, as was the case today, included binge watching Netflix.

She grabbed the six pack from the seat next to her and headed to the side door. She knocked, but walked in without waiting for an answer. She found Martha and Heidi in the kitchen. Bowls of popcorn, snack mix, and M&Ms took up most of the small island in the middle of the room.

Nora chuckled. "Did you invite the whole neighborhood? I would have brought more beer."

Heidi rolled her eyes and tipped her head in Martha's direction. "Don't blame me. She has no self-control."

Martha huffed. "If you're going to binge watch something, you might as well binge."

Nora nodded. "She has a point."

"Please don't encourage her." Heidi shook her head but slid her arm around Martha's middle and squeezed.

"But I do think one shouldn't watch six hours of television straight without some heavy-duty carb loading," Nora said.

"Exactly." Martha took the beer from Nora and opened three. "And if we're entering a world where a lesbian can be on the Supreme Court, it will also be a world where I can eat all the Chex Mix I want."

They each took a bottle and a bowl into the living room, setting up a buffet of sorts on the coffee table. Martha picked up the remote and navigated them through the menu. Nora helped herself to a handful of popcorn. "This feels much more civilized than queuing it up at midnight."

"Agreed. We're too old for that nonsense." She hit play and Nora settled in for some mindless entertainment.

After three episodes—complete with heckling, commentary about wardrobe choices, and cheering a particularly steamy same-sex kiss—Martha looked over at her. "Stretch and pee break?"

Nora nodded. "Sounds good."

They wandered into the kitchen, taking turns using the restroom. While Heidi was in, Martha folded her arms and leaned back against the counter. "How's life at the inn?"

Nora shrugged. "Quiet, at least in relative terms. Weekends are still full, but I'm empty two nights this week and three next."

"Graham still there?"

"Yes. She's going to stay until Christmas. My sister and her husband are coming up and we'll do Christmas here."

"Oh, that'll be nice. I know you haven't gone there the last couple of years."

Nora rolled her eyes. "Much to my sister's chagrin. I hate traveling in the winter, though, and it's a surprisingly good week for business."

"Well, this seems like a win for both of you. Anything else going on?"

Nora's mind went immediately to Will. Not that she would admit that. Even if Martha and Heidi were her best friends, there were some things she simply didn't confide. Will, and whatever feelings she stirred up, fell squarely in that category. "Not much."

After saying that, she realized the other, non-weird reason Will was on her mind and almost laughed at her hypervigilance. "I'm using the down time to freshen a couple of rooms. New paint, waxing floors."

"Did you hire someone?" Martha raised a brow. "I know how much you hate that sort of thing."

She thought back to her halting attempts to do some of the initial work on the inn. She'd already become friends with Martha and Heidi. They'd shown up one day to help out and found her half covered in paint and swearing at a paint roller. Not her finest moment. "Sort of. Graham wanted some projects to earn her keep and one of her friends from the fleet was looking for winter jobs to tide her over."

Heidi emerged just as Nora finished her sentence. "Who's looking for winter jobs?"

"Graham's friend that Nora hired to do some painting at her place."

"Ah." Heidi nodded. "Is she Graham's age?"

Nora shook her head. "Older than Graham, but still on the young side. At least compared to us old biddies."

Martha wagged a finger. "We are not biddies. We are women in our prime."

Heidi leaned forward and looked at her suggestively. "Is she gay? Is she hot?"

Nora rolled her eyes. "You're incorrigible. I doubt she's even thirty."

"You didn't answer my question."

"I shouldn't assume it, but she's probably gay. She seems it."

Heidi nodded again. "Good looking?"

Nora ran fingers through her hair and looked at the refrigerator. She didn't want to lie, but she had no intention of articulating just how attractive she found Will. Doing so would ensure that Martha and Heidi would want to talk of little else. And since she was doing her best to think of Will less rather than more, that was the last thing she wanted to do. She shrugged. "In a way. Kind of fresh and wholesome looking I'd say."

"So, girly?"

"Oh, no." Nora thought about the way Will's pants hung on her hips. The muscles in her arms. The way the super short hair on the back of her neck begged to be touched. She made an involuntary noise that she had to quickly cover up with a cough.

"So, she is hot."

Nora sighed. "She's got to be twenty years younger than us and she's working for me. Two very compelling reasons for me not to have an opinion on the matter."

Martha shrugged. "But that doesn't stop you from having one. It's human nature. And if you're being reticent, you probably think she's attractive."

Nora reminded herself that she liked having friends who were astute, and direct. "She happens to fall into the category of women I find attractive, yes."

"Category of women?" Heidi shook her head. "I think you might be trying too hard."

"If I am, it's because I'm smart enough to know I have no business being attracted to her."

"But you hired her." Martha folded her arms.

"Graham asked me to. If anything, I think Graham might have a thing for her. And if the feeling is mutual, I'd just as soon see for myself what she's all about."

"You do realize that makes no sense. And on top of that, Graham is an adult."

There was little Nora hated more than feeling irrational. "Well, what's done is done and I'm going to get some rooms painted in the process. Can we get back to the show now?"

Heidi nodded, but Martha gave her a serious stare. "I think you should focus less on how you think things should be and more on how they are. Or even how they could be."

Nora returned the intense look with a bland one. "That's very profound, Martha. Thank you."

Martha smiled smugly. "You're welcome."

Heidi led the way and they filed back into the living room. After the sixth episode, they decided to order Chinese. By the time Nora headed home, she felt stuffed, lazy, and content. Even if her mind kept wandering back to Will and what it would be like having her in the house for days at a time.

❖

Will hefted what felt like the millionth box and carried it down the ramp of the moving truck. She passed Darcy on the short path into the house and smiled. "Just the mattress left."

"Hurray." Darcy lifted her arms and waved them feebly.

Will carried the box into the house and set it in the corner of the living room. Emerson jogged down the stairs and the two of them walked out to the truck. They found Darcy wrestling with a queen sized mattress. "Not a one person job," Emerson called to her.

"I know." She'd managed to pull it forward and against her, which muffled the sound of her voice.

Will and Emerson climbed into the truck and went to either end of the mattress. "Why don't you go check on Liam and your parents?"

"Excellent idea." Darcy stepped back. "Are you two sure you have it?"

"We're fine." Will was beat, but with the end in sight, she had a surge of energy. "Home stretch."

She and Emerson maneuvered the mattress down the ramp and into the house. The stairs proved trickier, as they had to fold it over slightly to round the corner. Still, they got it into the master bedroom and set it on the box spring that had been brought up earlier. Emerson took a deep breath. "Thanks. I thought we might not make it for a second."

Will laughed. "Right?"

Darcy came in, followed by Liam. Darcy's parents stood in the doorway. Darcy eyed the bed. "Is that it?"

Emerson nodded and Will swept a hand around the room. "Congratulations, you guys. You're officially moved in."

"Yes!" Liam ran the rest of the way into the room and flung himself onto the unmade bed. He flopped onto his back and spread his arms wide. "I'm exhausted."

"Who wants pizza?" Darcy asked.

Liam, who'd done his fair share of carrying things after getting out of school, popped up without a second of hesitation. "I do."

Emerson turned to Darcy. "If you call it in, Will and I will return the truck and pick it up."

Darcy leaned in and kissed her on the cheek. "Deal."

Will and Emerson put the truck back together and piled into the front seat. Emerson started the engine and Will let out a big sigh. "I wish I had Liam's energy."

Emerson laughed. "You and me both. I can't thank you enough for helping today."

"You say that like there's a chance I wouldn't."

"You know what I mean."

Will propped an elbow against the window and looked at Emerson. "I do, but one of my favorite things about moving here is stuff like this. Holidays and family dinners are nice, but I'm really in it for—"

"The manual labor?" Emerson turned onto Route 6 toward Truro.

"Being there for each other. That really feels like family to me."

"See, that's really nice. I'm sorry I teased you."

They drove the short distance to the service station that doubled as a U-Haul rental and traded it for Emerson's car. Then they stopped by the pizza place Liam insisted was the best. By the time they got back to the house, Darcy's parents were gone and Liam lay flopped on the sofa.

"They were going to stay for dinner, but I could tell they were toast. As much as they love our company—"

"And pizza," Liam interjected.

"And pizza. I offered them the chance to call it a day and they jumped on it."

Emerson turned to Will. "I'm sorry. I should have said the same to you."

Will shook her head. "You won't get rid of me that easy. I'm starved."

Liam hefted himself from the couch and darted over to give her a high five. "I like the way you think."

They ate pizza on paper towels with cans of soda. Will had to laugh because Liam was clearly in hog heaven. She thought back to the days when life was that simple. After two slices, Liam began to fade. His eyes got droopy and he kept jerking himself awake.

"How about we call it an early night?" Darcy asked.

Liam nodded. "Yeah."

"I could put your sleeping bag on your bed instead of sheets. It'll be like camping, and you can wait until tomorrow for a bath."

"Yes!"

Emerson smiled at them. "If you do that, I'll clean up here and unearth the coffee pot for the morning."

Darcy smiled. "You have the best ideas."

Emerson stood and Will followed her into the kitchen. "Let me help you unpack some essentials. There's nothing worse than rifling in boxes when you're trying to put a meal together."

"I'm no dummy. I'm not going to refuse the help." They started with Darcy's boxes. First, because she had all the makings of a functional kitchen. Second, because all of her boxes were neatly labeled KITCHEN. "Remember how I said I could float you some money if things got tight over the winter?"

"Yeah." Will had no intention of taking her up on it, but she still appreciated the offer.

"I'd like to amend that. I might have a couple of odd jobs around here you could help me with and I'd insist on paying you for your time."

"I'm always happy to help. Free of charge. You're my sister and you've helped me more times than I can count."

"Eureka." Emerson pulled out the coffee pot and set it on the counter. "We've helped each other."

Will angled her head to one side. "Let's be honest, you're generally much more together than I am."

"Maybe, but you've always been better with your hands."

Will wiggled her eyebrows suggestively. "So I've heard."

Emerson rolled her eyes. "You know what I mean."

"I do." For all Emerson's talent as an artist, she did not do well with other tools or media. She'd once attempted to assemble an IKEA desk on her own and it was so mangled, Will had to take it all apart and start over. "What kinds of projects?"

"Every room will have to be painted and Darcy has convinced me we can reface the kitchen cabinets and replace the counters ourselves."

"She's probably right. I led a workshop on refacing cabinets at the store once."

"You did?"

"The regular guy was sick. I had his notes. It's really minimal carpentry. Take off old doors, paint or refinish the frames, put on new doors."

Emerson chuckled. "You make it sound easy."

"It's way easier than replacing them." Will looked around. The cabinets looked tired, but sturdy. "We can totally handle it."

"How do you feel about making a loft bed? Liam wants his to be raised so he can have a giant desk underneath."

"Of course he does." The more she got to know Liam, the more he reminded her of Emerson as a kid. "If we find a good set of plans, I'm sure we can handle it."

"Okay, see, now I'm getting excited. Please let me pay you so you'll have enough time to help me with these things. I can work around your job at the inn and any others you take on."

The idea of spending much of the winter with Emerson, and the rest of it with Nora and Graham, had major appeal. "Modest payment. Maybe. Just so I can eat well. Do you have tools?"

Emerson cringed. "Not really. I know I'll have to buy a few. I'm also thinking I can borrow some from Darcy's dad."

"Perfect. Well, my weekends are free." She tapped a knuckle on one of the cabinet doors. "How about I come over next week and take a closer look at these guys?"

"That would be great."

"And we can take some measurements in Liam's room. That way, I can start doing some research into possible plans."

Emerson smiled. "You do that and I'll make lunch."

"And by make, do you mean warm up something delicious that Darcy brought home from work?"

Emerson nodded without hesitation or shame. "Yes. Yes, I do."

"Then I'm in."

"Excellent."

"You do own a tape measure, right?"

"In one of these boxes?" Emerson smiled sheepishly. "I'm pretty sure there's one in Darcy's tool box."

Will narrowed her eyes. "It's pink, isn't it?"

Emerson shrugged. "I plead the fifth."

"So, we'll also do an inventory of tools and make a list of what you need. Then you can decide what to buy and what to borrow."

"You're so efficient."

Will chuckled at the descriptor. It wasn't one Emerson usually used for her. "I have my moments."

When she got home, Will took a shower and climbed into bed with her computer. Although the kitchen was probably the priority, she started looking at plans for building loft beds. As long as Liam didn't want any fussy detail work, they could build some really cool setups. She bookmarked a few she liked, including a couple of different desk and shelf configurations underneath.

She wasn't opposed to painting, but she hoped Nora had something similar in mind. Not a loft bed, obviously, but something special that would let Will show off her skills. At this point, she'd take pretty much anything that would make Nora think highly of her.

Chapter Six

The night before her first day at Nora's, Will set her alarm to go off extra early, but still woke before it went off. She dressed quickly, had a cup of coffee and a package of Pop-Tarts. Then she paced back and forth between the kitchen and living room, not wanting to be awkwardly early. Why was she nervous?

She rolled her eyes, knowing exactly why she was nervous. She was about to spend the entire day with Nora. Okay, that was probably a bit of an overstatement. She was going to spend the day with Graham, working at Nora's house. But she was certain to spend more time with Nora today than she had previously. Add to that, she'd be doing work for Nora. Even though Nora had agreed to hire her, Will got the feeling she'd done so under duress, or at least nudging from Graham.

She didn't want to be some hapless seasonal worker relying on the generosity of others to be able to support herself. And she most definitely didn't want one of those others to be Nora. Will hadn't figured out why, but she had a suspicion that Nora didn't like her. An extra degree of coolness in her eyes when Nora looked at her, maybe, or the reserved way she spoke.

Not that the coolness or reservation on Nora's part made Will any less attracted to her. If anything, it heightened it. It probably wasn't healthy if the attraction stemmed from the fact that Nora didn't seem too keen on her. Will shook her head. No, she'd found Nora striking the moment she laid eyes on her. Sure, the aloofness might have made her even more appealing, but at least it wasn't the cause.

God, how pathetic. Will had never been skilled at picking relationships. She had a penchant for older women, women who seemed sophisticated and confident. Not that there was anything wrong with that, but those same women never seemed to see her as an equal. That left her either admiring from afar or always scrambling to keep up. Or, in the case of Kai, letting herself get pushed around. And now here she was, obsessing over a woman at least ten—maybe more like fifteen—years older than her who was the aunt of her good friend. She wondered vaguely what was wrong with her.

She didn't wonder for long. A glance at the clock on the microwave told her that she'd paced and processed for close to twenty minutes and now ran the risk of being late. She grabbed her things and headed out.

On the walk to Failte, the wind gusted, causing dead leaves to swirl on the street. It might be sunny, but the warmth of early fall had vanished. Will zipped her jacket and stuffed her hands in her pockets, wishing she'd poured the last of the coffee into a travel mug. Maybe Nora would have some and share.

Will reached the front gate, thinking of the first time she'd been there. It felt longer ago than the few weeks that had actually passed. Even with most of the bushes and vines hibernating until spring, it looked inviting and well-tended. The crushed shell path crunched under her boots. At the front door, she hesitated again. Since guests of the inn came and went freely, it seemed weird to knock. Of course, strolling in unannounced did, too.

Before she could settle on one or the other, the large wooden door swung open. Graham smiled at her from the other side. "Hi."

"Hi."

"I thought it was you coming up the walk. Come on in."

Will followed her into the foyer. "Are you ready to get to work?"

"Can't we have a cup of coffee first?" Graham's tone was playful.

Will breathed in the aroma. Yes, she definitely wanted a cup. "I think it's considered better to work first and earn a coffee break."

Graham shook her head. "Who knew you'd be such a task master?"

"I know she's your aunt, but I'm still trying to make a good impression." Will didn't add that she wanted Nora to think of her as more than just Graham's friend.

Graham angled her head and gave Will a puzzled look, as though such a thought had never occurred to her. "Yeah, okay. Sure."

Great. Now she was the killjoy. "I just mean—"

"I appreciate your diligence." Nora appeared from the dining room.

Will cleared her throat, feeling even more awkward at having been overheard. "Good morning."

Nora dried her hands on a towel and offered a smile that was, if not warm, kind. "Good morning. I promise that I will judge you on the quality of your work, not how many cups of coffee you drink."

Will blushed. Yep, awkward. "Thanks."

"In fact, why don't I pour three cups that we can take upstairs while we discuss the work to be done?"

Graham leaned over and kissed Nora on the cheek. "You're the best."

Will, though tempted to do the same, refrained. "I really do appreciate the sentiment, and the coffee."

Nora looked her up and down and nodded before turning around and heading back to the kitchen. Will couldn't be sure, but it felt like she might have just passed a test. She took a deep breath and stuck her hands in her pockets.

"Relax. She's sweet."

Will nodded. Not the word she would use. Not that Nora couldn't have a sweet side, but that's not what Will saw when she looked at her. Or wanted to see, really. She liked Nora's perfect posture and reserved air. Almost as much as she liked to think about what might be simmering below the surface. And what it would be like to tap into that, to have it directed at her. For the second time, Will cleared her throat.

"Do you need some water or something?"

Will laughed. Fortunately, Graham didn't have a window into her thoughts. "I'm okay, thanks."

Graham rolled her eyes. "You need to relax."

Ha. If only it was that simple. "Yes, ma'am."

Graham opened her mouth, probably to protest being called ma'am, but was interrupted by Nora calling to them from the kitchen. "Will, how do you take it?"

Will sighed. In another life, she might turn the question into playful banter or, even better, open flirtation. Another life. "Black is fine for me. Thanks."

Graham crinkled her nose. "You and Aunt Nora are two peas in a pod."

Nora emerged with three cups and handed one to each of them. Will peered into Graham's cup, its contents light enough to be tea. "Is that even half coffee?"

"Shut up." Graham nudged her in the ribs.

Nora led the way upstairs and into a bedroom. All of the furniture appeared to be antique and lovingly cared for. The decor was elegant, if dated. It would appeal, perhaps, to an older traveler, but could stand a good freshening up. Of course, that might be Nora's style. "So, what are you thinking?"

Nora walked to the center of the room. "The floors are in decent enough shape that I'm not going to do anything with them. The furniture is as well. But I haven't redecorated since I opened ten years ago, so I'm going for a full update."

"Nice," Graham said. Will nodded.

"I've already picked out new bedding and rugs. Window treatments. Your job will be to move the furniture to the center of the room, remove wallpaper, and paint."

Nora had said as much when she offered Will the job. Even if part of her had hoped for something more involved, the other part was relieved. Simple projects were harder to mess up. And as much as she liked Graham, Will had the feeling she hadn't done much in the way of DIY. "Do you have the paint already?"

Nora looked around the room. "I've got the color picked, but I'm waiting to see the condition of the walls before I buy. I'm hoping we can do paint and primer in one."

"Good call."

"The thing is that the room is booked for this coming weekend. I need to know if you can do all the work in three days."

Will glanced at Graham, who looked nervous all of a sudden. Will smiled. She could do it alone in that amount of time. As long as Graham was even minimally helpful, they'd be fine. "Not a problem. We'll get the walls stripped and prepped today. Can you get the paint by tomorrow morning? Or give me the specifics and I can pick it up?"

Nora waved a hand. "I'll go out this afternoon once you decide on the state of things."

"Sounds good. We'll get cracking."

Nora pointed to a pile on the floor. "That should be all the supplies you need. If something is missing, let me know."

"Thank you." Will looked at Graham. "You ready?"

Graham nodded, now looking more eager than nervous. "Ready."

"I'll leave you to it."

Nora disappeared and Will tried not to be disappointed. She chided herself. Nora had hired her, not invited her over for tea. She finished her coffee, which might be the most delicious coffee she'd ever had, and looked at Graham. "Furniture first?"

"Sounds like a plan."

They moved the bed away from the wall, then positioned the rest of the furniture around it. She had Graham cover it while she got on the step ladder to remove the window treatments. Once that was done, she turned her attention to tools. Whether Nora had done it before, or had simply done her homework, it looked like she'd thought of everything. She pulled a paper scorer out of the package and handed it to Graham. "Can you run this all over the wall while I mix up the paste dissolver?"

"Yes?"

Will took it back and did a quick demo. "Like this."

"Oh." Graham took it back and offered a confident smile. "Yes."

At noon, Nora decided to check the progress of the work and offer lunch. She climbed the stairs and heard laughter coming from the room where Graham and Will were working. She crept toward the door, stopping short of the threshold, and listened.

"I'm just saying you're precocious. I didn't kiss anyone—boy or girl—until I was fourteen," Graham said.

"It was all innocent stuff, I swear. I didn't have sex until college." Will's reply sounded more playful than defensive.

"With?" Graham let the question linger.

"A graduate student. The teaching assistant in my Western Civ class."

"What year were you?"

"Freshman." There was a pause and then Will added, "I didn't get any farther than that."

"Farther than sex?"

"Farther than freshman year."

"Oh."

"It just," Will hesitated. "It just wasn't for me."

"That's cool. I sometimes wish I'd been too cool for school. I was the biggest nerd."

Nora tensed. If Will so much as hinted that Graham's education wasn't worth it, she'd fire her on the spot.

"Emerson was like that. I was athletic, popular, but I always wished I could be more like her."

"You could always go back." The youthful optimism in Graham's voice made Nora smile.

"I think that ship has sailed. It's okay, though. I like working with people, and with my hands. I do all right."

The last statement gave Nora pause. She'd made it through college, but barely. More because it was important to her parents than any intrinsic motivation. They'd hoped she would become a teacher. She'd gone along with it until she got her first glimpse of student teaching. She'd almost had a panic attack at the prospect of standing in front of thirty kids all day. Now, she staunchly supported higher education. But if she was being honest, it hadn't really been for her either.

Wanting to cut off any further trip down memory lane, she called out a greeting and went the rest of the way into the room. The furniture had been moved and draped with sheets. The curtains were down and Graham was wiping a wall down with a sponge. "I see you two are making good progress."

Will looked to Graham, who said, "Someone told me we were working on a deadline."

Nora chuckled. "Oh, right. Still, it's looking good. How about a lunch break?"

"Thank God. I'm famished." Graham pressed the back of her hand to her forehead.

Nora looked to Will. "Will?"

"I'm fine to take a break. I feel like I should tell you, though, that your walls have some rough spots and some stains."

Nora sighed. Of course they did. "Is it a couple of extra hours bad or I need to cancel this weekend's reservation bad?"

Will flipped her hand back and forth. "Somewhere in the middle. I can definitely get it done, as long as you don't mind me coming early and going late the next couple of days."

Nora appreciated the attitude. "I don't mind at all. I'll pay you for the time, obviously, but we can also work out some kind of overtime for your trouble."

Will lifted a hand. "No need. I'm truly happy for the work and I want it to be done right."

"Me, too," Graham said.

Nora glanced at Graham, having forgotten for a moment she was there. "Thank you. I'm not above getting pulled in, too, if needed."

"But we still get lunch, right?"

"Of course. I'm not a tyrant."

Graham dropped her sponge in the bucket at her feet and crossed the room to give Nora a hug. "You're a benevolent boss."

Nora chuckled. "Will, you're free to come and go, but you are also welcome to join us. It's just soup, but there's plenty of it."

"I would love that." The genuine gratitude in her voice caught Nora off guard.

They sat at the dining room table, talking about everything from Graham's thesis to how Nora came to own the inn. Will asked lots of questions, seeming to be as interested in Nora as she was Graham. Nora didn't know what to make of it. Not that she had to.

When they'd finished eating, Nora shooed them back upstairs to keep working while she cleaned up and made a trip to the hardware store. She picked up the paint, along with the putty and special primer Will suggested. By the time she got home, it was close to four and her walls were bare and ready to go.

Will accepted the supplies. "Patching holes is sort of a one-person job, so I'll do that before I go. Then we can sand and start priming in the morning."

"I'll keep you company," Graham said.

Nora sighed. A small part of her wanted to linger, enjoy playful conversation and not think about anything else. But that's not who she was, and on top of that she had things to do.

"I appreciate your staying late. I'll be downstairs if you need anything."

Nora went to the small office nook she had set up in a corner of the kitchen. She booted up her computer and opened the reservation book, selecting recipes and making lists in preparation for the weekend. Occasionally, she heard laughter from upstairs and found herself, not jealous, but envious perhaps, of the easy rapport. She shook her head. That was ridiculous. Between her friends and her guests, she had plenty of that. She didn't need— or even want—that with someone like Will.

CHAPTER SEVEN

Will and Graham finished two rooms before Nora had to put the projects on hold for the holidays. Not only did she have a full house for Thanksgiving, the weeks leading up to Christmas were more booked than not. They might be able to get the third upstairs room done the second week of December, but she'd have to wait and see.

Graham had taken to helping her in the kitchen. The girl didn't have much talent in that arena, but she was an eager learner. And she didn't mind dishes. There were always plenty of dishes. Today, Nora was giving her a lesson in French toast.

"Would you mind if I invited Will to Thanksgiving dinner?"

Nora sighed. She thought this might be coming. Too bad she didn't plan what she would say. "I'm not sure—"

Graham planted her hands on her hips. "Why don't you like her?"

Nora stopped whisking the egg mixture in front of her. "I don't not like her."

Graham raised a brow. "Could've fooled me."

Nora resumed whisking. It looked like they were having this conversation whether or not she wanted to. It didn't mean she didn't need to get breakfast on the table in an hour. "I just have a bad feeling about her."

"That is such an unfair thing to say. You don't even know her."

"Neither do you."

"Do you want this bread sliced?" Graham gestured to the loaf of Challah sitting on the island.

"That would be great. Thank you."

Graham started on the bread, going at it with a fierce determination that made Nora smile. "I know her better than you do."

"But still not very well. Someone her age shouldn't be showing up in town for no reason and working a job any high schooler could do."

"She came to town because her sister lives here."

That made it better. A little.

"And you've already said she does excellent work. Work, which I might add, I definitely couldn't have done alone."

"I was thinking of her other job, but you've made your point."

"I think she was in a bad relationship and was looking for a fresh start."

As far as Nora was concerned, volatile relationships—the kind that blew up and made someone want to leave town—screamed trouble. She'd learned that lesson years ago firsthand. "Just don't think of her as some lost puppy you can rescue."

Graham frowned. "I won't."

"Good." Nora took the bread and started dipping it. "I know her type and trust me when I say you don't want to get involved."

Graham huffed. "I still don't think she should be alone on Thanksgiving. Do you?"

"If she came to town because her sister is here, I'm guessing she won't be alone."

"Oh."

"The fact that didn't occur to you is what makes me worry." For some reason, it felt easier to focus on Graham's potential feelings rather than her own.

"What is that supposed to mean?"

"You've got this idea of her in your head. You can't go through life dealing with people based on your romanticized notions of them. You're asking to get hurt." She'd done just that when Jordyn came to town, falling for the fantasy of a budding musician who acted like Nora was her muse.

"Don't you think you're being a little dramatic?"

Nora slid a tray of bacon into the oven. "No, no I don't."

Graham narrowed her eyes. "Is this about Will, or Jordyn?"

Nora turned back to her. She'd never discussed Jordyn with Graham. Graham had been visiting for much of the summer she and Jordyn were together. Jordyn took Graham under her wing, playing the part of cool older sister to a T. Fortunately, Graham had already gone home by the time Jordyn vanished. Nora was curious about how much Graham knew, but she didn't want to ask. "I don't know what you mean."

Graham looked at her in a way that seemed far more adult than Nora liked to think of her. "I'm not asking you to give me all the details. I just know something bad went down. I don't think it's fair to hold whatever she did against Will."

She should have known. Even at sixteen, Graham had been perceptive. Still, Nora held her ground. "I'm not holding anything against Will. I'm simply saying there's a certain kind of woman you have to look out for. It's a lesson I'd rather you not have to learn the hard way."

Graham shook her head. Nora thought she might argue the point. Instead, she sighed in a way that felt like admitting defeat. "Is there anything else you want help with?"

"No, thank you for doing the bread. Don't be angry with me."

"I'm not. I'm," she shrugged, "sad I guess. I hate that you're so quick to see the worst in people."

That bristled, far more than Nora wanted to admit. More than Graham being annoyed with her for being practical, realistic. "There's nothing to be sad about. I've lived more years than you and I've seen more. People with trouble in their pasts are rarely above reproach. I'm sorry if you don't like that, but it's human nature."

"Okay." Graham sighed. "I'm going to go out for a run. I'll be back in a while."

Nora felt badly for deflating her. "Do you want breakfast before you go? It will be ready in about twenty minutes."

"I'm good. Thanks, though. Take care of your guests and I'll see you later."

Graham disappeared in the direction of her room and Nora went about finishing breakfast. Graham's words continued to play in her mind. Had she been too heavy handed? No, Graham was young and almost painfully optimistic. Nora had done little more than give her a reality check. If being the occasional voice of reason could spare Graham some of the bad choices she'd made in her life, it would be more than worth it.

With that settled, she went to the dining room to check the coffee and greet the guests who had already made their way downstairs. When Graham got home, she'd encourage her to invite Will to dinner. It would make Graham feel better and the chances of Will actually coming were slim.

❖

As much as Will appreciated the invitation to join Graham and Nora for Thanksgiving, she wasn't about to pass up the chance for a real family holiday, the first in longer than she cared to admit. She pulled into Darcy and Emerson's driveway and smiled. They'd been in the little house in Wellfleet for less than a month. Although she'd yet to help Emerson with some of the projects they'd discussed, they'd settled in and were excited to host their first holiday dinner. She grabbed the bottle of wine and her first attempt at a kugel and headed to the front door.

Before she had the opportunity to knock, the door flew open. Liam stood on the other side, decked out in khakis, a sweater vest, and a bow tie. "Hi, Will!"

"Hey, Liam. Happy Thanksgiving. You're looking very dapper today."

He stood a little taller at the compliment. "Thanks. Emerson and I got matching outfits."

Will chuckled. "Nice. I hope your mom took a picture for posterity."

He narrowed his eyes. "What's posterity?"

Will angled her head. "It means—"

"Liam, would you please let our guest in the house before you start interrogating her?" Darcy appeared in the foyer, wiping her hands on a dishtowel. "Sorry, Will. Please come in."

Will stepped inside and nudged the door closed with her hip. She handed Darcy the wine. "No, no, it was my fault. I used a word and Liam asked what it meant."

"Ah. And what word is that?" She lifted the bottle. "Thanks for this, by the way."

"You're welcome. Posterity."

"She asked if you took a picture of me and Emerson for posterity."

"I didn't, but I definitely should. Thanks for the reminder."

Will grinned. "Of course."

"But what does it mean?" Liam's voice took on a hint of exasperation, which made Will laugh.

"It means the future or, I think more specifically, future generations. Mostly, you say it about something you want to preserve or have remembered in the future."

Liam nodded slowly. "Cool."

"What's going on?" Emerson joined them in the small entryway. "What did I miss?"

Will looked at her sister. As promised, she wore an outfit identical to Liam's. Way preppier than her normal style, it made Will enjoy it all the more. "We were talking about your holiday attire. And making sure there's photo evidence of it." Will expected Emerson to groan, or at least roll her eyes. When she didn't, and merely smiled and said something about it being a good idea, Will shook her head. Things sure had changed. Since she couldn't remember seeing her sister happier, it seemed like a definite change for the better. "Let me and all three of you can be in it."

They filed into the living room and Emerson picked up her camera from the coffee table. She was in the process of handing it to Will when Darcy spoke. "How about we let Will get comfortable first?" She took the pan of kugel and headed to the kitchen. "Take off your coat and stay a while."

Emerson took Will's coat and smiled. "Sorry. Liam and I get carried away sometimes."

"No apologies needed. You two are adorable."

Darcy returned and Will took a bunch of photos, stopping with the arrival of Darcy's parents. Emerson poured wine and Darcy put the finishing touches on dinner. When they sat down at the table, a housewarming gift from Darcy's parents, Will happily took her seat next to Liam. Dishes were passed and, in lieu of a formal blessing over the meal, Darcy invited everyone to share the things they were grateful for while they ate.

Liam went first, rattling off the cutest list that included everything from learning how to throw a curve ball to his new house. Darcy's parents were very sweet. The things they said about Darcy, and about Emerson becoming part of their lives, gave her a pang for her own parents. When it was her turn, Will took a deep breath. "I'm grateful for all of you, and to be here. Here, at this dinner, but also here on the Cape. A year ago, I couldn't have imagined this would be my life and now I can't imagine being anywhere else."

Emerson went next, saying something about each person around the table. Darcy did the same, and by the time she finished, everyone was wiping at their eyes and sniffling. Which, in turn, made everyone laugh. Emerson picked up the platter of turkey and passed it to Will. "I think that's our cue for seconds."

Will stuffed herself and laughed until her stomach ached. She couldn't remember the last time she felt so much like part of a family. Despite wanting to get to Nora's, she didn't want the meal to end. They lingered around the table for a long while. Finally, Emerson shooed Darcy and her parents out to the living room. Will joined Emerson in the kitchen to clean up. It was the perfect cap to the meal—sharing chores like they'd done for so many years.

With dinner done, leftovers tucked away, and Liam sound asleep on the sofa, Will felt good about taking her leave. She hugged Darcy goodbye and Emerson walked her out. They'd had a dusting of snow overnight, but it had melted and temperatures were near forty.

"Thank you so much for coming," Emerson said.

Will smiled. "Wouldn't miss it."

"I still can't believe we bought a house."

Will raised a brow. "You're not having second thoughts, are you?"

"No, no, nothing like that. It's amazing. Just a little surreal."

"For what it's worth, I've never seen you happier."

"Thanks. It means the world to me that you're here, that you decided to stay."

"If it weren't for you, I don't know if that would be the case." The reality of that stayed with Will. She didn't want to be dramatic, or overly sentimental, but Emerson had been so much more than a sofa to crash on. Without being pushy or parental, Emerson had given her the space and the support to find herself. Even when she'd known she needed to get away from Kai, Will had no idea just how lost she'd become.

"And if it weren't for you, I don't know if I would have had the guts to take things with Darcy to the next level."

"I guess we're even, then."

Emerson grinned at her. "Good. That means I can ask a favor."

"Anything. Well, almost anything. What is it?"

"Help me pick out a ring?"

The meaning of Emerson's request sank in. She grinned. "Most definitely. Although I refuse to count that as a favor."

"Thanks." Emerson pulled Will into a hug. When she stepped back, she narrowed her eyes. "Wait, are you crying?"

Will blinked rapidly to prevent any tears from falling. "Not at all."

Emerson's face took on a look of concern. "Is something wrong? Are you not cool with me proposing to Darcy?"

Will shook her head, then punched her sister in the arm. "Of course I'm cool with it, you dolt. I'm just being mushy about it."

Emerson chuckled. "Save the mushy for when she says yes."

"Not that I think you have anything to worry about, but okay." Will glanced at her watch.

Emerson raised a brow. "Got somewhere to be?"

"Graham invited me for dinner. I told her I'd stop by for dessert after I left your place."

"Graham? Or Nora?"

"Graham did the inviting, but I think Nora was behind it."

Emerson merely shook her head. "Go. Have fun. We'll discuss this more thoroughly soon."

Will shrugged playfully. "If only there was something worth discussing."

With that, she climbed into her car and backed out of the driveway. The sun was beginning to set and there was virtually no traffic on Route 6. She flipped on the radio and found a station already playing Christmas music.

The inn emitted a welcoming glow. She passed it and found a parking spot a little ways up the street. She walked up the gravel path, thinking more about Nora than dessert. She didn't hesitate this time to walk right in. Inside, the guests seemed spread out between the dining and sitting rooms. Looked like she made it just in time.

"You came."

Will turned in the direction of Graham's voice. "Of course I did. You said there'd be pie."

Graham shook her head and smiled. "So. Much. Pie. Come with me."

She followed Graham to the buffet in the dining room. She had no idea what had been served for dinner, but if the dessert spread was any indication, it had been a feast for the ages. "Wow."

"I know. I'm trying to figure out if I can eat one of everything."

It seemed unlikely. Will lifted her gaze and looked around the room for Nora, but didn't see her. "Where's your aunt? I want to be sure to thank her for the invitation."

"She's probably in the kitchen."

Will looked at the swinging door that led to the kitchen just as Nora came through it. As if on cue, Will's stomach tightened and her mouth went dry. Did she have to be so freaking beautiful? Will got the sense she wasn't even trying, but the deep green blouse and skirt that fell to her knees just about brought Will to her knees. She swallowed and tried to focus her attention on the desserts.

The sight of Will, standing at the buffet with Graham, stopped Nora in her tracks. She'd known Will would be there, but it didn't seem to stop Nora's reaction to her. Her very inappropriate, inconvenient reaction. She squared her shoulders and tried to shake it off. "Hello, Will. I'm glad you were able to join us."

Will made eye contact with her and smiled. "Thank you for inviting me. I feel like I should confess, though, that I've technically already had dessert."

The casualness of the comment offset the intensity in Will's eyes. Nora took a deep breath and waved a hand. She could do this. "There are no rules on Thanksgiving, at least when it comes to pie."

"That's good to hear. When it comes to sweets, I have absolutely no shame." Will added a wedge of cheesecake to the slice of apple pie already on her plate. "And your spread is a thing of beauty."

Graham laughed and Nora smiled. She couldn't deny Will was charming. What she wanted to know was whether or not there was an angle to it. And since Graham didn't seem to have a suspicious bone in her body, Nora had to be suspicious enough for the both of them.

"Ms. Calhoun, would it be possible to get a glass of milk for Brandon?"

Nora turned her attention and found Amy, one of her guests, smiling at her. "Of course. And, please, call me Nora."

"Thank you, Nora."

Nora went into the kitchen for the milk. By the time she returned, Will and Graham were chatting with Martha and Heidi. Great. That's just what she needed. Convinced things would be better if she chaperoned, she crossed the room to join them.

"We hear you've got two of the upstairs rooms done," Heidi said.

Nora nodded. "They look great. You'll have to stop by when there's no one in them to check them out."

"And that would be…" Martha raised a brow.

"I've got a couple of empty weekdays in mid-December."

"We're hoping to get the last upstairs room painted before I leave," Graham said.

"But it's okay if you don't." Nora still didn't like the idea of Graham feeling like she needed to earn her keep.

"Did you know Will builds stuff?"

Nora looked from Martha, who'd spoken, to Will. "You do?"

"Nothing major. Bookshelves mostly." Despite the modesty of her words, the smile Will flashed was all confidence. It gave Nora a ripple of pleasure she did her best to ignore.

Graham chimed in. "She's helping her sister build a loft bed for…"

"Liam, my nephew. At least I imagine he'll be my nephew soon enough."

"Interesting." Martha narrowed her eyes and nodded.

Nora caught one of her guests trying to make eye contact with her. She hated to leave this conversation—she was learning things—but guests came first. She excused herself to find out what they needed.

One task turned into five and, before she knew it, her friends were getting ready to leave. She thought Will might linger, but apparently she'd picked up a few hours at one of the stores for the busy shopping weekend. The three of them walked out together, but not before Martha could elbow her in the ribs and angle her head at Will suggestively. Nora rolled her eyes, but laughed, and sent them on their way.

CHAPTER EIGHT

After checking out the last of her guests, Nora locked the front door and made the short walk to The Flour Pot. Martha stood out front, studying something in the window of the shop next door. "I hope I haven't kept you waiting," Nora said.

"Not at all. Heidi's working today and I came to town early to get groceries and take a stroll."

"Woman of leisure, eh?"

"I've got a double shift this weekend, thank you very much."

"Well then, you've more than earned a lunch date. Shall we?"

"After you." Martha bowed dramatically.

Nora walked into the café. The warm air and aroma of freshly baked bread enveloped her. She inhaled deeply. "I love the smell of bread someone else has baked."

Martha elbowed her in the ribs. "That's exactly how I feel every time I come to your house."

Nora laughed. They walked up to the counter and greeted Alex.

"Hello, ladies. What can I get for you today?"

Nora perused the menu board. "Soup for me. Tomato basil I think."

Martha nodded slowly. "Same. And coffee."

"Yes. Me, too."

"Coming right up." Alex totaled their order. Martha paid, insisting it was her turn, then they carried their lunch to one of the empty tables.

"I forget how quiet it gets at this time of year. I should come into town more often."

Nora sampled her soup. As with most of the offerings at The Flour Pot, it was delicious. "You should."

"Especially since you're more tied down."

Nora didn't like to think of it as being tied down, but winter often came with less flexibility in her schedule. She had fewer guests, but no staff to back her up. That meant she only got out when she had no guests at all. "You know you're always welcome at my house."

"I do, but it's nice to have someone else do the cooking, isn't it?"

Nora swirled a piece of sourdough bread in her soup. "It is."

"So, I owe you a thank you."

"You're welcome. What for?"

"Heidi and I decided to hire Will to paint our kitchen and living room."

Nora choked on her soup. She cleared her throat and took a sip of coffee, grateful to avoid a full-on coughing fit. "You did?"

"Why do you sound so surprised? I thought things were going well."

"Yes, but…" But what? There was no reason for her to be surprised. Or to have a problem with it. But something about it didn't sit well with her. She didn't like the idea of Will spending time with her friends. It felt like Will was creeping more and more into her life.

"Is there something you didn't tell us? Are you concerned about something?"

"No." Nora was concerned, but not in the way Martha meant. She shook her head, trying not to reveal just how annoyed the news made her.

"Are we taking her away from work at your place? I thought you had guests on and off through Christmas."

"You aren't taking her away from me. It's—" What was it? Martha looked at her expectantly. "It's what?"

Nora drummed her fingers on the table. "It's weird. That's all."

Martha dunked a piece of bread in her soup. "You yourself said she did good work. Not to mention being nice to look at while doing said work."

Nora looked at her food, suddenly not hungry. "Jesus, Martha. She's practically a child."

"I don't think she's as young as you think. Besides, I'm not trying to sleep with her or anything."

Nora rubbed her hands over her face. "That's not what I meant."

"So, what did you mean?" Martha narrowed her eyes for a moment, then sat up straight and opened them wide. "You're trying to sleep with her."

"Are you out of your mind?" She couldn't decide if she found Martha's insinuation ridiculous or insulting.

Martha lifted both hands. "Sorry, sorry. Not trying. But you want to. And it's pissing you off."

Nora folded her arms. "I think she wants to sleep with Graham. That's what's pissing me off."

"Oh." Martha nodded slowly.

"And I'm pretty sure Graham has a little bit of a thing for her. I don't want Graham to fall into the same trap I did." That was it. Nora kept a nice cushion around her heart, so it couldn't possibly be her own feelings that had her riled up.

Martha's expression softened. "What makes you think it's a trap? Or that Graham would fall into it?"

"You don't think Will looks like Jordyn?" Other than her sister, Martha was the only person who knew her entire history with Jordyn, from the whirlwind affair to the fact that it crashed and burned, taking the bulk of her savings with it. They had an unspoken agreement not to discuss it, but Martha could sense when shadows of the heartbreak crept in.

Martha took a deep breath and Nora got the feeling she was choosing her words carefully. "There's a faint resemblance, maybe, but nothing more."

"Physically, yes. But beyond that. She appeared out of nowhere and took some random seasonal job. Now she's sticking around and insinuating herself into Graham's life."

Martha shook her head. "I didn't get that sense at all. When she was at our house, she spent half the time talking about her sister and the work she was doing at her and her girlfriend's new house."

Nora frowned. The little she knew of Will's sister had come from Graham. Of course, she went out of her way not to be alone with Will. Maybe she was overreacting. "I didn't know that."

"Nora, what's really going on?"

She appreciated that Martha didn't lay it out there for her, or presume she knew exactly what Nora was feeling. Still, she had a way of getting right to the point of things, leaving Nora little place to hide. "She's gotten under my skin, I guess. Reminds me of Jordyn. And I'm not sure if I should be worried on Graham's behalf or my own."

Martha nodded sympathetically. "That, at least, I can understand. And I'm sorry."

Nora allowed her shoulders to slump. "I just hate being susceptible to it."

"Are you talking about actual risk or the fact that your brain can't help but to go there?"

"I guess it's both. I thought I was done with drama and intrigue."

Martha put her elbow on the table and propped her chin on her fist. "Are you sure you aren't borrowing trouble?"

"I'd rather borrow it than be caught unaware."

"That's fair. But I hate for you to be worrying about something that is probably nothing."

Nothing. Nora repeated the word in her mind. It was nothing. Graham would be gone soon. And Will wouldn't be in her house or in her mind anymore. Why didn't that make her feel better? "You're right."

"Thank you." Martha smirked, but then looked at Nora with concern. "Are you sure you're okay?"

Nora nodded. "Absolutely. I'm sorry if I overreacted. I'm excited for you to redecorate."

"Me, too. Even if part of me is worried Heidi will get a bee in her bonnet and want to redo the whole house."

"It can be addictive."

Martha shook her head. "Please don't tell me that."

They finished lunch and walked along Commercial Street. Nora window-shopped. She'd bought Graham's Christmas gift, but still needed something for her sister and brother-in-law. At Martha's car, they exchanged hugs. "We're on for New Year's, right?"

Martha grinned. "Wouldn't miss it. Are you sure there's nothing we can bring?"

"Sure. It's the one time of the year I throw a party that's more for my friends than my guests. I want you to have a good time."

"We always do. Speaking of, did you invite Will?"

She hadn't, but she imagined Graham would want to. Maybe she could extend the invitation to Emerson and Darcy. She'd wanted to meet the woman who did the cooking at the Flour Pot. For that matter, she should invite Alex and Lia, too. "I will. The more the merrier, right?"

Martha gave her a quizzical look, but only said, "So I hear."

A flurry of last-minute bookings prevented Will and Graham from tackling the final room upstairs. Will hung out with Graham a couple of times, but Nora remained elusive. Will didn't doubt Nora was busy, but she missed seeing her.

On one of those days, a snowy afternoon mid-December, Will and Graham hunkered down in the library with books and cups of hot tea. They'd shared lunch with Nora, but after issuing an invitation to her annual New Year's Eve party, she cited work and vanished into the kitchen.

"You'll come to the party, right?" Graham's face looked more worried than hopeful.

"Of course I'll come. Why wouldn't I?" Nora had included Emerson and Darcy, and commented that she planned to invite Lia and Alex as well.

Graham sighed. "Things have been a little weird is all."

Will kept her face blank. "Weird how?"

Graham sighed again, this time with an exasperated look on her face. "You and Nora. You're perfectly normal until you're in the same room together. And then you both get quiet and awkward. Every time."

Will knew what Graham was referring to. The problem was that she had no idea why or what to do about it. She was starting to worry Nora could barely tolerate her. And it wasn't even like Will had made a pass at her and been shut down. On top of that, Nora's dislike of her seemed to alternate with genuine friendliness. The inconsistency got worse as time went on rather than better. Even still, Will craved being around her. And every now and then, she'd swear she caught Nora staring at her with something that looked an awful lot like desire. It was confusing. "I don't know what you mean."

"Yes, you do. I know you don't want to talk about it, though, and that's fine. As long as you're coming."

"I am."

"And you'll bring your sister and Darcy, too?"

"I will. Although I hope Nora didn't feel obligated."

"No." Graham laughed. "I think it might have to do with wanting us to feel like there are some people our age there."

Now Will laughed. "It's a nice gesture, but I doubt that's the reason. I'm pretty sure I'm closer to her age than yours."

Graham frowned. Actually, it was more of a pout.

"What?"

"You're not that much older than me."

Will scratched her temple. "How old are you?"

Graham crossed her arms. "Aren't you not supposed to ask a lady that?"

"I don't think the rules apply when said lady is under the age of twenty-five."

"I could be older than twenty-five."

Will raised a brow.

"Fine. I'm twenty-three."

"And I'm thirty-four, so there."

"Well, Aunt Nora is forty-eight, so I still win."

Will tried to hide her surprise. She wouldn't have pegged Nora as much—if at all—over forty. Not that it made Nora any less appealing. It did, however, make her point moot. "You'll learn that age difference matters less as you get older."

Graham looked at her earnestly. "I don't think it matters so much now."

"That's fair." Will nodded. "I've always had the hots for older women."

Graham gave her a funny look. "Really?"

Will shrugged. She wasn't about to talk to Graham about her crush on Nora. "Just a thing, I guess."

Graham smiled shyly. "I know what you mean."

For some reason, that made Will feel better. She left Graham to work on her thesis and drove over to Emerson's. They were putting the final touches on Liam's loft bed Christmas present before he was out of school. "I think we should put it together in the basement," Will said when she arrived.

Emerson looked incredulous. "That sounds like a massive amount of extra work."

Will shook her head. "It really isn't. All the real work is in cutting, sanding, and painting."

"Don't forget pre-drilling."

Will chuckled. They'd had a lengthy conversation on the merits of pre-drilling. "Exactly. We won't fully tighten everything downstairs. Or secure it to the wall, obviously. But then Liam will get to see it and not just the sketch."

"That would be really cool. He asked for a loft bed, but he has no sense of what he's actually getting. I'd love to see his face the first time he sees it."

"Christmas morning, you could send him downstairs. It would be such a surprise. And the fact that it's fully assembled in the basement would blow his mind."

"Right." Emerson nodded slowly, then grinned. "How in the world did it get down there?"

"So, we can do it?"

Emerson laughed. "I love how you're even more excited about this than I am. Thank you for that."

Will shrugged. This project was sort of the Holy Grail for her—creative, working with her hands, spending time with her sister. On top of that, she got to take the lead and play expert. That never happened in her life these days. "I am. No shame. I'm hoping Liam will let me hang out with him."

"He adores you already."

Will smiled. Liam did seem to like her. She'd never wanted kids of her own, but being the cool aunt was shaping up to be one of her favorite things. She wondered if Nora felt that way about Graham. "The feeling is definitely mutual."

Chapter Nine

Between all the holiday bookings and Graham's parents coming in for Christmas, more than a week passed where Will didn't see Nora or Graham at all. She did her best not to mope, or to dwell on the fact that Graham would be heading back to school soon.

Spending time with Emerson helped, as did Liam's absolute delight in his new bed. In addition to getting it assembled in his room, she and Emerson tackled the cabinets and replaced the bathroom vanity. But even as she helped Emerson check items off her list, Will missed her work at the inn. And she definitely missed Nora.

By the time Nora's New Year's party rolled around, Will had worked herself into a state equal parts excitement and nerves. She adjusted her tie and assessed herself in the mirror. Even with it being the middle of winter, she was in better shape and had better color than she'd had in years. Not that it did her any good. The few times she managed to be in the same room as Nora, she hardly gave Will the time of day. Will shook her head. She sure knew how to pick them.

Still. Tonight would be fun. Besides getting to see Nora and Graham, Darcy and Emerson were coming. And Alex and Lia from the café, whom she'd met, but only briefly. The party promised to be the kind of swanky affair that she dreamed about more than she ever got to attend.

Will checked her watch. Emerson and Darcy were due to pick her up any minute. She slipped on her new wingtips, grateful she had a ride instead of having to trudge through the snow. Her phone pinged just as she finished buttoning her coat. Instead of responding, she headed out.

The ride to Failte took all of three minutes and they were early enough to get a parking spot right across the street. The lights Will had helped to hang right after Thanksgiving twinkled, reflecting off the snow and giving the house and front garden a magical, sparkly feel. She led the way up the front steps and into the foyer. Jazz played and a few people already gathered in the sitting room, sipping drinks.

Will took Darcy and Emerson's coats and pointed them toward the sitting room. She headed down the hall toward the closet just as Graham emerged from the kitchen.

"You're here." Graham's face lit up and she pulled Will, coats and all, into a hug.

"Wouldn't be anywhere else." Will returned the hug as best she could. If she could get half that enthusiasm from Nora, she'd be beside herself.

"Aunt Nora will be so happy. She was afraid you might not make it."

Will fought the urge to scowl. Why would Nora say that? Or think it? "Nowhere else I'd rather be."

Graham took the coats and hung them in the closet. "I'm going to push these to the back to make more room. That means you'll have to be the last to leave."

"Twist my arm."

Graham didn't twist, but she did link her arm through Will's for a second and give it a squeeze. "Let's get started with a cup of good cheer."

Graham led the way toward the dining room. Before Will could follow, Nora appeared in the hallway. She locked eyes with Will and stopped short. Like she was surprised Will was there. Or disappointed. "Hello."

Will offered a bright smile and tried not to stare at the way Nora's silvery blue dress made her look like a movie star. "Hi. Thank you so much for the invitation. You look fabulous."

Nora returned the smile, but Will couldn't help but feel like it was forced. She squared her shoulders, determined to have a good time. And hopefully the party vibe might help Nora relax a little. Although, since she was the host, that wasn't likely. "Thank you for coming. Did you bring your sister?"

Will nodded. "She and Darcy are in the sitting room. It was so generous of you to invite them as well."

Nora's features softened. Was it the mention of Emerson, or the compliment about being a generous host? "I'm looking forward to meeting them."

"I may have told Darcy about your lobster bisque. Be warned that she might try to sweet talk the recipe out of you."

Nora smiled then, a real and genuine smile. Why couldn't Will inspire that? "Perhaps she and I could trade secrets."

Will swallowed. Although there was nothing suggestive or sexual about Nora's comment, she couldn't stop her mind from going there. She forced away the thought of sharing a different kind of secret with Nora. "I'm sure she'd be open to a barter."

The front door opened and more guests arrived. Nora excused herself to greet them. Will headed to the dining room to find Graham. She'd expected an impressive spread, but this exceeded even her imagination. "Wow."

Graham laughed. "Are you really still surprised?"

Will chuckled in return. "I shouldn't be."

Graham poured wine and they rejoined Emerson and Darcy, who'd found drinks and claimed a spot near the window with Lia and Alex. Will kissed Lia lightly on the cheek and extended a hand to Alex. "It's good to see you again."

"Likewise," Alex said.

"We were just congratulating them," Darcy said with a wide smile.

"On?" Will looked at Lia and Alex, who seemed to be bubbling with happiness.

Lia patted her stomach. "Starting a family."

"Oh, my God. Congratulations." Even without being close to them, Will's heart filled with joy. Before moving to Provincetown, so few of her friends were lesbian. To have not just lesbians, but lesbian couples and families around every turn made her happy.

Alex and Lia got pulled away, leaving Will and Graham with Emerson and Darcy. "Are you two going to have more kids?" Graham asked.

Will watched the unspoken exchange between her sister and Darcy. Eventually, Darcy lifted a shoulder and smiled. "It's not off the table, but we're focusing on one thing at a time."

Emerson slid a hand around her waist. "What she said. I think I have to convince her to marry me first."

Graham sighed. "I can't wait to fall in love."

Will nodded. "You and me both."

Conversation turned from love to Graham's return to school, projects at Emerson and Darcy's house, and other things. Each time there was a lull, or anytime she thought no one would catch her, she looked around in search of Nora. With seemingly no effort, Nora worked the rooms. She laughed and talked and touched people on the arm or shoulder. She refilled glasses and opened bottles of wine. On more than one occasion, she vanished into the kitchen, only to reappear moments later with another tray of food. She never broke a sweat.

At one point, she drifted over to their little group. She graciously accepted compliments, waved off offers of help, and negotiated a recipe trade with Darcy. Everything about the conversation was easy and light. Nothing like Will's attempts to chat up Nora one on one. But it was hard to be bothered about anything when Nora smiled and laughed and, once, rested her hand on Will's arm as she made a point. No, Will could think of nothing but how she might get more of this Nora.

But even as she reveled in it, Will knew Nora wouldn't linger. Will watched as she kept one eye on the door. The moment it opened for a batch of new arrivals, Nora excused herself.

After greeting friends from one of the real estate offices in town, Nora continued to circulate. She'd enjoyed talking with Emerson and Darcy more than she'd expected. Whether it was their work or Darcy's son, they seemed older to her, more settled. She could have sworn Graham told her Will was the older of the two, but she must be mistaken. Of course, in the context of that conversation, Will had been perfectly fine—witty, easy to talk to even.

Nora uncorked another bottle of Cabernet and let her gaze wander. Like a magnet, it went right to Will. Will caught her eye and smiled. God, she had a nice smile. Nora glanced away. When she looked again, Will's attention was directed at her sister. Nora gave herself permission to study her, just for a minute.

She certainly cleaned up nicely. The blue dress shirt made her eyes seem even more blue. The gunmetal gray tie matched her pants and made her look far more grownup than Nora had come to think of her. If she didn't know better, if Will wasn't friends with Graham and had simply showed up at her party, Nora might be tempted to indulge in a little flirtation. The kind that would make Tisha proud.

Nora shook her head. Her imagination was getting the better of her. After she'd ensured the food didn't need replenishing, she made a point of moving out of Will's line of vision. Or maybe more accurately, making sure Will was out of hers.

Shortly before midnight, Nora weaved her way through the downstairs rooms with glasses of champagne. When she was confident everyone had something to toast with, she climbed the first couple of stairs and called for everyone's attention. All eyes turned toward her. After checking her watch, she started the countdown. She called out thirty seconds, then twenty. At ten, everyone joined in. She returned to the main floor just as calls of "Happy New Year" filled the room.

Cheers went up. A few people had come with noisemakers. She watched friends and couples embrace, friendly kisses and some with a bit more heat behind them. She watched Will kiss Graham on the cheek and felt a wave of relief that it looked nothing more than platonic.

She exchanged hugs and friendly kisses with Martha and Heidi, then Graham. As she turned away from Graham, Nora found herself face to face with Will. She saw the surprise she felt mirrored in Will's eyes. But more than that, she saw something more. Desire? Was that possible? Nora's pulse ratcheted up.

Will smiled. "Happy New Year."

Every other person in the house melted away. It was her and Will and a shimmery aura of potential. Nora leaned in and, for a second, thought Will would kiss her. Really kiss her. In that second, Nora realized how badly she wanted her to.

But as quickly as the moment came, it vanished. Will kissed her lightly on the cheek, just as she had done with Graham. Relief and disappointment coursed through her, along with a jolt of electricity. Although brief—and in no way sexual—the contact made her heart thud in her chest and left her lightheaded.

Nora grasped the banister and tried to get her bearings. She just needed a minute to collect herself. Fortunately, everyone seemed caught up in the celebrations. She escaped to the kitchen.

Once alone, she was able to take a few deep breaths. She held onto the counter and closed her eyes. Slowly, the dizziness faded.

"Are you okay?"

Nora opened her eyes to find Martha standing in the doorway, concern etched on her face. "I'm fine."

"You don't look fine. You're all flushed. And I saw you book it in here like something was on fire."

Damn it. "I felt a little overheated. All the people, I think. And the champagne."

"In all the years I've known you, you've never been a very convincing liar. You should give it up."

In spite of being cornered, Nora laughed. "And in all the years I've known you, you've been a know-it-all."

"I don't know all, but I do know you. What's up?"

Nora pressed the back of her hand to her cheek, trying to will away the flush she knew was there. "Nothing serious or bad, I promise. Can we leave it at that for now?"

Martha studied her for a moment. "If you promise to fill me in later. The fact that something's affected you, and you don't want to talk about it, makes it important enough to tell your best friend."

She had a point. Had the tables been turned, Nora would have felt the same. "That's fair. At the moment, I have a house full of guests and I need to get back to them."

Martha pushed open the swinging door and made a flourish with her arm. "By all means, madam hostess."

In the few minutes she'd been gone, several of those guests had started collecting their coats. Nora stationed herself by the door to thank people for coming and wish them a good night. Among those leaving were Emerson and Darcy, but Will wasn't with them. Nora resisted the urge to look for her among the remaining guests.

By one, nearly everyone had left or, in the case of her overnight guests, retired to their rooms. She didn't mind. It was hours past most of her friends' bedtimes. Hers as well.

Martha and Heidi lingered at the door and seemed to be the last to depart, except for the fact she still hadn't seen Will. Would she leave without saying goodbye? Rude, but maybe for the best.

"Bridge next week, yes?" Heidi asked.

"At your place. I'll be there."

"And you'll spill," Martha said.

Heidi raised a brow. "Spill what?"

"Nothing." Nora rolled her eyes. "Your wife exaggerates."

Martha huffed. "We'll see about that."

They left and Nora looked around. No sign of Graham. She wondered if she and Will had sneaked off somewhere. Instantly perturbed, Nora squared her shoulders and headed to the kitchen. She'd work off a little of her annoyance before bed and make a dent in the cleanup. It would make breakfast service in the morning easier anyway.

She stopped in her room long enough to slip out of her shoes and dress. She changed into a work shirt and capris, along with mules she wore around the house. When she stepped into the kitchen a moment later, she found Graham and Will side by side at the sink.

"What are you two doing?"

They turned in unison. "Dishes," Graham said.

"I can see that. Perhaps a more appropriate question is why."

Will smiled at her and Nora experienced an echo of the feeling she got when Will had kissed her earlier. "You threw an amazing party. We wanted to show our appreciation."

She would have expected as much from Graham. Nora wondered if Will had expressed interest in cleanup duty or if she'd been roped in. "Really, a thank you would have sufficed. You're still wearing your nice clothes."

Will shrugged. "We borrowed a couple of aprons. Now, are you going to keep giving us a hard time or put things away as we wash and dry?"

Will's tone seemed mildly flirtatious. Nora tried not to fixate on it. "I'll put things away. I'll also find a way to thank you both for doing all this work you didn't need to do."

"Um, you've put a roof over my head for six months. I think I'm the one who owes you." Graham finished drying a punch bowl and handed it to her.

Nora took it into the dining room and tucked it into the china cabinet in the corner. It was one thing for Graham to say that, but what about Will? What was her angle? She returned to the kitchen and started putting away the platters Graham had stacked.

"And you've given me a job," Will said, as though reading Nora's mind. "I feel like you took a chance on me and I appreciate it."

That was true, but probably not for the reasons Will thought. "You've earned every dollar I've paid you. In fact, I'll pay you for tonight as well."

Will smiled at her again. Again, it gave Nora a flutter of something she'd rather not think about. "Absolutely not. This is strictly volunteer."

Nora stopped trying to reason or argue with both of them. She focused on getting her kitchen, as well as the dining room, back in order. In between putting away bowls and platters, she cleared the few remaining plates and glasses from the rest of the downstairs. In less than an hour, they were done. "I still feel badly that you did all this work, but I'm grateful."

Graham draped an arm over her shoulder. "We were more than happy to help. Now you get to sleep for three whole hours before you start up again."

"You have to get up in three hours?" Will seemed horrified by the idea.

"I've got three couples who'll be expecting breakfast. I'll probably sneak in a nap tomorrow afternoon. It's the one day a year it feels justified."

Will's face relaxed, but she still didn't seem satisfied. "Can I help? I could crash on a sofa for a couple of hours and be good to go."

The eagerness in her voice, and the sincerity, softened Nora. "Really, you've done enough."

"Unless," Graham removed her arm from Nora's shoulder and went over to bump Will's, "you're simply angling to stay over. I know you rode over with Emerson and Darcy."

"I…"

The look of discomfort on Will's face softened her further. "You are most welcome to stay. I can even offer you a bed." The subtext of Nora's words hit her and she continued. "The room next to Graham's is empty. Please, take it. It's the least I can offer."

"Stay." Graham nudged Will again. "You can help with breakfast then go tromping out in the snow."

"You can have breakfast," Nora amended. "No help required."

Will seemed to think on it for a moment. "I would never pass up an opportunity to spend the night at Failte." Then she smiled. It held the same confidence as when she'd talked about building things—charming and dangerous as hell.

Nora swallowed. What had gotten into her? She nodded briskly, afraid her thoughts might be showing on her face. "Excellent. Graham, will you show Will where everything is? Both of you feel free to sleep in tomorrow. Thank you for everything."

Nora took one final look around the kitchen, nodded, then headed to her room. Will watched her leave, then turned her attention to Graham. "Thanks for scoring me a sleepover."

Graham shrugged. "The room's empty. And you really shouldn't have to walk home at two in the morning."

"Without boots."

"Especially without boots." Graham led the way to a bedroom off the main hall by the stairs. She opened the door and bowed. "After you."

Will entered the room as Graham flipped on a light. It was close to twice the size of Graham's room, with a four-poster bed, an antique dresser, and a plush chair in the corner. "I don't think I've ever slept in a room this nice."

"Wait till you feel the mattress." Graham walked past her and undid a latch on a door. "I'll be right back."

Graham left the room, leaving Will to wonder where she'd gone. A minute later, Will heard a clicking sound and the door Graham had unlatched opened. "Hi."

"Ah. I get it."

"Aunt Nora installed locks on both sides when I came for the summer. She didn't want guests to think someone might have access to their room."

"Or you to worry about curious or confused people stumbling into yours." It was kind of a genius setup.

"Exactly. You want something to sleep in?"

Sleeping naked probably wasn't advisable, so Will nodded. "That would be great."

Graham disappeared again and returned with a pair of sweatpants and a shirt that had Chatham written on it in the shape of a shark. "This is the most boyish thing I have."

Will smiled. "It's perfect. Thank you."

Will took the clothes, but Graham didn't step back. They stood like that for a moment, neither of them speaking. Will tried to think of something funny that would break the awkwardness that seemed to be growing by the second. Before she could, Graham came even closer. Will knew what was coming, knew she needed to prevent it. She froze.

The press of Graham's lips, soft and tasting lightly of champagne, jerked her back to her senses. She pulled away. "Graham."

Graham's eyes opened. Surprise quickly morphed into embarrassment. "I'm sorry."

Will pushed through her own surprise and mustered a smile. "Don't apologize. Please."

Graham shook her head. "I am, though. I don't know where that came from."

Will wanted to believe her. It was much easier than—and far preferable to—any other explanation. "New Year's can do that to a person."

Graham smiled brightly. "Exactly."

"So, we're cool?"

"Totally cool." Graham backed away in the direction of her room. "Do you need anything else?"

Will didn't want to make things weirder by asking Graham if she was sure she was okay. Instead, she offered a smile. "I'm good. I'm sure I'll be out the second my head hits the pillow."

"Okay. Cool." Graham nodded vigorously. "Night."

"Night." Graham closed the door.

Will waited ten seconds in case she came back. When she didn't, Will undressed and put on the T-shirt. She eyed the sweatpants, then pulled back the covers and brought them into the bed with her. That way, she could get them on quickly if she needed to. She settled herself in and felt the mattress mold to the shape of her body.

Oh. It was nice. She could definitely get used to this.

She realized the overhead light was still on, so she got out of bed, flipped it off, and got back in. Better.

Will sighed into the darkness. Despite telling Graham she'd fall right asleep, she took a moment to process her night. Starting with that weird kiss. Will didn't know exactly how much Graham had to drink, but she'd probably gotten at least a little bit buzzed. Will didn't judge. She'd had plenty of her own ill-advised advances after one too many beers, especially in her twenties. Hopefully, everything would be normal by morning. And hopefully, Graham wouldn't be nursing too terrible a hangover.

Feeling like the matter was settled, she turned her thoughts to the party itself. It had been great—sophisticated without being stuffy. Exactly the kind of party she wanted to throw with Kai. Only Kai got so stressed about everything being perfect and they would end up having a huge fight before the guests arrived and it would put a damper on the whole evening. Nora struck her as a perfectionist, but not someone who lost her cool on a regular basis.

Of course, she'd seemed a little flustered when Will wished her a happy new year. Which was odd considering Will had simply kissed her on the cheek. Oh, she'd wanted to do more. It had taken every bit of self-restraint she could muster not to bury her hands in Nora's hair and pull her close and...

Will coughed. Even though she was alone, something about having those kinds of thoughts about Nora in a bed in Nora's house made her feel weird. Like she was being too forward, or somehow disrespectful.

She chuckled at her strange sense of propriety. Emerson had accused her of being chivalrous. She'd also accused Will of letting that sense of chivalry lead her into bad situations, accept things that were otherwise unacceptable. Will didn't like to think of it that way, but it certainly played into how out of hand things got with Kai.

Although no one was in the room to see her, Will shook her head. Kai was behind her. In front of her, Nora. Whether or not things with Nora went anywhere, thinking about her was a much better way to spend her time. She closed her eyes and thought about the smoothness of Nora's skin and the subtle fragrance of her perfume when Will got close to her. She thought about what it would have been like to slide a hand around her waist. Respectfully, of course.

Those were the thoughts she took with her as she drifted off to sleep.

CHAPTER TEN

After New Year's, Graham had only a few days before heading back to school for her final semester. Nora helped her pack, including a couple of boxes that would need to be shipped. She'd miss her, but Nora was proud of her for finishing a master's degree. Hopefully, she'd find a job that kept her on the East Coast, so their visits would be sporadic and not nonexistent. As they drove along Route 6 to Boston, Nora kept those thoughts to herself. As much as she might like to have Graham close, she wanted her to end up wherever she had the best opportunity.

Graham, who'd been surprisingly quiet for the first half of the drive, turned to her. "You should hire Will to help out."

Nora took her eyes off the road long enough to give Graham a bland stare. "Really?"

Graham folded her arms in exasperation. "Are you trying to tell me you're unhappy with the work she's done already?"

Nora sighed. "She's done very good work."

"Exactly. We didn't even get to all the painting. I know you have more you want done. And you yourself said January is dead."

"I know." She couldn't admit that the prospect of spending time alone with Will left her uncomfortable. At least not out loud. She'd come to terms with the fact that she both found Will attractive and didn't trust her. Saying as much to Graham would only make matters worse.

"What? I can see the wheels in your head turning."

"Maybe you're right." The words were out of her mouth before she could stop them.

Graham narrowed her eyes. "Right about what?"

"Right about taking Will on. I'd hoped to get all the painting done, but with help, I might be able to refinish the stairs, too." In explaining to Graham, Nora convinced herself it was true. She wanted the work done, after all. And she certainly had the self-restraint not to do anything stupid.

Graham beamed. "See? It would be great to take care of all of that while things are quiet."

Nora nodded. "You give me her number and I'll reach out to her tomorrow."

"I'll do you one better." Graham pulled out her phone.

"Don't call her now."

"I'm just sending her a quick text. Give her a heads up."

"Just send me her number. I'm capable of sending a text." Nora returned her attention to the road and hoped she wasn't making a mistake.

Graham rolled her eyes. "Fine. It's not like I won't text her about something else anyway."

"I wish you weren't so attached to her," Nora couldn't help saying.

"Why not? She's a great person."

Nora fell back on her initial assessment, although it felt less and less accurate. Or fair. "She's a person who's a lot older and yet a lot less settled than you. I worry she might take advantage of you."

Nora glanced at Graham, who rolled her eyes dramatically. "I wish."

"Graham."

"I'm serious. She's hot. And sweet and funny. She could take advantage of me any day of the week." Graham huffed out a sigh. "Not that she's interested."

Nora had no intention of acting on her own attraction, but Graham's comment was like a giant bucket of ice water to the face. And to her libido. Which was probably for the best. "You can do better than her."

"I don't know why you would say that." Graham crossed her arms defiantly. "You're worse than my mother."

She hadn't meant to sound so callous, or to start an argument. Nor did she want Graham leaving on a sour note. "I'm sorry. I just think you're a very special person and you deserve someone who is smart and ambitious and will worship the ground you walk on."

That seemed only to make her pout more. "You talk like I'm some kind of precious thing. I'm not."

"That's not what I meant." Nora floundered for an exit strategy.

"I'm a woman, just like you. And I want to be wanted, not worshiped." Graham turned in her seat and fixed Nora with an intense stare. "Don't you?"

If there was one thing she wanted to talk about less than Graham's love life, it was her own. "Not high on my list these days."

"Maybe it should be."

Nora laughed at the absurdity of Graham's assertion. "I appreciate the sentiment, but I think I'm okay."

"You're great. That doesn't mean you don't deserve a girlfriend. Or at least an affair."

"Margaret Graham Connor, bite your tongue."

"Nora Bridget Calhoun." Graham made a show of sticking out her tongue, then biting it. "I'm still right."

As much as she might not want to have this conversation, it broke the tension that had threatened to take over their final hour together. She could put up with a little teasing for a worthy cause.

At Logan, Graham waved off her offer to park and go into the terminal with her. "I'm fine. I'll call you when I land."

Graham hugged her and Nora allowed herself to hold on for an extra moment. "It's been wonderful having you here these few months. I'm going to miss you."

When Graham pulled back, her eyes were glassy with tears. "Me, too. Thank you for everything."

Nora squeezed Graham again, then hurried back into her car. Graham offered a wave and hustled into the terminal out of the cold. On the drive home, Nora tried not to think about how empty the house would be. On one hand, she looked forward to the quiet of January and February. It was the only time of year she had whole stretches with no guests to tend. And as much as she loved her work, there was something magical about taking long baths, drinking coffee in the library in her robe, and eating grilled cheese and tomato soup for days on end.

But for the first time in as long as she could remember, Nora wasn't looking forward to it. The prospect of so much alone time made her lonely. Ridiculous. Given her line of work, alone time was the closest thing she got to vacation. She refused to be mopey about it.

Then again, maybe she'd have less alone time than usual. The prospect of having Will around—without Graham—gave Nora a feeling of uneasy anticipation. She might cling to the notion that her only interest in Will was the work she'd do, but in the car, alone with her own thoughts, she knew better. Even as she admitted it to herself, Nora brushed it aside. She was perfectly content with her life exactly as it was. Even if the list of people thinking she needed to have an affair—Tisha, Martha, now Graham—continued to grow.

On a matter of principle, she stopped by the little gourmet market before heading home. She picked up some nice cheese and a baguette, some olive tapenade and a bar of chocolate with sea salt. She was going to go home, open a bottle of wine, and have a nice dinner in front of the fire.

When she got home, Nora did just that. She lit a fire and a couple of candles, opened a bottle of Bordeaux she would normally reserve for guests, and made a little picnic for herself. She ate dinner curled up on the sofa and refused to feel anything but content. Instead of heading to her room, she topped off her wine and went upstairs to the master suite. She'd indulged in a king-size bed for the space, a relative rarity in a P-town inn, but had not ever used it herself. Tonight, that would change.

She smiled at it on the way to the bathroom, where she drew herself a bath in the antique claw foot tub. She slid into the hot, sudsy water and sighed. Why didn't she do this anytime she had an empty house?

Nora pulled herself out before the water had a chance to grow cold. After toweling off, she picked up her nightgown. It was halfway over head when she paused. When was the last time she slept in the nude? Not being able to answer meant she was clearly overdue. She padded into the bedroom naked, peeled back the duvet and the crisp white sheets, and slipped in.

Heaven.

Or, it was heaven until Will's face popped into her mind. No, that wasn't entirely accurate. She had Will's face in her mind, but also the rest of her. Strong, dexterous hands. Narrow hips. Small, firm breasts.

Nora shook her head into her pillow. She had no idea whether Will's breasts were firm. And she had no business imagining one way or the other. Or wondering how it would feel to have Will's body pressing her into the mattress.

Nora huffed and turned onto her side. Clearly, she'd been celibate for too long. That had to be it. Will just happened to be the most attractive woman she'd seen in a while. She couldn't begrudge her imagination for working with what it had.

Nora rolled onto her back. What would it feel like? She pressed the palms of her hands to her breasts. As her nipples began to harden, she wondered if Will's hands would be rough. Probably. The idea sent ripples of desire down her spine. She sighed, shifting her hands so that she could roll her nipples between her fingers. She pinched and tugged, imagining Will above her, teasing her with tongue and teeth.

What would it be like?

By the time she ran a hand down her side and between her legs, Nora was slick with arousal. She slid one, then two, fingers up and down, grazing her clit each time. She lifted her knees and opened herself a little wider. Wide enough for Will to settle between her thighs. When she eased her fingers into herself, she moaned. She closed her eyes tighter and bit her lip. Will's face remained in her mind, a look of fierce concentration etched into her features.

Nora's hips rose to meet her hand. Her thrusts became harder and faster and she pushed herself toward release. The familiar pressure began to build. God, she hadn't come in so long. Just a little bit more and she'd be there.

The orgasm crashed over her. Nora groaned under the intensity of it. Her whole body quaked.

When she finally came down, she was breathless. Her muscles felt weak and trembly. She lay there for a long time, letting her body shiver with the aftershocks.

Her pulse slowly returned to normal; her breathing steadied. Although her body was relaxed, her mind raced. She might tell herself it was a natural—overdue, even—release that her body needed. But she knew better. Will had stirred things in her that had long been dormant. And even if she felt a moment of satisfaction now, she'd awakened something with a far bigger appetite. An appetite she couldn't possibly indulge.

She turned the worry over and over in her mind, willing a solution to come. Normally, doing so would keep her up half the night. But between the wine and the bath, not to mention the orgasm, her body had other ideas. She drifted off in a matter of minutes.

Nora woke, surprised it was light out. She didn't remember falling asleep, nor did she stir even once during the night. She couldn't remember the last time she'd slept so well. She stretched, enjoying how loose her muscles felt. And then she remembered what she'd been doing before she fell asleep.

What had felt brazen the night before made her sheepish in the light of day. Not that she'd ever feel shame for touching herself—she was far too liberated for that. But how it had come about. How much thoughts of Will had been a part of it. What the hell was wrong with her?

Nora stared up at the ceiling. It was fine. It didn't matter. It wasn't like Will, or anyone else, knew what passed through her mind. And it had been ages since she'd felt compelled to take care of herself in that way. If anything, she should make a point of doing it more often. That way, it wouldn't feel so significant.

Feeling like she'd settled things, she climbed out of bed. She needed to strip the bed, but that could wait until she'd had a cup of coffee. She caught a glimpse of her naked self in the mirror. And put on some clothes.

After coffee and breakfast, she got to work. She spent a couple of hours getting the suite and a second room ready for the guests she had coming in that afternoon, another hour at her desk paying bills and planning upcoming menus. By then, it was time to get ready for happy hour. With only four people staying, she opted for some goat cheese tarts that were a bit fussier than her usual fare. She put a bottle of Chardonnay on ice and set out a bottle of Syrah for anyone who wanted red.

Despite the self-imposed business, her mind had continued to wander to Will and to Will's inexplicable hold on her imagination. The first couple arrived around four and the second shortly after. She got them situated with keys and information, then sent them to get settled and freshen up. She got a fire going in the sitting room and arranged the snacks and drinks on the table under the window. It didn't take long for the room to fill with laughter and conversation. The two couples—both pairs of middle-aged lesbians—hit it off right away. Nora was happy to not be needed to keep the conversation going.

She almost accepted an invite to join the women for a walk down Commercial Street and dinner. But that was one boundary she liked to keep between herself and her guests. Holding on to it seemed important all of a sudden.

With the house momentarily empty, Nora made herself a light dinner and returned to her desk. Before turning to her computer, she picked up her phone and found a text message from Graham.

Miss you already. I might have to come for spring break. Have you talked to Will?

Nora drummed her fingers on the desk. Part of her wanted to wash her hands of Will altogether. But doing so felt like defeat. In addition to having Graham harangue her, she'd have to figure out how to do her remaining winter projects without help. On top of that, she had a nagging feeling that, when it came to Will, out of sight would not equal out of mind. She copied the number Graham had sent her into a new message. *Graham tells me you might be interested in some additional work over the next couple of months.*

She returned to her conversation with Graham, assuring her she had reached out to Will and would keep her posted. Before she hit send on that message, she had a reply from Will.

Absolutely. I have a few other projects, but my schedule is flexible. Let me know what works best for you.

Nora shook her head. Responsive and professional. That mattered far more than the way work pants hung on her hips or the way she always left Nora wondering whether or not they were flirting.

She arranged to meet Will late Monday morning. The inn would be empty for three days and they could decide what could be accomplished in the time they had. The exchange left her feeling almost giddy. In response, Nora pulled out a notebook to make a wish list of projects—shampooing the rugs, refinishing the stairs, and maybe even installing shelves in the linen closet. That, she told herself firmly, was something to be giddy about.

CHAPTER ELEVEN

Will was wide awake by five a.m. It seemed, even with nowhere to be until ten, her internal alarm clock remained consistent. It didn't help that her mind was running six ways from Sunday with thoughts of Nora. Will was equal parts excited and nervous to see her. The fact that Graham would no longer be part of their interactions made her wonder. Would things between them be flirty? Or would they be awkward?

She needed to make a good enough impression that Nora would take her on. The coolness of their first few meetings had faded, but Will still didn't know how to read what felt a lot like sexual chemistry between them. Not to mention the fact she remained unconvinced that Nora fully liked her. Yet.

Thinking about how to take their interactions to the next level occupied Will while she took a shower and considered her closet. She didn't want to look like she was trying, but she did want to impress. She settled on gray pants and a maroon sweater with a plaid oxford underneath, then spent a little more time than usual on her hair. Not that it would survive the twenty-minute walk under a knit hat, but still.

When she emerged from her room, she found Kaylee standing in the kitchen with a cup of coffee. She was already dressed in scrubs for work. "Don't you look fancy," she said.

Will frowned. "Really? I was hoping for casually polished."

Kaylee grinned. "That, too. Fancy is a relative term. I usually see you in jeans and flannel."

"Okay." That made her feel slightly better. "I think."

"What's the occasion?"

"I have a job interview. Well, sort of. You know that B&B Graham's aunt owns?"

"Yeah. You did some work there before Christmas."

"Graham went back to school last week, but her aunt asked if I might be interested in some other projects. I'm meeting her this morning to talk about it."

"Cool."

"So this isn't too much?" Will moved her hand up and down to signal her outfit.

"Definitely not."

Will didn't mention her desire to look nice for Nora. "Thanks. So, you're early shift today?"

Kaylee nodded. "All week, in fact. It's so civilized."

Will walked over to the coffeepot to pour herself a cup. "Nice."

"I'll make dinner tonight if you'll be home."

Will inhaled the aroma of the coffee before taking a sip. "If you're making dinner, I'll make a point of being home."

"Requests?"

"Chef's choice." Will was a decent cook, but Kaylee had far more talent. Unfortunately, her schedule often prevented her from doing much with it.

Kaylee set her cup in the sink, then went to the rack by the door to pull on all her winter gear. "I'll stop at the store after work."

"And I will do the dishes and love you forever."

"Good luck with the pseudo interview." Kaylee opened the door. A gust of frigid air whipped in, along with a little bit of snow. "God, I hate winter. See you tonight."

"Bye." Will didn't relish going out in that either, but at least she had a good reason. She refilled her coffee, then grabbed the last packet of Pop-Tarts from the cabinet. Kaylee had convinced her to give them up as a New Year's resolution. Whether or not she kept it remained to be seen, but Will made a point of savoring them in case they were in fact her last.

With time to kill before she needed to be at Nora's, Will opened her laptop. She had no idea what kind of work Nora would have in mind, but it never hurt to go in with some ideas. Since Darcy had introduced her to Pinterest, it was now her go-to for random ideas. Even if Emerson made fun of her for it. She pinned a bar of hooks made out of old keys and another made from door knobs. She also searched for shelves and storage cubbies for closets and other small spaces. For some reason, she thought Nora would appreciate anything that made her life tidier.

That was one of the things about Nora she found most attractive. She loved how in control Nora seemed—of all aspects of her life. Will liked the order and wanted to be part of it. But she also wanted to muss her up a little, tempt Nora into being carefree. She wondered for the millionth time whether Nora could, in fact, be tempted.

When it was time to go, Will bundled into her heaviest coat. She added a hat and scarf, then pulled on her winter boots and a pair of gloves. She opened the door and blinked against the biting wind. Her thoughts echoed Kaylee's comment. She hated winter.

Nora heard stomping on the porch and figured it must be Will. She headed to the front of the house and, sure enough, Will was stepping over the threshold into the foyer. She took off her hat and shook her hair. "Good morning."

"Good morning. I didn't realize it was so bad out."

"More wind than snow." Will stuffed her hat and gloves into her coat pockets and bent over to untie her boots. "You don't mind me in socks, do you?"

Nora appreciated that Will would take off her boots. "Of course not. Let me take your coat."

"Thanks. And thanks for reaching out."

Nora hung the coat. "I made fresh coffee and I've got some pastries leftover from earlier. Can I interest you in either?"

"Yes, but only if you promise not to judge me for eating two breakfasts." Will flashed a smile that was more playful than concerned.

"Never." Nora led the way to the dining room, ignoring that flush of warmth that had filled her cheeks. She poured two cups and gestured to the platter on the buffet. "Help yourself."

Will put a Danish on a saucer and joined Nora at the table. "If I had this in the house every day, I'd weigh a thousand pounds."

Nora smiled. "I indulge, but in moderation."

Will quirked a brow. "Why do I get the feeling you're talking about more than pastries?"

Okay, this definitely felt like flirtation. And heaven help her, she liked it. Nora swallowed. "A good rule to live by, I'd say."

"Agreed." Will's eyes remained playful.

They needed to get down to business before she embarrassed herself. "So, there is one more room I'd love to get painted."

Will pulled a tiny composition book from her pocket, along with a pen. She opened it to a blank page and jotted a few words. "Okay, that's doable."

"I've also been planning to refinish the stairs."

Will nodded. "I'll be honest, I haven't done that before. I do know my way around a sander, though, and I've worked with both oil and water-based stains."

"That's good enough for me. I was around when the floors were last done. I didn't do the work, but I asked a lot of questions for future reference."

"Great. Anything else?"

"Do you build? I want to put some shelving in the laundry room and maybe a closet."

Will's eyes lit up. "It's funny you should say that. I was looking at some storage solutions online this morning."

"Storage solutions?"

Will shrugged sheepishly. "I worked at a big box store. I may have soaked up the lingo."

"Right. Well, I've eyed some of those systems, but I never could justify the cost."

"There are some really cool things you can put together yourself that are much less expensive." Will took out her phone and, after a few taps, flashed the screen at Nora. "Things like this."

The photo was of a linen closet, beautifully organized with shelves, dividers, and bins. "You can do that?"

"It's a lot easier than it looks, especially if you install it directly into the closet."

Nora imagined her hopelessly full linen closet upstairs. Part of the problem was that she kept too much in it, but the other was that she'd haphazardly crammed a small bookshelf into it to act as shelves, which resulted in a lot of wasted space. "I love it."

"I hoped you would."

Will had spent time thinking about her—her inn, at least—ahead of time. Nora turned that over in her mind, unsure of what to make of it. "It sounds like we've got more than enough work to get you started, then. Let's talk payment."

Will sat up a little straighter. "I'm happy to do it by the project or by the hour. Whatever you're more comfortable with."

She'd seen Will work enough to know that she didn't dawdle. "Let's say the hour, then. I'd rather things be done well than quickly."

Will nodded. "Sounds good."

"I still have guests most weekends, so weekdays are best for me. And we'll have to plan so that most messes can be cleaned up or hidden by Friday afternoons. Does that work for you?"

"I'm doing a few things at The Flour Pot on Mondays when they're closed, but that's my only scheduled thing. I've also got some projects at Emerson's place, but the timing there is flexible."

For someone without steady employment for the off-season, Will came across as organized and hard-working. Again, Nora was struck with the notion she'd been too quick to judge her. "I'll prioritize what I want done and we can tackle one thing at a time. When are you available to start?"

Will smiled. "How's tomorrow?"

Again, Nora got the distinct feeling Will was flirting with her. And again, Nora had to admit, she rather liked it. Even if she didn't really play along, it didn't mean she had to shut Will down at every turn. There wasn't any harm in that, was there? "Perfect."

"I'm an early bird. What time is too early for you?"

Was that a challenge? "I'm up by five most days."

"Same. How's seven?" Will asked.

That was much earlier than she'd come when Graham was around. Interesting. "Fine by me. I'll provide coffee, but I only have pastries when there are guests."

"That's probably for the best. My roommate is a nurse and has decided I need to start drinking smoothies."

Nora laughed at that. She'd never joined the smoothie craze, but she understood it. "She probably has a point."

"We'll see. She said I could start without adding greens. I'm not even sure what she means by that."

"I have a feeling you'll find out." Did Will always have this sense of humor? Nora found herself wondering again about Will's age, among other things.

Will sighed dramatically, but gave Nora a look that said they were in on the joke together. "Anyway. While I'm here, do you want to show me the closet in question? I didn't bring a tape measure, but if I see how big it is, I can give you an idea of what's possible."

"Only if you promise not to laugh at what I have rigged up in there now."

"Your secrets are safe with me."

Will managed to make the statement seem suggestive. Instead of fighting the flutter, Nora enjoyed it. "I have a measuring tape if you'd like."

Will shook her head. "Let's take a look at it for now. Since I'm painting first, I'll have plenty of time to get exact measurements."

Nora led the way upstairs to the tiny hall closet. She opened the door and stepped back so Will could see. "You can be honest. I can take it."

"Oh, this isn't bad at all. I was expecting chaos."

Nora laughed, both relieved and charmed by Will's comment. "It's chaotic by my standards."

"From what I can tell, you've got some exceedingly high standards." Will looked at her in a way that made Nora think she wanted to kiss her.

Nora swallowed and took another step back. Surely, she was imagining things. She had to be. "So I've been told."

Will continued to look at her. Nora would swear Will was staring directly at her mouth. "I admire a woman who isn't afraid to know what she wants."

Nora licked her lips. Her throat was suddenly parched. She needed to break this weird tension suddenly between them. Even if she was the only one who felt it, she was afraid something was about to happen. Something that would put a crack in the invisible boundary she needed to maintain. "I'm glad you don't think I'm too fussy." Nora turned and walked down the hall and down the stairs. She figured Will would follow, but she didn't trust herself to look back. The uneven creaking behind her confirmed it.

"Not at all. I think we're good to go for now. I won't take any more of your time today."

Nora wondered if Will was in a hurry to leave or if she sensed the weird chemistry suddenly in the air. She walked Will to the door. "Thanks again for coming out in such bad weather."

"If I stayed home when it snowed, I wouldn't venture out until April. Or so people keep telling me."

"You have a point. Nonetheless, I appreciate it." There. That was nice, normal conversation.

Will finished lacing her boots and stood. "I'll see you in the morning."

"I'll look forward to it." It was the kind of thing she'd say anyway, but she meant it. Really meant it. She barely resisted shaking her head.

"Same here."

Will left and Nora remained standing in the front hall. What exactly had she just gotten herself into? She squared her shoulders. Nothing, or at least nothing more than she'd agreed to. It would be nice to have some projects done that didn't involve a whole crew or a massive drain on her savings. Her attraction to Will didn't have to change anything. Especially since Will would never know.

Nora considered going upstairs to prep the room about to be painted. Will could do it, but the less prep she had, the sooner she would finish and be able to start on other things. Since Nora was especially excited about the other things, she headed upstairs to get to work.

CHAPTER TWELVE

Will stepped off the ladder and surveyed her progress. She'd finished installing the braces for the inset shelves in the linen closet, but had decided to put a coat of white paint on everything before installing the actual shelves. Not a necessary step, but combined with the LED light she'd put above the door, the closet would feel bright and clean in addition to organized.

When she heard Nora on the stairs, she glanced at her watch and smiled. 12:30 on the dot. Time for lunch.

She didn't want to assume Nora would offer her lunch every day, but she was getting to the point of wondering why she bothered to stuff protein bars and apples in her bag each morning. She also didn't want to assume those lunches signified anything, but she had a hard time not reading meaning into their increasing number of shared meals. At the very least, they were getting to know one another better. Will hoped it might be more than that.

Although Nora didn't seem inclined to share many details of her personal life, she had opened up more than in the beginning. By the same token, the more she learned about Will, the less intent she seemed on maintaining a cool facade. That mattered. Will hated the idea of people disliking her. She went out of her way to be nice. But Will also had bigger plans. Well, if not plans, hopes. Despite assuring Emerson she wouldn't get in over her head, Will held onto a hope that she and Nora might have something more. Nora might not see it yet, but if she was growing to like Will, that certainly improved Will's chances.

"It looks like you're going to finish that this afternoon."

At the sound of Nora's voice, Will turned and smiled. "I think so."

Nora came up behind her for a closer look. "Is it wrong to be so excited about a closet?"

Will shook her head. "Not at all. Having things organized and tidy has a calming effect on the mind. Giving yourself ways of making that easier just makes sense."

Nora nodded. "That's a nice way of looking at it. Thanks."

"There is an entire industry built around storage solutions."

"Again, that sounds much more compelling than pretty closet shelves."

"Since I painted those pretty shelves yesterday, all I need to do is put a couple of coats of paint on the walls and braces and we can finish the installation."

Nora allowed herself to smile in anticipation. "It sounds like you're at a perfect stopping point for lunch."

Although tempted to say yes, Will wanted to get that first coat of paint on before taking a break so it would have a chance to dry. "I would love to join you, but I need about half an hour to get to a good stopping point. Will that work?"

Nora waved a hand. "I'm in no hurry. Come down whenever you're ready. I'll be in the kitchen."

"Sounds good. Thanks."

Nora headed downstairs and Will returned her attention to the closet. She popped the lid on the can of white enamel she used for the shelves and got to work. Because she'd painted the interior of the closet before, it only took about twenty minutes to paint the strips of wood she'd added and touch up the few spots she'd scuffed. She slid her brush into a plastic bag so it wouldn't dry out.

In the kitchen, she saw no sign of Nora. The island she usually used for food prep was completely covered in boxes and bags and cans of food. Several canisters in different sizes lined the counter. A moment later, Nora emerged from the pantry with her hands full. She added to the pile on the island and looked at Will. "Hi."

"I could help with that, you know."

"Oh, you're going to." Nora had a playful gleam in her eye. Will raised a brow. "How so?"

"Your comment about the closet got me to thinking about the pantry. I make a point of cleaning it out once a year, but I thought this might be the perfect time to implement—what did you call it?—a storage solution."

Will laughed, in part because she loved that Nora got excited about closet renovation. More than that, though, was Nora being playful. That had to be a good sign. "I think that sounds like a fine idea."

"Excellent. But first, lunch."

Will went to the sink to wash her hands. "I hope you don't feel obligated to feed me every day. Don't get me wrong, I love it. I just don't want you to feel obligated."

"There's always plenty." Nora turned away to take plates from the cupboard. With her back turned, she added, "And the company is nice."

Will wished she could see Nora's face. But even without it, she smiled. "I enjoy it, too."

As usual, they sat adjacent to one another at the table in the dining room. Nora had warmed up plates of shepherd's pie for them and Will was doing her best not to inhale hers. It required more restraint than she cared to admit.

"You have some paint in your hair."

Will looked up from her plate to find Nora studying her. Instinctively, she touched her fingers to her hair. Sure enough, she felt the roughness of dried paint on a patch of it near the front. "I should wear a hat."

"Other than winter hats, I don't think I have one I could lend you. I have some bandannas. You could use one as a kerchief."

Will laughed. "I appreciate the offer, but I'm not sure my butch sensibilities could handle a kerchief."

Nora laughed as well. "Fair enough."

"You have such a great laugh."

Nora raised a brow.

"I mean it. It's warm and authentic. I try to think of ways to inspire it without making a complete ass of myself." The words were out of Will's mouth before she'd thought about them. But she meant it and didn't regret saying so.

Nora's expression softened. "I guess I have a tendency to be serious."

"Have you always been that way?" Will meant the question in a lighthearted way, although she was curious as to how Nora would answer.

Nora furrowed her brow and frowned. "Mostly. I've always had goals and a pretty intense focus to accomplish them."

"Emerson was the same way. So determined. Such a rule follower." Even in Will's accomplished high school days, she'd done what came easy. Discipline had never been a virtue she could claim.

Nora tipped her head to the side. "There's something to be said for following the rules."

Will couldn't be sure, but she sensed a ruefulness in Nora's tone. It made Will want to erase all her worries, show her a more carefree way of being in the world. "There's also something to be said for throwing caution to the wind."

Nora smiled slightly, but her face reflected a deep sadness. "I tried that once and it did not end well."

"What happened?" Something told Will that if she knew the answer to that, she'd have the key to understanding how Nora worked.

Nora blinked a few times and her face changed. The vulnerability of a moment before vanished. In its place, the cool poise Will had come to know so well. "Just some foolishness on my part. It cost me dearly at the time, but I learned my lesson."

Will wanted desperately to know more. She decided to press her luck. "Foolishness can prove very seductive. I've had my fair share for sure, along with the consequences."

"Is that so?"

"Sure." She might not enjoy talking about Kai, but she figured she owed it to Nora to be honest. Besides, being open might make Nora more inclined to reciprocate. "I fell for a girl who made me feel like the center of the universe."

"Seductive indeed."

"Kai worshiped the ground I walked on. She made me feel like a hero—strong, handsome, like I could save the world."

"And then?"

Will sighed. "And then anytime she didn't feel like the only and absolute center of my universe, we fought."

"Ah. The jealous type."

"Yeah. At first it felt like a compliment. She thought I was so incredible that anyone who met me would be attracted to me."

"But?" Nora's face was kind, like she might already know the answer.

"But the compliments turned into accusations, and the accusations came with threats. At first, she'd pick fights, insist I was looking at another woman or flirting with customers at the store where I worked." Will swallowed, looked down at her hands. "After a while, the fights got physical."

"Oh, Will."

"Not abusive, or at least not like you're probably thinking."

Nora tried to keep her face calm. As far as she was concerned, physical fights were the definition of abuse. Not to mention the emotional abuse that came with that level of jealousy and possessiveness. Did Will not see that, or was she trying to downplay it now? "It sounds like her behavior crossed the line."

Will nodded. "It did. I mean, she hit me a couple of times. It didn't leave a mark, but I know that's unacceptable."

Unacceptable was putting it mildly. But if her own experience was anything to go on, indignation wouldn't make Will feel any better. Nora reached across the table and took her hand. "I'm so sorry."

"Thanks." Will nodded. "I won't excuse or condone her behavior, but part of it was my own doing. When it was good, it was really good. I stuck around longer than I should have."

"Don't feel badly. The pull of a charismatic personality is a powerful force."

"Isn't that the truth? So, what about you?"

Nora sat quietly. She'd told so few people about Jordyn. But Will had opened up about something just as painful. Even more, she talked about the decisions that got her there. Something about that resonated. Nora wanted to assure Will she wasn't alone in making bad choices. She took a deep breath. "I was swept off my feet, too. She was passionate and had a fiery temper. She made it seem like I was the best thing that ever happened to her and made me feel like, together, we could conquer the world."

"Until?" Will's face showed genuine concern, not a desire for a juicy story.

Nora pressed on. "Until she raided my bank account and vanished."

"Oh."

"I never saw or heard from her again." Even now, after all this time, it made her chest tighten to think about what she could have lost.

"Did you involve the police?"

Nora shook her head. "I'd put her on the account, so it would have been hard to make a case. And I was humiliated."

"What did you do?"

"I'd sunk almost everything into this place, so there wasn't all that much to steal. I borrowed some money from my sister to make ends meet, worked for two seasons without hiring any extra staff so I could pay her back."

"You could have given up, but you didn't. And look how far you've come."

Not wanting a shared moment to turn into pity, Nora lifted her chin and squared her shoulders. "And I do my best not to look back. Well, with the exception of remembering how foolish I was."

Will smiled. "It's good to remember. And to remember that one bad experience doesn't speak for all women, or all relationships."

Nora was less sure about that, but she didn't want to come across as bitter. "It's good that you haven't hardened your heart. It's easier said than done sometimes."

"Agreed. So…" Will trailed off, seeming to defer to Nora on where to take the conversation next.

Nora's mind churned with Will's disclosure, on top of the fact she'd just shared a part of her past she typically held close. She didn't like the swell of emotions, or the intimacy of this much sharing. She plastered a smile on her face and stood. "So, I'll let you get back to work."

Will's face reflected surprise at the abrupt shift. To her credit, she stood as well, and didn't press it. "Do you want me to look at the pantry now?"

Although it made sense, Nora needed a few minutes to collect herself. Alone. "I've still got plenty of cleaning to do. You go finish upstairs. We can talk whenever you're done."

"Okay. Did you decide on shelf liner? I can lay that for you once the shelves are in."

Nora could handle that herself, but giving it to Will would keep her busy a little longer. She picked up the bag full of rolls and handed it over. "That would be great. Thank you."

Will peered inside the bag. "Should only take a couple of hours."

"Let me know if you need anything."

"Of course."

Will smiled at her. Nora couldn't tell if it was encouraging or sympathetic. Neither sat well. She turned away and busied herself with picking up plates from the table. Will went back to work and Nora returned to the kitchen. She did the few dishes, then stood looking at the chaos of pantry items covering every available surface. She considered doing her usual cleaning and putting everything back. Suddenly, the idea of working in close quarters with Will on yet another project made her uneasy.

Why had she chosen to confide in Will? Will hadn't even pushed, really. She'd merely asked. And Nora answered like it was no big deal. Will had made it seem like no big deal.

Nora shook her head. Each day she spent with Will seemed to open a new door, shed light on another dim corner. She'd initially applied that analogy to learning more about Will, but it seemed to be working both ways. That should give her pause. But, in spite of herself, she wanted more and more to see where it would lead.

CHAPTER THIRTEEN

With the linen closet done, Nora had Will tackle the downstairs guest room next, figuring the stairs would require a solid week of not being used. Even with that large project remaining, she was pleasantly surprised by how much they— Will—had accomplished. Nora headed to the laundry room with a basket of towels, wondering if her room might deserve a fresh coat of paint, too.

As she walked past the basement stairs, the sound of running water made her pause. She looked down at the laundry in her hands. It was her first load of the day, so it couldn't be the washing machine. She set down the basket and opened the basement door. The sound grew louder. That couldn't be good.

She flipped on the light and started down the stairs. The sight of a puddle, rapidly inching toward her, stopped her in her tracks.

"Will?" After calling her name, Nora realized how much panic was in her voice.

She heard footsteps overhead. "Is something wrong?"

"There's water everywhere." Yep, panic.

Will came the rest of the way down and joined Nora on the small patch of floor that remained dry. "Do you know where it's coming from?"

Nora shook her head. She tried to channel the calm, logical part of her mind, but couldn't get it to work. "I have no idea."

Without waiting for Nora to say more, Will sloshed in. The water only came up the side of her work boots, but it didn't do anything to assuage Nora's anxiety. Her basement wasn't wet; it was flooded. No, flooding. Present tense. And she had no idea how to stop it.

"It looks like your water heater." Will had disappeared around a post, but her voice carried clearly to where Nora stood.

Nora braced herself and followed, trying to ignore the way water immediately soaked through her canvas house shoes. "The water heater? How do you know?"

She rounded the corner and saw Will on her hands and knees next to the water heater. Meanwhile, water poured out of the top of the tank. "If I can shut off the supply, it should stop."

How did she know that? And how was it she remained so level headed when water was gushing right above her head? "Okay. It's, um, I think the valve is behind there maybe?"

Will stood up. "I got it." She reached over and turned the knob located on the pipe coming out of the top of the tank. The water slowed to a trickle, then stopped.

"Oh." Why was Will on the floor, then?

"I just wanted to shut the gas off first. If there's any back flow of water into your gas line, you've got even more problems on your hands."

"Right." Again, how did she know that? "Um, thank you."

Will shook her head. "I stopped the water, but I haven't fixed the problem. Your water heater is toast."

Nora looked from Will to the tank, then back to Will. This time, curiosity won out. "How do you know?"

"Because this is almost always how they go."

"Hmm." The fact of it didn't surprise her. She hadn't replaced it when she bought the place and her inspector had indicated it was close to ten years old then. But she'd never experienced a blowout before. For not ever being a homeowner, Will seemed to know exactly what was going on and what to do about it. Nora realized, had Will not been there, she'd be standing in her even more flooded basement trying to Google how to make the water stop. "You stopped the flood. That counts as saving the day in my book."

Will smiled in that way she had—full of charm, but with a trace of shyness. Combined with her dirty hands and soaked pants, the result was enough to kick Nora's heart rate up a notch. No, it was the adrenaline of the last twenty minutes. Thinking about Will that way at a time like this was beyond ridiculous. Wasn't it? Nora realized Will said something and she'd missed it. "I'm sorry?"

"I said you're going to have to get someone to come in and replace it. That's far beyond my level of expertise."

"Oh, of course. I wouldn't expect you to." Nora could not stop staring at Will. Nor could she stop her mind from imagining what it would be like to peel off her wet clothes. Would she be soft underneath, or hard? Probably the perfect balance of the two. Nora swallowed. "I'll call a plumber."

"It's not an emergency, but you won't have hot water until you do. You can decide how urgent that is."

Nora laughed. "Pretty urgent, as far as I'm concerned. I'll go look up a number now. I…let me get you a towel."

"That would be great, thanks."

Nora led the way upstairs. She went into her linen closet and grabbed a couple of bath towels. She returned to find Will sitting on the stairs to the basement. "I'm just taking off my boots so I don't track water all over the place."

Nora looked down at her own feet. Soaked. And a trail of wet footprints leading down the hall. "Don't worry about it."

Will accepted the towel and started dabbing at her pants. "The least I can do is not drip."

Nora's shoulders slumped. "I'd offer you a shower, but without hot water, it seems rather cruel."

Will stood. "I'm okay."

"How about you let me throw your pants in the dryer at least. It should only take a little while to get them mostly dry."

"Um, sure."

The implication of her words hit her. "I didn't mean...I probably have a pair of sweatpants that would fit you."

Will grinned, then. Nora would have been hard pressed to classify it as anything but suggestive. She felt a sudden and compelling need to escape. "I'll be right back."

Nora fled to her room. She found a pair of light green joggers in the bottom drawer of her dresser. Not Will's style by any means, but she figured they'd do for the moment. She brought them out to where Will had been, but she was gone.

"In here." The voice came from the small powder room.

"Ah." The door opened a crack and Will's arm came out. Nora stepped close enough to hand her the pants. Through the opening, she caught a flash of leg and what appeared to be striped boy shorts. God, why did she have to look? "Here you go. Hand me your things and I'll get them going."

Will handed her the khaki work pants and a pair of very wet socks. "Thank you so much."

Grateful for another task, Nora went to the small laundry room off the kitchen. Although part of her wanted to wash them first, that would only prolong the time Will had to stay. And it was already getting late. She threw them in the dryer and set the timer. She then turned her attention to her phone and finding someone who would bring her a new water heater. She started with the company who'd installed her garbage disposal and replaced the kitchen faucet a few years prior. She dialed the number and said a prayer that they had an after-hours service.

"Richie's Plumbing, this is Shirley."

Thank God. "Hi. I'm Nora Calhoun. I own Failte Inn here in Provincetown and my water heater just died."

Fifteen minutes later, Nora had learned all about the advances in tankless water heaters and had chosen a brand new energy efficient model. It cost twice as much as merely replacing what she had, but would more than pay for itself within a year.

And she'd never have to worry again about running out of hot water when she had a full house. "So, can you come tonight? I'm willing to pay extra."

"Normally, that wouldn't be a problem, but we pulled our guys from the road an hour ago. The storm is getting bad."

"It is?" When she'd checked the weather that morning, the worst of the Nor'easter was supposed to bypass them.

"I can squeeze you on the schedule tomorrow. I think that's the best you're going to get."

"Yes, okay. That's fine." Nora's mind raced. She could go without hot water for twenty-four hours, especially with no guests scheduled for a few days. But if the snow was bad enough for a business to close, what the hell was she going to do about Will?

"Should be around two in the afternoon, but we'll call you when someone is on their way."

"Great. Thank you." Nora hung up the phone, but remained standing in the dining room. She couldn't send Will out into a blizzard. Especially since Will had stopped the disaster in her basement from becoming truly catastrophic.

Will came into the room, looking adorably awkward in Nora's pants. She looked out the window and sighed. "It's getting bad out there."

Nora came up beside her. "Worse than bad. The plumber can't come until tomorrow because they don't want any of their crew on the road."

Will turned toward her, breathed in her subtle perfume. For probably the millionth time, she fought the urge to lean in, find the exact places on Nora's skin where she'd dabbed it. "Oh, man. That's not good."

"I feel bad sending you out in it. The snow is probably up to your knees already."

Was Nora flirting with her or being conscientious? Will turned to face her and cocked a brow. "Why do I feel like we're having a 'Baby, It's Cold Outside' moment?"

Nora flushed and looked away, but didn't deny it. After a moment, she brought her gaze back to Will's. "You really will freeze out there."

Will had no idea what Nora was offering, or what she had in mind. But whatever it was, Will didn't hesitate. "Are you asking me to stay?"

The question came out in a more suggestive tone than she intended and Will hoped she hadn't scared Nora off. Nora cleared her throat. "I mean, I'm offering. If you don't want to venture out in this. I have plenty of rooms. Obviously."

Although her words denied any trace of desire, the stilted delivery gave Will hope. At this point, what did she have to lose? Even if nothing happened, staying meant more time with Nora. It also meant not having to go out in a blizzard. "I would love to stay."

Nora nodded, all business. "Good."

Before Will could decide what to say next, the dryer buzzed. "Wow. That was fast."

Nora went to retrieve Will's things. She handed them to her. "You're welcome to keep the sweats if you'd like."

Will smiled and looked down. The pants left a good four inches of Will's long legs exposed. "I appreciate the offer, but I'm not sure high waters are my best look."

Nora angled her head. "I don't know. I think they're sort of cute."

Okay, that had to be flirtation. "I'll be right back."

Will changed pants again and returned to the living room. Nora looked her up and down, quirked a brow. "I guess that's better."

"I...uh." Will's usual confidence abandoned her. The prospect of venturing into uncharted waters with Nora thrilled her, but stirred up nerves in the process. "Since I'm staying over, I could start sanding the stairs."

Nora shook her head. "You've already put in a full day of work. I don't expect you to do any more. You relax and I'll make dinner."

"I appreciate the offer." Will crossed the room and put a hand on Nora's arm. "You don't need to take care of me like one of your guests, though. What if I made you dinner?"

Nora's face was incredulous.

"I can cook, you know. As a matter of fact, I enjoy it."

"I didn't mean—"

"I know. I'm offering anyway. You've fed me plenty of times since I started working here. It'll still be your ingredients, but at least let me prepare them for you for a change."

Will could see the wheels turning in Nora's mind. Was she deciding whether or not to trust Will in her kitchen? Or was it something more? Eventually, she said, "Only if you really want to."

Will smiled. "I do."

"Do you want help? Or me to show you where things are?"

The idea of a supervisor made Will nervous. It also defeated the purpose of her taking care of dinner. "I think I can manage. I promise it won't be anything fussy, since boiling water for dishes is no one's idea of fun. Why don't you go relax for a little bit? You've been working today, too."

Nora looked at Will, considered arguing with her. Will had worked circles around her. Yes, she was getting paid, but still. She didn't want to seem contrary, though, or like a control freak. Knowing she had those tendencies was her best defense against them. "I suppose I could build a fire. Especially since no one will be getting a hot shower."

Will's eyes lit up. "I would love that. We can eat in the sitting room, at the little table."

It did sound nice. Not romantic. Cozy. She could do with a little cozy. "Okay."

Will started toward the kitchen, but turned back. "You don't mind me in your kitchen, do you?"

Nora shook her head. Even if it freaked her out a little, she had no intention of owning it. "Not at all."

Will smiled. "Just checking."

Will disappeared down the hall and Nora went to the fireplace. She meticulously laid the wood, set kindling underneath. She got it going, then stood and looked around the room, wondering if it was too ambitious a project to replace the wallpaper. Maybe she'd talk to Will about it over dinner. Whether or not they did it, it would be good to have something to talk about.

The idea of a leisurely meal with Will made her uneasy. Even though they'd shared more lunches than she could count. Even though Will had confided in her and somehow got Nora to confide in return. It was because she knew Will would be staying over. And unlike New Year's Eve, they'd be in the house alone.

Annoyed that she was getting herself all worked up, Nora sighed. Maybe a glass of wine would help her relax. She went to the small cellar she'd created under the stairs, then realized she had no idea what Will was preparing for them. She'd just pop her head in and ask.

She was almost to the door when she caught the strains of music. She stilled so she could make out what it was. Billie Holiday. And Will was singing along, badly. A flutter swept through Nora's chest, catching her off guard. Willing herself not to be charmed, she pushed through the swinging door.

She found Will standing at the stove, stirring a pot and swaying to the music. Her hair was a mess and her work pants hung on her hips in that ridiculously sexy way. Nora swallowed. No, she wasn't charmed; she was something far more dangerous. She opened her mouth to speak, but no words came out. Before she could find her voice, Will turned, jumped, then dropped the wooden spoon she was holding.

"God, you scared me." Her tone was more amused than annoyed.

"Sorry. I—" Nora cleared her throat. "I was going to open a bottle of wine, but decided I needed to know what we were having."

Will picked up the spoon and carried it to the sink. "No worries. I sort of forgot I wasn't alone."

Great. She couldn't get Will out of her head and Will lost track of the fact Nora was even there. "Smells good." It did smell good, like garlic and bacon.

"Carbonara."

"Impressive."

"It's one of those dishes that seems fancier than it is. And it doesn't make too many dishes."

Nora nodded. She'd made it once or twice. It wasn't part of her regular rotation because of the calories, but she did always have the ingredients on hand. "I approve. I also think a nice oaky chardonnay is in order. May I pour you a glass?"

Will's smile seemed shy all of a sudden. "That would be nice."

Nora busied herself with getting a bottle from the cooler, glasses from the buffet in the dining room. She pulled the cork and poured two glasses. She handed one to Will. "Anything I can do to help?"

"Just waiting for the pasta."

"Okay. I'll...I'll get out of your way, then." Nora retreated from the kitchen. She stopped in the dining room to pick up some napkins and utensils from the sideboard. Back in the sitting room, she set them out. She'd pulled out candles and was striking a match before she caught herself. She blew it out quickly. This was not a romantic dinner.

She'd just tucked them back away when Will walked in carrying two plates. "I see you set the table. I just need to grab my wine."

"I'll get it." Nora hurried from the room, using the moment alone to take a deep breath and center herself. By the time she returned, Will had angled the table so they both could enjoy the fire. Nora took the seat opposite her. She set down the glass, as well as the rest of the bottle from the kitchen, and picked up her own. "This looks delicious."

Will shrugged. "It's nothing special, but it tastes good."

"I'll take that any day over fussy and bland." Nora smiled. See? There was nothing wrong or weird about this. Just dinner. Even if her cheeks were flushed and she had a hard time taking her eyes off Will's hands.

"Agreed. Thank you for letting me putter around your kitchen. It's much nicer than the one in my apartment."

"I'm glad you enjoyed it. And thank you for making me dinner. It's not often that happens."

"I'm extra glad I stayed, then."

They ate in silence. Will seemed uneasy. It made Nora feel badly, thinking her coolness toward her had a lot to do with it. Will hadn't actually done anything to warrant suspicion. If anything, she'd proved herself hardworking and good-natured. Thinking that she'd jumped to conclusions, and treated Will unfairly, gave Nora a pang of guilt. She shouldn't have been so quick to judge, even if she'd never said a word about it to Will. "So, are you glad you stayed in P-town? Nor'easters notwithstanding?"

Will smiled and shifted her shoulders in a way that seemed more artless than world-weary. "I am. I didn't realize how much I missed being close to my sister. And my life here isn't anything spectacular, but it's my own. That's more than enough for me right now. Even with Nor'easters."

The choice of words gave Nora pause. Had circumstances been different, had she not had her own family to rely on in difficult times, she could be no better off than Will was now. No, she could be worse. The idea threatened to make her sentimental. To give her hands something to do, she picked up the wine and refilled their glasses. "I'm glad it's working out for you."

After finishing their meal, Nora tried to do the dishes, but Will insisted on helping. When they were done, Nora looked around the kitchen. Dinner had calmed her nerves some, but a certain electricity remained in the air. More than anxious, it left her with a lingering sense of anticipation. "I'm thinking this weather might call for one more glass of wine. Can I interest you in joining me?"

"I think you could talk me into it."

"Red this time?"

Will nodded affably. "That would be great."

Nora went to the cellar and pulled out a Pinot Noir. She poured glasses and, without any sort of verbal exchange, they moved to the sofa facing the fire. Nora sat, tucking her feet under her. "I hate to admit it, but I don't often build fires when there aren't any guests in the house."

"I know what you mean. I'm like that with cooking. It feels like a lot of effort just for one."

Whether it was being hunkered down against the storm or the third glass of wine in her system, Nora felt strangely uninhibited. Free. "That and it feels self-indulgent."

Will angled her head and studied Nora. "Not good at pampering yourself, are you?"

Nora rolled her eyes, but chuckled. "Something like that. Let me guess. You have it mastered?"

Will laughed. "Not even close. I was always the girl who couldn't sit still, couldn't relax."

"Really?" Not what she expected. The idea of having such a trait in common left Nora unbalanced, even more than she already was.

"Moving here was a turning point for me. I'm trying to slow down, appreciate each day."

Nora struggled to do that herself. "And it's working?"

"Like I said earlier, I think P-town is good for me. Not to mention all the great friends I've made."

Nora swallowed. "Graham, you mean."

"Graham is beyond great. On her own, but also because she's the reason I met you."

The look in Will's eyes told her they were no longer talking about friendship. "Will."

Will glanced away, then back, locking eyes with Nora. "You're an amazing woman, Nora. I love that I've gotten to know you." She paused, as though choosing her next words carefully. "Of course, that's only made me even more attracted to you."

Nora's pulse quickened. She felt like she was on the precipice, with her body screaming one thing and her brain another. Jump or scramble back from the edge. "I…"

Will reached over and took her hand. "I'm just putting it out there. You don't have to do anything with it. Unless you want to."

CHAPTER FOURTEEN

Nora didn't speak for a long moment and Will began to fear she'd read the signals wrong. She'd meant what she said. She didn't want Nora to feel any pressure to reciprocate. But, God, did she want Nora to reciprocate.

Nora reached for her wine just as Will did. The movement brought their faces close. No more than two or three inches separated them. Will's gaze moved from Nora's eyes to her mouth, then back. She swallowed, unable to initiate the kiss she wanted so badly, but equally unable to pull away. Nora seemed to be under the same spell. They stayed like that for what felt like an eternity. Her skin grew warm. A swell of anticipation rippled through her.

And then it happened.

Slowly, Nora closed the space between them. Will leaned in. She'd waited for this moment, wanted this moment, for so long, almost couldn't believe it was happening. She placed a featherlight kiss at the corner of Nora's mouth, half expecting to be swatted away. But Nora didn't swat her away. She didn't pull back. Instead, she turned her head slightly so that their lips were in perfect alignment. Will took that as an invitation and kissed her again. This time, she traced her tongue along Nora's bottom lip.

It was just as soft as she imagined and tasted faintly of wine. The combination invaded her senses, made her want to slow down and speed up. She wanted to find a way to stop time, commit each and every detail to memory. Because she had no idea where it would go or how long it would last.

Nora, however, seemed to have other intentions. She fisted one hand in Will's shirt, placed the other on the back of Will's head. She angled her mouth and took the kiss deeper. Will allowed Nora to take the lead. She reveled in being wanted, taken. It still felt a little unreal and she wanted to soak it in, make sure she wasn't imagining it.

When Nora pulled away, Will felt the absence sharply. She blinked and found Nora's green eyes searching her face. "What is it? What's wrong?"

Asking seemed preferable to begging her not to stop.

Nora licked her lips, swallowed. She tried desperately to sort out what Will might be thinking, or feeling. Although her mind had the soft edges of a couple of drinks, her thoughts were clear. Will had kissed her. She'd started it. But then she seemed to back off. It left Nora feeling like maybe she'd imagined it. Or, perhaps worse, that Will had thought better of it once they'd started. "I need to know what you're thinking right now."

"I'm thinking about how long I've waited for this moment. And I'm thinking how it's even better than I imagined."

Could that be right? Despite her own attraction to Will, she'd not imagined it would be reciprocated. Sure, Will had flirted, but she'd been focused on the idea that Will might be interested in Graham. She'd not allowed herself to really think about there being anything between them.

"I'm also hoping you'll let me do it again. And again and again after that."

Nora shook her head. This had to be a terrible idea. She couldn't believe it to be anything else. Even if she wanted it more than anything in recent memory.

"Okay. I'm sorry if I read the signals wrong," Will said.

"No."

"No?"

"No, you didn't read the signals wrong."

"Oh. You were just shaking your head, so I—"

Nora didn't let her finish. She feared if she didn't act now, the flash of courage might vanish. And if it did, so would any chance of seeing what might happen. She pressed her lips to Will's mouth, hoping the interruption hadn't ruined the moment.

Will's response was instant. She resumed the kiss, with even more passion than before, if that was possible. The intensity of it made Nora gasp. Will took advantage, sliding her tongue into Nora's mouth. Nora's heart flipped in her chest and heat gathered between her thighs. Will seemed at once to tease and take, coax and demand. Nora basked in the sensations, feeling intensely alive.

Will shifted, gently pushing Nora onto her back. Will positioned a knee between her legs and it took all of Nora's will power not to arch her hips against Will's thigh. Will braced one hand on the arm of sofa. The other crept under Nora's sweater. The feel of Will's fingers on her skin sent Nora into overdrive. She'd forgotten how immediate arousal could be, how much it could consume both her body and her brain.

But even through the haze, a bit of reality pushed through. If they were going to do this, it wasn't going to be on the floor of the sitting room. Or the sofa. It didn't matter how nice the fire was. "Let's go upstairs."

Will stopped kissing her neck long enough to look at her. She seemed to search Nora's face for some sort of hidden meaning. But then she eased herself off the sofa and stood. "Lead the way."

Nora stood as well and took Will's hand. They'd use one of the guest rooms. That would be nicer. It would be less personal, too, and come morning, she might appreciate that. At the top of the stairs, she turned left and led them toward the king suite. If she was going to be reckless, she might as well do it in style.

At the threshold, Will hesitated. Nora felt equal parts relief and dread. "What is it?"

She could see Will swallow as she searched for words. "I just want to be sure this is what you want."

It was Nora's turn to hesitate. Will was giving her an out. If she chose not to take it, whatever happened next would be squarely her decision. There'd be no pretending otherwise. Even with the weight of that understanding, she couldn't bring herself to do it, to stop whatever this was even before it began. "It is."

Will smiled. "Good. Because it's what I've wanted from the moment I first saw you."

She let that sink in. "You're exaggerating."

Will shook her head. "It was the first time Graham brought me here, the night of the rehearsal dinner. You walked into the hall wearing a dress and an apron and I had to pick my tongue up off the ground."

Nora thought back to that day. She'd thought of Will as just another one of Graham's strays. No, that wasn't fair. She'd felt an attraction, too. But she'd shoved it aside, dismissed it. And it had worked for a while, sort of. Until recently. The idea that Will had those feelings, had held onto them for months, left her with a strange mixture of pleasure and unease.

"Does that make you uncomfortable?" Will's face morphed into one of worry.

In lieu of an answer, Nora leaned in and kissed her. She opened the door to the suite, and pulled Will gently inside. She stopped near the bed, then turned to Will. She kissed her again.

"I'm going to take that as a no."

Nora slid her hands under the hem of Will's shirt, pulling it up and over her head. She repeated the process with the thermal shirt she wore underneath. Will's torso was pale in relation to her face and arms. Pink nipples stood erect from her small breasts.

Before she could touch, Will's hands began inching up her sweater. Nora had a moment of self-consciousness when she thought about her body, toned still but not as perky or tight as it had been in her youth. "I—"

Will dropped the sweater on the floor. "You are perfect."

Will trailed fingers up her sides to cup her breasts. Nora's nipples strained against the lace of her bra, aching for the touch she'd told herself for so long she didn't need. She leaned into it, trying to convey her desire without saying it out loud.

Will reached one hand around, unhooking her bra with a single flick. Nora smiled at the smoothness of the move. She was about to comment on it when Will brushed her thumbs over her nipples. Nora gasped.

"Are you okay?"

Nora nodded. "Yes." Should she confess just how long it had been since she'd been with someone?

"Do you want to tell me what you like? What you want?"

Nora shook her head.

"Okay. Then tell me if there's something you don't like, or something you want me to do different."

She nodded, then said a silent prayer that her lack of words wasn't a turnoff. She simply didn't think she could get her brain and mouth to engage in such a coordinated effort.

Will kissed her, a slow and languid kiss that demanded all of her attention and quieted the stream of questions in her mind. When Will slid her hands into the waist of her leggings, she didn't flinch at the prospect of being entirely nude. Will worked them down, then stood. She looked Nora up and down and Nora's skin warmed in the heat of her stare. "Utterly perfect."

Nora reached for the button of Will's pants. With the button and zipper undone, they fell without nudging. Underneath, Will wore a pair of snug navy and light blue striped boyshorts. Nora dispensed with those as well, allowing her hands to linger for a moment on the tight muscles of Will's ass.

When they were both naked, Nora stood for a moment. The slight buzz she'd enjoyed when they started kissing had vanished. And while she appreciated being in possession of her full faculties, she longed for the soft edges and eased inhibitions. But before she could think too much, Will's arms were around her.

Nora sank into the embrace—the heat of Will's body, the smoothness of her skin, the gentle friction of their bodies sliding against one another. Will reached over the bed and pulled the duvet back, then eased Nora onto it. The coolness of the sheets sent a chill through her, but Will quickly joined her. It was hard to know which sensation delighted her more, the warmth or the weight of Will's body pressing into her.

Will kissed her mouth, her jaw, the length of her neck. She dipped her tongue into the hollow of each collarbone before zigzagging down to her breasts. For what felt like an eternity, Will stayed there. Soft circles with her tongue gave way to teasing flicks; gentle bites paired with possessive sucks. She arched into it, buried her hands in Will's short curls. She made noises that surprised her, but somehow seemed to communicate things to Will.

When Will began to slide further down her body, Nora had a flash of something she could only describe as an out-of-body experience. It felt like she hovered over the bed, could see their bodies writhing on the crisp white sheets. This was her final chance to back away. She could still stop this before it went all the way. The sane part of her mind could still prevail.

And then Will's tongue pressed into her.

Nora shot off the bed, almost to a fully upright position. Will shifted her mouth slightly, just enough that Nora could hear her speak. "Easy. Relax. I've got you."

She lay back down and took a deep breath, willing herself to be calm. Will pressed into her again, but shifted slightly to avoid her hypersensitive center. Will's tongue was soft, but the tiniest bit rough. Her strokes were light, but she moved with purpose.

Will dipped inside and every muscle in Nora's body tightened. And then her tongue eased up, spreading slick heat and just the right amount of pressure. "Oh. God."

"Mmm."

The sound Will made created the slightest vibration. Before Nora could stop herself, she went tumbling over the edge. She cried out, tried to stop her body from bucking too wildly.

Will looked up. "Wow."

Nora flushed, embarrassed that she'd come as quickly as a horny teenager. "Sorry."

Will crawled up the bed until their faces were level. "What on earth are you apologizing for?"

"My," Nora swallowed, "lack of restraint."

Will ran a hand down her body. "Then I think the phrase you're looking for is 'you're welcome.' Because that was amazing and I am awash with gratitude. You might be the sexiest woman I've ever been with."

"I just—"

"You just nothing. I could come just thinking about you. So unless you're saying you're done—"

It was Nora's turn to interrupt. "No. I'm most definitely not done."

Nora rolled so that they were facing. She might regret all of this come tomorrow morning, but tonight was a different matter. She'd started something and she intended to finish it. Well, maybe finish wasn't the right word. She would see it through. And if the look on Will's face was any indication, they were just getting started.

She shoved aside any anxiety about being out of practice and began an exploration of Will's body with her mouth. She closed her eyes, soaking in the taste of Will's skin, the faintly masculine scent of her soap. Will was much more muscular than Jordyn had been. It helped to chase away any shadows of memories that threatened to creep into her consciousness. She took her time and enjoyed herself, taking Will's movements and noises as all the encouragement she needed.

She made her way down Will's body, lingering at her navel, then the patch of light brown curls. When she closed her lips around Will's clitoris, she felt it pulse against her tongue. The sensation, and the salty sweet taste of Will's arousal, made her own muscles clench. She'd forgotten that pleasing a woman was almost as delicious as being pleased.

To Will's credit, she lasted longer that Nora did. Nora alternated long strokes of her tongue with gentle flicks. When she started to suck, she heard Will swear. The swears continued, interspersed with Nora's name and the word yes over and over. Nora wanted to keep her like this, but she craved the feeling of Will coming undone.

When she felt Will tense, followed by a quivering in the muscles of her legs, Nora quickened her pace. The heat that poured out of Will nearly gave Nora another orgasm. By the time Will's body stilled, Nora was insanely aroused and breathless.

In what felt like only seconds, Will propped herself up on her elbow. "That was amazing. And sexy as hell."

Nora, feeling extra brave, smiled. "I was thinking the same thing."

"Please tell me I can have you again."

Nora swallowed. There was something to be said for the energy level of a thirty-year-old. "Yes."

With remarkable speed, Will sat up, then got into a kneeling position. Nora made her way back up the bed. Will remained kneeling, her gaze moving up and down Nora's body. "I could look at you for hours. Do you mind if I stay like this? I want to watch the way you respond to me. I want to see you when you come."

Speechless again, Nora nodded. Will spent a few moments caressing Nora's breasts, her ribs. The touch was gentle, unrushed. But it did little to lessen the pulsing ache. Nora wanted so badly to be filled. When she thought she couldn't take it another minute, she succumbed. "Please."

Will smiled at her and eased her knees apart. She settled herself between them. She used her left hand to spread Nora open. Being so exposed gave Nora an odd feeling—sexy, but vulnerable. But before she could process it, Will slid two fingers into her.

"Fuck."

"Oh, I intend to."

Nora opened her eyes to find Will staring intently at where their bodies were joined. The intensity of Will's concentration took her breath away. But then Will started moving her hand and Nora couldn't see or think or do anything other than feel the way Will moved inside her. She closed her eyes and gave herself over to it.

Having come once made it easier for Nora to hold her orgasm at bay. She focused on the friction of Will's fingers, the press of her knuckles. She moved with Will's hand, against it. When Will's thumb brushed over her, Nora arched into her. "Oh, yes. Will."

Will continued her thrusts. Not fast, but with enough force that Nora felt like she was filled with each one. The pressure built slowly this time, intensified by squeezing Will's fingers, trying to pull her closer. When the vibration began in her abdomen, Nora didn't fight it. The pleasure rippled through her, quenching a thirst she didn't know she had.

It took a long moment for her vision to clear. Nora worked to catch her breath and calm the trembling in her muscles. All she could think about was Will's body. Wanting to reciprocate, but also wanting to touch and to explore. To see if she could have the same effect Will had on her. She sat up and covered Will's mouth with her own.

Although the kiss was intended for Will's pleasure, the effect had Nora feeling aroused all over again. When she finally broke it, Will cupped her cheek in her hand and smiled. "Relax. There's no rush, no pressure."

Nora had to laugh at her own eagerness. Clearly, it had been too long. She leaned in and kissed Will again, but lightly this time. "But you have no idea how badly I want you."

"If it's half as badly as I've been wanting you, then I take it back. You may have your way with me." Will flopped onto her back and spread her arms wide.

Nora laughed. She'd never been with someone who was playful when it came to sex. Even the early weeks and months of her relationship with Jordyn—when all they seemed to do was have sex—things had been intense, but never playful. She rolled on top of Will. "I'm not going to turn that down."

Nora took her time exploring Will's body. It was the perfect balance of hard lines and soft curves. She was strong, but not overly defined in that way people who obsessed about exercise were. Nora touched and tasted, reveling in each sound that came from Will's lips, each contraction of muscle as Will moved with her, against her.

She grazed fingers along Will's ribs, over her breasts. She teased her nipples, loving the way they hardened under her hand. This, this was the part of being with a woman she missed most. There were countless ways of achieving an orgasm, but nothing could replicate giving pleasure.

When Nora eased into her, Will trembled and whispered her name. The playfulness was gone. In its place, a quiet need.

Nora went slowly, wanting to draw her out, make the moment last as long as possible. When Will began to writhe, Nora bit her lip. She increased the force of her fingers, along with the pace. Will rode her hand in a way that was beautiful to watch.

When Will clenched around her and called out her name, Nora almost lost it. Unguarded and primal, the way Will came filled a void inside her she didn't even know was there. Before Will could open her eyes, Nora wiped at her own. The worst thing in the world would be for Will to see her being overly emotional.

When Will did open them, Nora was smiling—going for a mixture of confident and satisfied. "Hi."

"Hi." Will blinked a few times. "Holy crap."

"Yes, something like that."

Will shook her head slowly. "I can't believe that finally happened."

Finally. Not the word Nora would have chosen.

"You're okay, right?"

Nora nodded, appreciating being asked. "I'm good."

"Come here." Will motioned with her hands.

Nora allowed herself to curl up next to Will and be wrapped up in her arms. Tomorrow would be soon enough to figure out what all this meant. And what she was supposed to do about it.

CHAPTER FIFTEEN

Will woke alone in the giant bed. She reached a hand across the sheets. Nora's pillow was cold, so she'd been gone a while. Worried she'd slept unreasonably late, Will sat and looked around for a clock. The small one on the bedside table told her it was barely seven. That was a relief. She wondered what time Nora got up.

Anxious to see her, Will climbed out of bed and pulled on her clothes from the day before. Even upstairs, when she opened the door, the aroma of coffee greeted her. Will breathed it in with appreciation. She couldn't remember the last time she'd been somewhere and not been the first one up. It felt weird, maybe, but not without its perks.

She found Nora in the kitchen, holding a mug with both hands and staring out the window over the sink. "Good morning."

Nora looked at her with an expression Will couldn't decipher. She nodded, but didn't smile. "I think we got over a foot of snow."

"Really?" Will went to the window and peered out. Sure, that much snow in such a short period of time was problematic, but it didn't make it any less beautiful. "Wow. We got snow in Maryland, but never like this. This is gorgeous."

"From inside, at least. Would you like a cup of coffee?"

The flat tone of Nora's voice gave Will pause, especially when her own feelings bordered on giddy. "I can get it."

Will got a cup from the cabinet and helped herself. She resumed her spot next to Nora in front of the window. Nora immediately looked down at her own cup, then turned away. She walked over to the pot and refilled it. Will returned her gaze to the window, but was aware of Nora's proximity. Or more accurately, her seeming refusal to be in close proximity.

"Is everything okay?" Will hoped she was imagining it.

"Yes."

When Nora didn't elaborate, Will considered letting it go. But last night was enough to put Will in a good mood for the next month. Nora was making it seem like no big deal or, worse, a big deal, but in a bad way. "I don't want to pry, but it doesn't seem like it."

She turned to face Nora, who was now leaning against the counter a good ten feet away. "I'm not sure last night was a good idea."

Oh. Will swallowed the lump in her throat and tried not to jump to conclusions. "I didn't force myself on you, did I?"

Nora shook her head vigorously. "No, I don't mean that. I was a fully willing participant."

"So…"

"So, we were sort of trapped together and there was wine and a fire and things just sort of happened. I'm not saying it wasn't good."

That was a relief. Will tried to lighten the mood. "From my vantage point, it was more than good."

Nora nodded. "It was. More than. I'm just saying it was ill-advised."

Will felt torn between defending what had happened between them and wanting to dissolve into the floor. She didn't know if she could handle being something Nora regretted. "I thought it was special."

Nora smiled, but it seemed to Will rueful. "It was. That's not the point."

"What is the point?"

"You work for me. I've got to be twenty years older than you. You're good friends with my niece. I could go on."

"I'm doing work for you, but I don't think of you as an employer. It's not like I'd ever sue you or anything. And I think it's more like ten years. As for Graham, I don't think she has anything to do with it." Will realized she sounded all worked up, so she stopped and took a breath. "If you aren't interested, say the word. I'll respect that. But if your qualms are about age or some kind of power dynamic, I hope I can convince you that I wanted last night. I've wanted it pretty much from the day I met you."

"How old are you?"

Was it a good sign or a bad sign that Nora zeroed in on the age difference? "Thirty-four."

"Oh."

"Is that good or bad?"

"Neither. Better, I guess, than I thought. I thought you might not be thirty."

Will chuckled. "I get that a lot. So, see? Not a big difference."

Nora narrowed her eyes. "How old do you think I am?"

Will knew Nora's age from her conversation with Graham, but knew better than to say so. She went with her initial impression. "I don't think you look a second over forty."

Nora gave her an incredulous look. "There's no need to patronize me."

Will swallowed. "Graham mentioned you were in your forties, but I was surprised."

She shook her head. "Closer to fifty."

"Is that really what's bothering you? The age difference?"

"Yes. No." Nora sighed. "It just feels sudden. And reckless. I don't do reckless."

"Okay. I get that. I'm not sure I agree, but I get it. Can we at least talk about it before you shut this down completely?" God, she hoped so.

Nora didn't seem convinced, but she didn't immediately say no. "All right."

"What if I made us some breakfast first? No one should have a serious conversation on an empty stomach."

Nora lifted a hand. "I can make breakfast. You cooked last night."

Will considered. "You make breakfast and I'll go out with the shovel. It's going to take a while to dig out, so we should do it in shifts."

"Only if you let me pay you."

Will cringed. She did not need Nora thinking about her as the hired help, especially right now. But she had a feeling if she put up a fuss, Nora wouldn't let her help with the snow at all. And there was a lot of snow. "I'd rather you didn't, but I don't want to argue."

Nora smiled and tipped her head to the side. "You're a quick learner. Don't do too much. If you can make a path to the front gate, that should be enough for the plumbers."

"I'll be back before you know it."

Will left the room and Nora stood for a moment. She drained her coffee and poured another cup. She pulled out ingredients for a frittata and tried to focus on the task at hand. Which worked for all of two minutes.

What the hell was she thinking? She wasn't, or at least she hadn't been last night when she gave in to the desire that had been nagging at her for weeks. She couldn't even blame too much wine. Sure, that had smoothed out her inhibitions, made it easier to ignore the hesitation that had kept Will at arm's length. But she'd known what she was doing.

Will had clearly known what she was doing. Even now, in the light of day and with a sobering cup of coffee—or three—the thought of the things Will did to her made Nora's toes curl. Will made her feel things she didn't even know she could feel.

Instead of extinguishing the pent up sexual energy, or releasing some of the pressure, sleeping with Will had only intensified it.

Nora returned to chopping vegetables with a vengeance. They'd eat breakfast, she'd listen to what Will had to say, and that would be the end of it. She was not a woman easily swayed. Last night notwithstanding.

An hour later, they sat at one end of the dining room table. Nora studied Will over the rim of her coffee cup. Her face looked fresh and relaxed, cheeks pink from the cold. Her hair had the sexy rumpled thing going on. She had to fight the urge to put her fingers in it. God, she was hopeless.

"I don't think we have to define anything right now. Or decide, for that matter."

Nora shook her head. "You make it sound so easy."

Will lifted a shoulder and smiled. "It's supposed to be."

"That's what people always say, but it's rarely true."

Will knew better than to dismiss Nora's concerns. Doing so would likely make her shut down altogether. And if she shut down, there was no doubt that she'd shut Will out in the process. "I understand that, better than most maybe. But we're on the same page from the get-go. That counts for something, right?"

Nora sighed and looked up to the ceiling. "You're going to go for the hard sell, aren't you?"

Will shook her head. "No sell. Well, maybe a little sell. I like you. I've been attracted to you from the moment we met. And if last night was any indication, the attraction is mutual."

"Oh, it's mutual."

Will grinned at that. "We're adults. No pretense, no agenda."

Nora considered. Could it really be as easy as that? Probably not. But maybe walking away completely wasn't necessary, either. Will had proved herself more than handy, not to mention good company. Nora swallowed. And the moment she let her mind wander to the night before, her insides went molten. Not to be cliché about it, but she'd honestly forgotten how good it felt to be with a woman.

Or maybe it had never been as good as it was with Will. Nora didn't want to think about that. It had too many implications. Implications that went beyond the possibility that Will had talent in the bedroom. Implications about how the two of them clicked. How they fit together in ways Nora didn't even know possible.

"You're shaking your head." Will frowned. "Do you not believe that's possible?"

Will was offering her a gift—good company and mind-blowing sex with no strings. She'd never been good at accepting gifts. She had a tendency to add strings or at least imagine them. But maybe this was her chance. "I think it's possible."

"But you're not interested?"

"Not uninterested."

Will raised a brow. "Keep talking."

Will seemed perfectly comfortable with whatever Nora was willing to give. Whatever boundaries she put in place. "Whatever happens between us is separate from whatever time you spend on the clock."

"Absolutely. I don't mix business and pleasure."

"And we're not dating. No courting either."

"Courting?"

"No flowers, no romantic dinners. That's not what we're doing."

Nora thought she saw a flash of something in Will's eyes, but it vanished almost as quickly as it appeared. "I will resist wooing you."

Nora indulged in a smirk. If Will had a sense of humor about this, it might actually work. "Is that terribly out of character for you?"

"Wouldn't you like to know?"

God help her, she would. But that was beside the point. No, not beside. It was the exact opposite of what she was trying to do. "I'll live. For the time being, I'll take what you're offering."

"Which is…"

Will's tone was a blend of playful and suggestive. Despite her best intentions, Nora found it sexy as hell. "Which is that you will continue to do work for me and the terms and conditions of that won't change."

"And?"

Nora swallowed again. This conversation should not be turning her on. "And we can continue doing what we did last night as long as it remains mutually agreeable to both of us."

Will nodded slowly. Nora had a moment of regret for putting it in such transactional terms. But before she could take it back, or elaborate, Will extended her hand. "Deal."

Nora couldn't tell if Will was poking fun at her way of phrasing the proposition or if she was on the same page. In the end, it didn't really matter. Will was agreeing to the terms she laid out. Nora took her hand and shook it. "Deal."

Before she could talk herself out of it, Nora stood to clear the table. Will followed her into the kitchen, positioning herself at the sink to wash dishes before Nora had a chance. Nora wrapped up the leftovers and topped off both their coffees.

When she was done, Will dried her hands and hung the towel. "So, when do we get to start?"

"Start what?"

"Our new arrangement." Will stepped toward her and put a hand on her waist.

Despite the thick sweater and camisole she wore, Nora swore she could feel the heat of it against her skin. She had a sudden image of Will tearing off her clothes, taking her on the kitchen island. Almost as shocking was realizing she'd let her. Her nipples tensed in anticipation. Heat pooled between her thighs. "Immediately."

Before she knew what was happening, Will's hand was gone. "Great. I was thinking I'd like to tackle the stairs. I know that has to be at least a full week of no guests, but I think we should commit to a time frame."

Nora blinked at the abrupt shift. Embarrassment over where her thoughts had been caused her cheeks to flush. She struggled to regain her composure. "I—"

Just as quickly as she'd pulled her hand away, Will was back. This time she slid both hands around Nora and pulled their bodies together. "I was kidding. What I really want to do is drag you back to bed right this minute."

"Oh." Surprise mixed with delight. And the initial flash of arousal intensified. "Well."

"I promise that I will get to your stairs and every other project you dream up between now and the arrival of spring. But if I don't get my hands on you soon, I might literally die."

In addition to how good the sex was, Nora realized how lovely it was to be wanted. Really wanted. The heat of Will's stare rivaled that of her hands. Hands that had crept under Nora's sweater and were now stroking up and down the slick satin of her camisole. "We can't have that."

"Shall I drag you to bed or would you rather I take you right here?"

As much as part of her wanted to be taken in the middle of the kitchen in broad daylight, reason won out. Even with no guests in the house, the front door was unlocked. It wasn't unheard of for a friend or delivery person who knew her to walk right in. The idea of it had a chilling effect on her arousal. She laughed. Apparently her recklessness knew some bounds.

"What?" Will looked alarmed.

"Nothing. Sorry. I would like very much for you to drag me to bed."

Will narrowed her eyes. "Are you sure? I want to respect your boundaries."

The sincerity in Will's voice struck her. Despite the confidence she wore when it came to sex, there was an earnestness about her that made her almost timid. Nora needed to remember that. It might make her like Will more, but it also made her a little dangerous. Even after everything, Nora had a soft spot for earnest types. She refused to let that make her vulnerable. "Let's go."

Nora slid out of Will's arms and took her hand. She made a point of playfully pulling her toward the stairs. Then she stopped. "Wait." Nora skirted around her and went to the front door. She flipped the deadbolt into place with a smile. "Better safe than sorry."

She turned back to Will, who gestured to the stairs. "Ladies first."

Once they were back in the bedroom, Nora lifted her arms and Will removed her sweater. She felt silly standing there in a cami and leggings. She went to slide down the leggings, but Will stopped her. "Please, allow me."

She also wished she was wearing sexier underwear. She had not anticipated that she and Will would have sex again, so she'd not given it a thought when she got dressed. She was going to have to up her game if they kept this up. And they'd pretty much just agreed to keep this up. The thought of it sent a ripple of laughter through her, the sort of giddy laughter that comes with being utterly careless.

"Am I tickling you?" Will stood up and looked into her eyes.

The gaze turned Nora's nervous laughter into pure desire. She no longer wanted to think about being reckless or negotiating rules. She wanted Will. Nora wanted her with a ferocity that took her breath away. "Just a little. I'm fine now."

"I'll try to be more intentional when I touch you." Will took the hem of the cami in her fingers and slid it over Nora's head.

"It's fine. You can do whatever." When did she lose the ability to form full sentences?

"I do like the sound of that." Will leaned forward and kissed her. If possible, it was even hotter than the last time. With the hesitation gone, Will's mouth covered hers. Not aggressive, per se, but confident. Will knew how to kiss a woman senseless and, now that she knew Nora wanted it, she didn't hold back.

Nora allowed herself to be swept up in the kiss. Her own hesitation was gone as well, giving her the freedom to focus on the sensation of Will's tongue sliding over her bottom lip, the gentle tug of her teeth. The only way Nora could think to describe it was a kind of slow urgency. Unrushed, but still laced with need. It went on and on.

❖

Will lifted her head and glanced at the clock. "That's too bad."

Nora looked at her, cocked a brow. "What's too bad?"

"It's after one. And if I'm remembering correctly, the water heater guys will be here soon."

"Shit." Nora bolted out of bed.

Will sat up. "Relax. Barely after one. They're not banging on the door now."

"But I may have missed a call from them. They could be here any minute."

"Okay, okay. I'm with you." Will pulled on her clothes and followed Nora downstairs.

Nora picked up her phone. Will watched her shoulders relax. "Nothing yet."

"Good. How about I go try to dig out our cars? I'm sure we'll need to go somewhere eventually."

That got Nora to smile. "You don't have to do all the shoveling. I'm able-bodied, you know."

"Oh, I know." She looked at Nora suggestively and Nora flushed. The rise of color made Will want to drag her to bed all over again. Sensing Nora wouldn't be as amenable this time, she started putting on her boots. "I'm just happy to help. I like it."

"Thanks. Why don't you focus on your car first? I'm sure you'd like to go home for a while. I can handle mine."

"I..." She probably shouldn't say it, but the last place she wanted to go was home.

Nora smiled at her coyly. "I'm not saying you can't come back later. I just thought you might like a change of clothes."

"Ah." Will's stomach fluttered with the delight of being wanted.

"I mean, I thought you looked great in my joggers, but you didn't seem to like them."

Apparently, Nora's playful switch had been flipped. Will tried not to think about how temporary it might be. "You just like looking at my ankles."

"Your ankles are fine, but I'm—"

The phone rang, cutting her off. As much as Will wanted to hear the rest of the sentence, she had shoveling to do. And the sooner she finished, the sooner she could go home. And the sooner she did that, the sooner she would be back at Nora's.

By the time Will got to her place, it was late afternoon. She took a quick shower, spending most of it wondering if she could talk Nora into shared showers at some point. After getting dressed, she packed a bag with some work clothes and clean underwear. She contemplated a semi-nice pair of pants, but settled on jeans and a sweater. She didn't want to jinx herself.

Before leaving, she checked her phone and realized she'd missed a text from Emerson.

Hope you're not too buried. Free for dinner or a drink?

As much as Will wanted to get back to Nora, she wasn't about to blow off her sister.

Things are good here and the roads are clear. Want me to come to you?

While she waited for a reply, Will sent a quick text to Nora. She was a little nervous that Nora would tell her not to bother coming, but she didn't. Nora may have worked in a comment about staying over making it easier for her to start working on the stairs, but Will didn't mind. The end result meant another night at Nora's. Her mind started spinning all sorts of images of Nora naked and under her, naked and on top of her, naked and—

I'll come there. Pig? Half an hour?

Will texted her agreement and drove the short distance to Commercial Street. Winter might bring Nor'easters, but it also brought infinitely easier parking. Will thought it might be a reasonable trade. Despite the cold, the Squealing Pig was warm and inviting. Several people sat at the bar and nearly half the tables were filled. Will smiled. It felt like a hometown bar.

Emerson arrived a couple of minutes later. In the short time it took them to exchange hugs and order beers, Will knew something was up.

"I asked Darcy to marry me and she said yes."

"Oh, Emerson. That's so awesome."

Emerson smiled, looking like happiness might literally explode from her at any moment. "Thanks."

"I'm so happy for you. Like, insanely happy." Will had helped Emerson pick out the ring, so there was no real surprise in the announcement. It made no sense that she should have such an emotional response now. Still, she had to blink back tears. "Although I've got nothing on you. Joy is radiating off you like heat from a fire."

"I didn't expect her to say no. But I don't think I've ever been more nervous in my life."

Will cleared her throat and grinned. "Not even your gross anatomy final?"

Emerson chuckled. "Not even then."

"How did you do it?"

Emerson took a deep breath. "Liam was at his dad's this past weekend. I made dinner, lit candles, the whole thing."

Will smiled. Emerson didn't have the same romantic streak Will did, but she had her moments. "Of course you did."

"And then I gave her the painting I did of Liam, her, and me."

Will's heart melted at the image. "Oh, that's good."

"I'd put a ring on Darcy's finger in the painting. It was a tiny detail, but one she noticed almost immediately."

Darcy was a queen of detail. That part didn't surprise Will at all. "And?"

"And she started to make a joke about it and I got down on my knee and asked her. By the end we were laughing and crying. And then Liam came home and we told him and there was more laughing and crying."

"Sounds like it was perfect."

Emerson nodded and got a reflective look on her face. "You know, it was."

"You'll have to let me take you both to dinner to celebrate."

Emerson leaned in and bumped her shoulder against Will's. "That's sweet, but you don't have to do that."

"I know I don't, but I want to. And I'm sure you're subtly looking out for me like you always do, but my finances aren't nearly as dire as I worried they might be." Which was true. Between Emerson forcing some money on her for the projects at her house and the work she'd pieced together for Alex, Nora, and Nora's friends, she'd make enough to get her to spring without having to worry.

"It's really nice of you. I'll talk with Darcy and we'll figure something out."

CHAPTER SIXTEEN

For the third morning in a row, Will woke to find herself alone in Nora's bed. She was beginning to realize that no matter how early she woke up, Nora invariably beat her to it. Hopefully, that meant Nora was an early riser and not uncomfortable waking up together. Hopefully.

She found Nora at her desk in the kitchen. The aroma of coffee and something magical baking in the oven enveloped her. "Please tell me I get to have some of whatever you're making."

Nora turned to her and smiled. "I'm baking it for you, so you can have as much as you want."

"I don't know what I did to deserve such spoiling, but please tell me so I can be sure to do it again and again."

"You finished the pantry, which allowed me to put everything away."

"Right." She hadn't thought about what a big deal that would be to a woman like Nora. "I'm sorry it took so long."

"Nonsense. The stairs are much more important. I'm just glad you were able to do it in between things drying and curing and whatever else-ing."

"I know, but I'm sure it was hard to have your kitchen in chaos for a week."

"Keeps me on my toes. Coffee?"

"I can get it." Before helping herself to a cup, Will crossed the room and gave Nora a kiss. It felt almost domestic, a fact that made her feel strangely content. "Did you sleep well?"

"Quite. You?"

"Very well. I always considered myself an early riser, but you seem to have me squarely beat in that department."

Nora shrugged. "Years of practice."

Will poured herself coffee and refilled Nora's cup. "Well, I'm impressed." Feeling brave, she added, "Even if part of me would like to wake up with you."

"I'm fairly restless once I'm awake. I never want to disturb you."

"I understand. Just know I'd never think of it that way."

"Point taken." Nora rose from her desk and went to the oven. She pulled out what looked like coffee cake, complete with crumb topping.

"Oh, that looks good."

"I'm afraid it has to cool a bit before I can cut it."

Will pouted. "That seems cruel."

"I think you'll live."

The playful conversation made up for waking up alone. It was also a stark contrast to their first morning together, when even before their talk, Nora had made her discomfort clear. "Fortunately, my tolerance for delayed gratification has improved."

Nora smirked, which Will found incredibly adorable. "Cute."

"Cute enough to be your Valentine?" The holiday was the following week and Will had been waiting for a way to work it into the conversation.

Nora's expression changed immediately. "What do you mean?"

"I don't know. I hadn't planned anything. But we could go out, let someone else do the cooking. Nothing too romantic, of course."

Nora gave her an incredulous look. "Do we have to go out?"

Will took a deep breath. Of course Nora wouldn't want to go out. "No. I don't want to pressure you or make you feel uncomfortable."

"Thank you. It's not that I wouldn't enjoy going out with you. It's something about Valentine's Day, you know. Small towns and gossip."

Will refused to let that bother her. "It's all good. There's plenty to be said for staying in."

"Do you only think about sex?" The words might be scolding, but Nora's tone was playful. It bolstered Will's confidence.

"Yes." Will shook her head. "No." Then she nodded. "Yes."

Nora laughed. The sound sent a flutter of joy through Will, made her think Nora was starting to relax, at least on some things. "At least you're honest."

Feeling bolder, Will leaned in and kissed her. "Will you let me make you dinner?"

"I should make you dinner, since I'm the one who doesn't want to go out."

"Or we could skip dinner entirely."

Nora batted at her arm. "You're insatiable."

Will leaned in again, bringing her face within inches of Nora's. "For you. But I think that's more your fault than mine."

"Stop." A flush of color rose in Nora's cheeks.

Nora might protest Will's more salacious commentary, but Will had come to see it as something she did on principle. She wondered if Valentine's Day was the same thing—what Nora thought she was supposed to do rather than what she might actually want. "So, we're agreed. We're staying in."

Nora nodded slowly, relieved and a little turned on. "Staying in." She let her mind wander to the possibilities and then reality hit her. "Wait."

"What?"

"I can't do anything on Valentine's Day. I have guests." How could she have let that slip her mind? That was the reason the stairs had to be done so quickly in the first place.

"Oh."

"I'm sorry. I don't know how I forgot." Which wasn't entirely true. The idea of spending the night with Will had distracted her. Nora shook her head, as though doing so might clear her mind and help her re-center.

"It's okay. Business comes first."

Although Will put up a casual exterior, she was clearly disappointed. Before she thought it through, Nora said, "What about another night? We could plan our own little stay in when it'll just be the two of us."

Will's face brightened. "That would be great."

Nora might tell herself this was just sex, but Will's reaction made it clear it was about more, at least on her part. Not that Nora was responsible for Will's feelings. Nor did it imply anything about her own. But the word relationship settled uncomfortably in her stomach and a myriad of warning bells and red flags flashed through her brain. "We'll have fun."

"So do you have people this coming weekend? Can I help with anything?"

She didn't need help, but having it would be nice. So would company. Nora hated to admit she wanted for either. But Will seemed so eager. She had a feeling saying yes would be as much for Will's benefit as her own. "Two couples arrive Friday and another Saturday. All are staying until Tuesday morning."

Will rubbed her hands together as though they were plotting something. "Do you do anything special?"

"Two people have requested flowers in their rooms. I'll do a fancier happy hour on the fourteenth and one man asked for a late night proposal arrangement in front of the fire."

"A proposal? That's awesome. I don't have anything at all slated for the next week. I am at your disposal."

"If you work, you have to let me pay you."

Will looked hurt by the statement. "That's not why I offered."

"I know, but I refuse to take advantage."

Will laced her fingers together and stared up at the ceiling. "I have a proposition for you."

Nora repressed a smile. "And what's that?"

"You pay me in meals and accommodations."

"What do you mean? Like for friends? We could work something out."

Will shook her head. "I meant me."

"I don't mean to be obtuse, but I don't understand."

"I'd love to hang out with you for the weekend. But something tells me you're not going to be keen on the idea of having that kind of sleepover while you have paying guests in the house. Assuming no one is using Graham's room, I could stay there. I'll work for my keep."

Nora narrowed her eyes. "You want to hang out?"

Will shrugged sheepishly. "I like spending time with you. And my one roommate who stayed through the winter is gone for a couple of weeks. And I'd be helpful—a win-win. It wouldn't be awkward."

Nora took a deep breath. Everything about this was awkward. But sort of sweet, too. Will was trying to spend time together and also respect her boundaries. In that sense, it was actually kind of perfect. "Yes. Okay. That would be really nice, actually."

"Yeah?"

"Yes. No one is in that room. And things around here are always easier with two pairs of hands." Will nodded, but didn't speak. She had this expectant look on her face that Nora found inexplicably endearing. "And I like spending time with you, too."

It was the right thing to say. Will broke into a huge grin. "I won't even ask for permission to sneak into your room after everyone else is in bed."

Nora felt another flutter, this one decidedly lower than the first. "Maybe you should."

She enjoyed watching Will sit up a little straighter. "Okay, then."

"Sneak in, I mean. You don't need to ask permission."

"Oh." Will look surprised, but in a good way. "I'll remember that."

"But first, I need to dust."

Will pouted. "Right. I'll help."

Nora laughed and waved her off. "I got it. Why don't you go home and pack for a couple of days? There will be plenty to keep you busy when you get back."

Will bounded up. "I like the sound of that."

When she left, Nora got out her cleaning supplies and got to work upstairs, since she wouldn't be able to get to those rooms once Will did the final coat of varnish on the stairs. She dusted and scrubbed, fluffed and freshened. While she worked, she turned over her current situation in her mind. Maybe she was blurring the lines some, but Will didn't need to know that. Nor did it have to mean anything or imply that things would go further than she wanted them. She remained squarely in control of her life and her choices. And that meant she was in charge of her future. As long as that stayed safely locked away, along with her heart, everything would be fine.

She'd just finished when the front door opened. She gathered her things and headed for the stairs. "Will, is that you?"

"It's not."

Nora groaned inwardly at the sound of Martha's voice. Not that she was unhappy to see her. No, she was annoyed at being caught expecting Will. Even if she could pass it off as a job. "Hi, Martha." She started down the stairs. "What brings you by?"

"I'm meeting Jan for lunch and I thought I'd stop over and check out your pantry."

Nora joined Martha at the bottom of the stairs. "I'm happy to show it off."

Martha followed her to the kitchen. "But if you're expecting Will, I can come back another time."

The tone was teasing and begged for a response, but Nora wasn't quite ready to give her one. "Nonsense. She's helping me get ready for the Valentine's crowd."

"Ah. It seems like she's turned out to be quite indispensable."

Nora opened the door to the pantry and stepped back so Martha could see. If asked point blank about her relationship with Will, she probably wouldn't lie. But at the same time, she didn't want to be caught up in a back and forth of double entendres. It was less about privacy, she realized, and more about cheapening what she and Will had. Even if she planned to keep some boundaries, she didn't want to make it feel cheap.

"She's taken on projects I didn't even know I wanted." Realizing she'd walked right into a double entendre without even meaning to, Nora laughed.

"Why are you laughing?"

"Nothing."

"Are you sleeping with her?"

The bluntness of the question caught her off guard. It shouldn't have, given Martha's style. But she thought she'd been discreet, subtle. Martha wouldn't ask if she didn't have reason to think the answer might be yes. "What makes you ask that?"

Martha shrugged. "You never did fill me in on the New Year's Eve party. And I've seen the way you look at her, a mixture of wistful and hungry."

Oh, that was not good. "Really?"

"Yes. And even more importantly, I've seen the way she looks at you."

Nora swallowed. "How's that?"

"Like she's completely in love with you."

The only time they'd all been in the same room, aside from New Year's, was an afternoon she spent at Martha's house. Will was working on something for Heidi the same day they had a bridge date. Surely, nothing in those interactions could have led Martha to such a conclusion. "That's ridiculous."

"I don't see what's ridiculous about it, especially if you're already having sex." Martha said it like it was the most obvious thing in the world.

Nora leaned back against the kitchen island. "Love doesn't have anything to do with it."

"But you are sleeping together?"

"Have slept together." For some reason, the distinction felt important.

"Multiple times?"

"A few."

Martha raised a brow. "Here? Is she staying?"

Nora knew that sounding defensive would only egg Martha on, but she couldn't seem to help herself. "She's stayed over a couple of times. We're not cohabiting or anything."

"I see." Martha nodded. "Well, now I know why you didn't want her working for us."

Nora stood up straight. "What does that mean?"

"It means you keep everything in your life neat and tidy. And nothing about this," Martha waved her hand to indicate the current topic of discussion, "is tidy."

She let her shoulders slump. "Tell me about it."

"No, no. That's my line."

"Funny."

"I'm serious. Are you having fun? Are you happy? And most importantly, is she any good?"

How had she gotten herself roped into this conversation again? "I plead the fifth."

"Not an acceptable answer."

"I—" Nora's protest was cut off by the sound of the front door and Will's called greeting.

"This conversation is paused, but not over." Martha poked her lightly in the chest. Then she grinned. "We're in the kitchen, Will. Nora was just showing off your handiwork."

Will joined them and Nora found her gaze bouncing between Martha and her. She didn't know what she was looking for. Perhaps some kind of unspoken conversation. But other than Martha studying Will a little more closely, nothing. If anything, Will's attention remained squarely focused on her. On top of that, she'd put her bag down somewhere before coming into the room. Intentional or not, Nora appreciated the discretion.

"Do you think you'll have some more time on your hands before spring? I'd love to put some shelves in one of our closets." Martha winked at Nora. Nora sighed and hoped Will hadn't noticed.

"Absolutely. I love projects like that."

"Organizational?" Nora asked.

Will smiled. "Small and within my skill set."

Martha crossed her arms over her chest. "Does that mean you don't do plumbing?"

"I can replace a faucet, but that's about it."

"Interesting. I might take you up on that."

Will nodded agreeably, seemingly oblivious to any subtext in the conversation. "Sounds good."

"Well, I'll get going. I don't want to keep you from your..." she trailed off and looked at Nora suggestively. "Projects."

Nora held the door open and Martha sashayed through. "Thanks for stopping by."

"I'm so glad I did. So many interesting developments."

Nora rolled her eyes. "I'll see you next week."

"You most certainly will. Bye, Nora. Bye, Will."

"Bye." Will smiled and waved, finally looking like she sensed something might be up.

Nora closed the door behind her and turned to Will. "She knows."

"Knows what?"

"About us. That we're sleeping together."

A look of alarm crossed Will's face. "I didn't say anything."

Nora shook her head. "I did. I mean, she guessed, so I merely confirmed. I just thought you should know, especially if you're going to do more work for her and Heidi."

"Oh." She stood quietly for a moment, making Nora wonder what she was thinking. Finally, she looked at Nora. "Is that okay?"

The concern in her eyes made Nora feel small. She'd dictated every parameter of their relationship and Will had let her. Suddenly, the idea of spending a few days together felt like a chance for her to let go of some of that control. She smiled. "It is. I'm a private person by nature, but not secretive. Martha and Heidi are my friends. And Martha could tell something was up, in a good way."

"Okay." Will smiled then, a genuine smile that reached her eyes. "I'm glad."

"It means they're both likely to give me a hard time for the foreseeable future, but I'll manage."

Will frowned. "Would they really do that? They seem so nice."

"Oh, they're nice all right. But we've been friends long enough that they have license to tease and generally harass me."

"Ah. Well, that's okay, then. That makes them practically family."

"You're always ready to see the best in people, aren't you?"

Will cringed slightly. "It's naïve. I know."

Nora shook her head. "Not at all. I think it means you have an open heart. That's a gift. Or maybe it's something you work really hard at. Either way, it's refreshing."

Will lifted a shoulder and offered a small smile. "It's gotten me into trouble a time or two."

"Which makes it all the more remarkable."

She was fully blushing now. "Thanks."

Nora decided to change the subject. "Did you bring things?"

Will nodded. "When I heard voices, I tucked it in the closet. I didn't want to make things awkward."

"I really appreciate that."

"I'll put it in Graham's room now."

Nora winced. "How about we don't call it Graham's room? Call it your room. Although, at this point, I'm not sure how much time you'll be spending in it."

Will grinned at that. "Okay."

Will got to work on the stairs and Nora continued her cleaning downstairs. She stopped around six to make dinner and tried not to think about how domestic it all felt. But when they sat down to eat, Will seemed to have a cloud over her head. "What's wrong?"

Will looked up quickly, as though surprised that Nora had spoken to her. "Nothing."

It probably wasn't fair, but Nora played the card she had. "If you don't like the meal, you don't have to eat it. You won't hurt my feelings."

As expected, the comment sent Will's head shaking. "It's not that at all. This is completely delicious." She took a hefty bite to prove her point.

Nora sipped her wine. "So it's something else."

Caught, Will's shoulders slumped. "I told you Emerson and her girlfriend Darcy got engaged."

"You did. I thought you were happy about it."

"I am," Will said quickly. "I just wish I could do something nice for them."

In a million years, Nora would not have guessed that's what was bothering her. "Like what?"

"Like take them out for a nice dinner to celebrate." She frowned. "But that seems so generic."

"What about an engagement party?"

"Yeah, that would be perfect." Will offered her a weak smile. "If I could pull it off."

"Why don't we do it here?" She couldn't imagine Will had a huge affair in mind.

"Really?"

Nora shrugged. "Sure. In case you hadn't noticed, I'm kind of an expert at throwing parties."

"Oh, I noticed. It would be impossible to spend time with you and not notice. I just didn't want to impose. I want to pay for it of course, I just can't afford anything too fancy."

Nora thought back to the one party she'd thrown with Jordyn. Jordyn had wanted to spare no expense, only the entire expense was on Nora's shoulders. The more she got to know Will, the more she regretted ever comparing her to Jordyn. "You can chip in for the cost of food and wine, and help with the labor. That will be plenty."

"I would love that. I hope you don't feel obligated, though. That's why I hesitated to say anything in the first place."

"Nonsense. The one time I met Emerson and Darcy, I liked them very much." Nora flashed back to the New Year's party, the one where Will had been merely a guest. "We could host it together."

Will sat quietly. Nora imagined her wrestling with whether she should read meaning into that last statement. It looked like a mixture of hope and hesitation in her eyes. "Together?"

Why not? It's not like they were the ones getting engaged. And it would be even more awkward to pretend there was nothing between them. She smiled. "Yes. Together."

"Wait. Do you mean together, together?"

Nora chuckled. "Yes."

Will looked up at Nora and studied her. To Will, everything about this screamed big, giant deal. But if Nora didn't think of it that way, Will didn't want to go there and risk Nora reconsidering. "That would be awesome. Thank you."

Nora narrowed her eyes at Will. "What are you thinking? I can see the wheels turning."

She didn't want to lie. She just needed to play it cool. "I'm thinking how excited Emerson and Darcy will be. And how much fun it will be to throw a party with you. As far as I'm concerned, you're the master."

Nora laughed again. "Not the master, but I do have a lot of practice. And I agree. Parties are fun."

Will, whose intentions really had been focused on doing something nice for Emerson and Darcy, now found her mind full of thoughts about her relationship with Nora. She imagined them dressed up and standing side by side. They'd bustle in and out of the kitchen, of course, as hosts should. But they'd also get to stand around and drink cocktails with other couples. It caught her by surprise just how much the idea of that thrilled her.

"You're caught up on the together part, aren't you?"

Did that mean Nora was, too? "No. I mean, yes. A little. But in a good way."

Nora raised a brow. "How so?"

Tread carefully. "I totally respect your privacy, but I'm excited by the idea of doing something with you that is something couples would do, something that is more than just the two of us."

"That makes sense."

Will swallowed. "Are you okay with it?"

"I am." Nora smiled and ran a finger down Will's arm, sending a shiver down her spine and a flood of warmth to her center. "Of course, I thought you liked all the things we did, just the two of us."

"Oh, I do." But that didn't stop her from longing for more. "This is definitely a case of one in addition to the other."

"You're not going to try to make out with me in front of a room full of people, are you?"

Will huffed and rolled her eyes to cover up the sting of Nora's comment. "I guess not."

Nora pulled her hand away, but smiled. "You know what I mean."

"I do." Even if it felt like things between them were two steps forward and one step back, at least the direction was forward. "I was teasing you. It's going to be small and low-key. And I promise not to get frisky in the middle of it."

Nora stood and disappeared into the kitchen. She returned a minute later with a notepad and a pen. "Okay, let's get started on details. Things are quiet here after Valentine's Day. I won't have more than an occasional guest until at least the middle of March. We'll need to confirm a date with your sister and get an idea of numbers from her as well. Once we have that, we can decide on food and stuff."

Will smiled and allowed herself to go back to being excited. They were going to have a blast.

By the time they finished eating, Nora had sketched out a couple of variations of a cocktail party for her to present to Emerson and Darcy. If she'd been impressed with Nora's party throwing prowess before, that sentiment was now magnified tenfold. The woman thought of everything. Literally, everything.

Chapter Seventeen

Valentine's Day came and went without a hitch. Even if Nora was hesitant at first, having Will around had been nice. More than nice. She was helpful and attentive and didn't seem to mind taking directions. On top of that, they'd had fun. And not just bedroom fun. They'd clicked in every possible way. The end result left her feeling maybe this wasn't such a bad idea after all.

Over the weeks that followed, they'd fallen into a routine of sorts. Will didn't spend all her nights at the inn, but she was there more than not. Nora liked it, even if she didn't like to think about how much. On mornings when there were no guests, that routine included a leisurely breakfast in the dining room—something Nora had never indulged in when alone.

On the morning of the engagement party, they were doing just that. But in spite of having everything organized and ready, Nora found herself fidgety. She drummed her fingers on the table. Will sat across from her, sipping coffee and working on a crossword puzzle. Nora chided herself for hesitating, for being self-conscious. "Will?"

Will lifted her head. "Yes?"

No point beating around the bush. "Do you like to strap?"

Will choked on her coffee, then sloshed the contents of her mug onto the newspaper. Nora cringed as Will coughed. Will finally stopped, then waved a hand between them to indicate the mess. "Sorry."

"No, it's me who's sorry. I shouldn't have brought it up. I don't know why I did."

"No, no. I have no problem with you bringing it up."

"Could have fooled me." It was mortifying. God, when had she gotten so out of practice?

"You caught me off guard. That doesn't mean my answer isn't yes."

Nora narrowed her eyes, unsure of whether to believe her. "Oh."

Will reached across the table and squeezed her hand. "My answer is definitely yes."

If the look in Will's eyes was anything to go on, she meant it. Nora swallowed. "Oh."

"Do you?"

Nora glanced down for a second to regain her composure. "Yes. I mean, not myself. To do the strapping, that is. I like to receive. If you know what I mean."

Will watched Nora fumble over her words, blush a dozen shades of pink. If the initial question had caught her off guard, the rest of this conversation turned her on. Nora's combination of forward and halting was charming, so unlike her usually sure way of doing pretty much everything. Add to that the subject matter itself. She loved to strap on. And since Kai didn't like it, it had been ages since she had. "Yes, I know."

"I'm sorry. I didn't mean to be so awkward about it. It's… it's been a long time, I guess, since I've negotiated these things."

Will nodded. "You don't have anything to apologize for. There is no easy way to talk about some of this stuff, at least at first."

"Right."

"If anything, I'm glad you broached the subject."

Nora didn't look convinced. "Really?"

"Really. I don't know if it's just me, but that's the kind of thing I wait for a woman to ask for, rather than putting it out there. That might be weird or, I don't know, old fashioned."

Nora shook her head. "No, I totally understand. It makes sense."

"So, yeah. That's something you like?"

Nora nodded, seeming to get shy again. "It's been a long time. Not just negotiating. Doing."

It was rare for Will to feel like the savvier, more confident one. It was kind of a turn on itself. "Same here."

Nora didn't seem to believe her. "You don't have to say that."

Will smiled. "It's true. The last woman I was with wanted nothing to do with it, so—"

"Oh. Okay."

The implications of their conversation sank in and Will wanted nothing more than to spend the entire day exploring the possibilities. She almost—almost—wished Emerson and Darcy's engagement party wasn't that night. "When I go home to get clothes for later, I could get what we need."

Nora swallowed and Will couldn't tell if she was nervous or aroused. "Yes, please."

They finished breakfast and worked their way through Nora's to-do list. Her meticulous, thorough to-do list. But if Will had any hesitation about the level of detail, it vanished when, at two in the afternoon, everything looked beyond perfect. Even most of the food was put together.

As much as she didn't want to leave, her dress clothes remained at her apartment. Along with other things she'd need before the night was done. She went home and packed quickly, then walked back to Nora's even faster.

She found Nora in the kitchen, already showered and in her robe, drinking a cup of tea. Will loved the casual intimacy of it. "Do you need any help in here?"

"Not a bit. You go shower. I'll be there in a minute to finish getting ready."

Will started to leave, but turned back. "Nora?"

Nora looked her way. "Yes?"

"Thanks again for this. I'm really looking forward to it."

"Me, too." Nora smiled, the kind of easy, genuine smile she'd not bestowed on Will when they first met. She'd been doing it more and more, but it still made Will weak in the knees.

It wasn't the first time Will brought a change of clothes to Nora's, but it was the first time she did more than take a quick shower and change. Nora had offered her use of one of the upstairs bathrooms, but Will opted to share Nora's. She told Nora it would save an extra cleaning, but truthfully, she wanted to be with Nora, to revel in the feeling of getting ready for the party as a couple. Even if she hadn't been able to coax Nora into the shower with her.

She stood in the bathroom, applying a small amount of wax to her damp hair. Nora sat at her dressing table in the bedroom in stockings and a slip, putting on makeup. Will lingered in the bathroom longer than she needed, enjoying the opportunity to watch. It was the sort of thing she'd had fantasies about, but never before had she been with a woman who actually embraced such an old-fashioned ritual of femininity.

After mascara and lipstick, Nora turned her attention to her hair. As much as Will loved it down, she knew Nora would want to pull it up and out of the way while she played hostess. She watched as Nora scooped it up and, in a matter of seconds, had it shaped into a twist and clipped in place. The result left Nora's neck exposed. Will licked her lips. Maybe up-dos weren't so bad.

Nora assessed herself then glanced up, catching Will's reflected gaze. "What?"

Will smiled, not really minding that she'd been caught staring. "Enjoying you."

Nora shook her head, but smiled. "You make me out to be far more interesting than I actually am."

"I beg to differ. I could watch you for hours."

Nora pushed back her chair and stood. Will clearly meant it as a compliment, but the intensity of Will's attention left her unbalanced. It felt at times like Will's affection bordered on adoration. It left her uneasy. "Well, you'd better snap out of it. We have work to do."

Will grinned and offered a playful salute. "I am at your service."

Nora slipped into the dress she'd picked out for the evening, along with a pair of low heels, then led the way from her bedroom to the kitchen. There wasn't all that much to do, given that they'd decided on a happy hour with hors d'oeuvres instead of a full meal. But being busy gave her somewhere to direct her energy, and Will's. Nora slid the wheel of Brie into the oven and set the timer, then started pulling things from the refrigerator. They moved the board of cheeses and dried fruit out to the buffet, along with crackers and sliced baguette and a tray of tea cookies. Nora opened the first few bottles of wine while Will arranged beer in a shallow tub of ice.

"What else?" Will put her hands on her hips and looked around.

"I think we're good."

Will glanced at the clock on the wall. "If I'd known there was so little left to do, I'd have dragged you to bed for a quickie."

Nora swatted at her with a pot holder. "Stop it."

Will pulled her into a kiss that made her knees wobbly. "I'm serious."

Nora did her best to tamp down the butterflies that seemed to be visiting her with increasing frequency. She would not get swept off her feet. Would. Not. "I am, too. People will be here any minute."

Will ran a hand down her back and gave her ass a gentle squeeze. "That's why they call it a quickie."

Nora opened her mouth to protest, but was interrupted by a knock on the front door. "That's probably your sister now. Go let them in."

Will pouted, but headed for the door. Nora watched her go. When did she start finding that sexy? She shook her head at the absurdity of it, then checked on the Brie. The pastry was puffy and brown, so she pulled it from the oven and moved it to a plate. By the time she carried it out to the dining room, Emerson and Darcy were taking off their coats.

Darcy walked over to her, beaming. "I'm sure Will has said so, but we can't thank you enough for doing this."

Nora returned the smile. "I love a party and you two are officially the most low-maintenance couple I've ever met."

Darcy laughed. "Could I get that in writing? I'm pretty sure low-maintenance is the absolute last word Emerson would ever use to describe me."

"Happily." Nora stole a glance at Emerson. Although she'd initially thought she and Will looked nothing alike, Nora realized now they had the same lanky body type and posture. So different from her and Colleen, who had similar eye and hair color, but not much else.

"I'm also hoping that, after this, you and I get to be friends. I'd love to trade recipes and kitchen stories."

The idea of being friends with Will's sister's soon-to-be wife gave her pause, but from everything she could tell, she and Darcy would get along great. She squeezed Darcy's hand. "I hope so, too."

Will and Emerson walked over to join them, but before they could start a conversation, the door opened. An older couple came in and Darcy introduced them as her parents. Gloria and James. Nora repeated their names to commit them to memory as she shook their hands. Alex from The Flour Pot and her wife Lia were right behind them, followed by a handful of people Nora didn't know. Nora slipped into hostess mode, pouring drinks and making sure the snacks stayed replenished.

She made a point of speaking to everyone, especially people she hadn't met before. In addition to putting Failte on the radar, she'd found networking a great way to stay on top of the new and growing businesses in town that she wanted to support. She also got the chance to reconnect with some passing acquaintances. Even without knowing Emerson or Darcy well, it turned out they had some friends in common.

Will disappeared from time to time, emerging from the kitchen with more ice or a fresh basket of pita chips for the buffet. Having the help was nice, but Nora found herself more struck by how much Will remained by her side. She would have expected it to feel clingy and smothering, but it wasn't. It felt like they were a team. A couple.

Will offered a brief toast. Emerson and Darcy said a few words, mostly expressing gratitude. By a little after eight, everyone but the guests of honor had taken their leave. Will helped Emerson and Darcy pack up the gifts they'd not expected to receive. Nora wrapped up some cookies for Darcy's son Liam, not so much because he needed cookies but because she wanted him to feel remembered. Darcy thanked her and they agreed to get together soon for tea and to talk shop.

The four of them hovered at the front door as Emerson and Darcy put on their coats. "I've never had such a nice party thrown in my honor," Darcy said.

Emerson nodded. "Agreed. What can we do to thank you?"

Nora waved a hand. "Not a thing. It was an absolute pleasure."

Darcy pulled her into a hug. "Well, you at least have to promise to come for dinner. Before things get too hectic around here."

"Absolutely."

Will hugged her sister, then Darcy. "I'm so happy for you both."

Emerson lifted a brow at Will. "Same."

Will flushed slightly and looked down. Nora took her hand and gave it a squeeze. "You two have a good night. And drive safely home." When they were alone, Nora turned her attention to Will. "So, what do you think? Success?"

Will smiled and seemed to get shy. "More than."

"Are you sure? You seem quiet all of a sudden."

"Absolutely. I'm not quiet, just happy."

Nora got the feeling Will was talking about more than a well-executed party. "You make an excellent cohost."

Will nodded. "I was happy to help, but let's be honest. It was all you."

"Nonsense. You did at least half the work. On top of that, you worked the room. That's the most important part, making people feel welcome and comfortable."

Will continued to nod slowly, as though turning that over in her mind.

"What is it?" Maybe she'd misread Will's response and something was bothering her.

"The one time Kai and I had a party, we had a huge fight right before, then another one after. She accused me of flirting with people she worked with. I'd sort of forgotten about that until just now."

"Ah. Let me guess. You did just what you did tonight—took care of your guests and tried to make sure everyone had a nice time."

Will looked at her and her eyes were shiny with tears. She blinked a few times so that none of them fell, but she couldn't hide the fact of them. "Something like that."

Although they'd talked about Will's former girlfriend before, it was only in that moment that Nora realized how toxic the relationship had been. Or how much Will carried the baggage of it with her. Nora gave into the urge to lift a hand to Will's cheek. "I'm sorry."

Will covered Nora's hand with her own and shifted it so that she could kiss the tops of Nora's knuckles. Everything about the night had been perfect. She had no desire to ruin it with talk of her stupid and naïve relationship choices. "You have nothing to be sorry for. Thank you for helping me pull off a better party than I could have imagined."

Nora angled her head. "It was a pretty great party."

"And now you're going to go take a bath while I clean up."

Nora planted her hands on her hips. "Absolutely not. We threw it together, we clean up together."

Will loaded the dishwasher while Nora put away leftover food and put empty wine bottles in the recycling bin. She hand washed trays and platters, handing each to Nora to be dried and put away. It didn't take long for the kitchen and dining room to be put back together. "So, does this mean we get to go to bed now?"

Nora smiled. "You didn't eat much. Do you want some dinner first?"

"Not even a little."

"Good. Me, neither."

Chapter Eighteen

Nora went to the bathroom to undress and wash her face. Will used the moment alone to get ready. Once she'd physically gotten herself situated, she tried to center herself mentally and emotionally. Not only was she about to be with Nora in a way that would take their intimacy to a whole new level, she was still riding the high of the party and all it seemed to imply about their relationship. The combination left her feeling a strange mix of invincible and tender.

The bathroom door opened and Nora emerged wearing the ivory silk robe Will had come to know and love.

"You are exquisite." Will slowly removed the robe, kissing and caressing as she went. Nora had a softness to her that felt different from their previous times together. Will couldn't put a finger on it, but she felt a huge responsibility—not just to please Nora, but to take care of her. Will gently eased her onto the bed.

Will didn't think she'd ever seen anything as beautiful as Nora was right then. Her skin glowed in the soft light of the lamp. Her hair spread on the pillow like a crown of gold. Her whole body seemed open, poised in a mixture of anticipation and desire. Knowing that anticipation and desire was for her made Will's head swim. She wanted Nora with a fire that threatened to engulf her. But even more than that, Will wanted to please her. She wanted to make Nora feel things no one had before. Part challenge, part promise—although it was hard to tell whether she meant that for Nora, or for herself.

Will took her time, kissing and caressing each inch of Nora's torso. She worshiped her neck and her arms, her hip bones, her thighs. Nora shifted slightly under her, not quite writhing, but moving against Will in a way that drove her crazy. When Will finally grazed her fingers over the small triangle of blond curls, Nora arched to meet her. Will braced an arm near her head and leaned in.

"Easy." Will whispered the command close to Nora's ear, but she didn't stop the movement of her hand. Nora relaxed, but began to squirm in earnest. "Are you ready for me? Do you want me inside you?"

Nora nodded, but without opening her eyes. "Yes."

"Look at me."

Nora's lids fluttered open. Her pupils were dilated. "Yes."

Will swallowed the lump that formed in her throat. The anticipation, she'd expected. The desire, too. The nerves, however, caught her off guard. Even more than the first time they'd slept together, a knot of uncertainty gripped Will.

"Please."

Will held Nora's gaze. "Sorry. I'm not trying to torture you."

Nora let out a ragged laugh. "Are you sure?"

Will chuckled. "Promise. It's just that this feels like a big deal all of a sudden."

Nora shook her head, almost imperceptibly. "No. It's just like before. Mutual enjoyment. Only more enjoyable."

Will smiled. She didn't want to let Nora see how much her words hurt. Will was so far beyond mutual enjoyment. Now wasn't the time to bare her soul. She needed to give Nora more time. Eventually, she'd have to see that what they had was so much more. In the meantime, Will resolved to do anything and everything in her power to bring them closer. And this was one of them. "I'll do my best not to disappoint."

Nora's laugh was low and sultry. It helped to ease the tension. "I'm sure you won't."

Will shifted on the bed, kneeling between Nora's thighs. Nora arched slowly in anticipation. Will positioned the head of the cock, rubbed it gently over Nora's sex. She could give Nora this. And maybe, just maybe, she could lay the foundation for what she really wanted.

Slowly, and with more care than she thought herself capable of, Will eased inside her. When Nora gasped, Will froze. "Are you okay?"

In lieu of words, Nora nodded. She bit her lip in a way that drove Will absolutely mad.

"If you want me to stop, you have to tell me."

Nora's reply was soft, but clear. "I don't—I won't—want you to stop."

Will slid the rest of the way in. She'd been so focused on Nora—her reactions, her desires, her pleasure—that she'd almost forgotten how incredible it felt to be with a woman like this. The sensations pulsed through her. Pleasure, of course, but also a heady mixture of power and responsibility. She'd often grappled with both those things, so the feeling threatened to overwhelm her.

No, she was going to enjoy this. And she was going to be sure Nora did, too.

Will focused her attention on Nora's face. She'd closed her eyes again and her head rocked gently from side to side. Will set a slow pace, wanting to make sure she wasn't too much for Nora, but also wanting to savor every second. She rested her hands on Nora's thighs, sliding her fingers up and down the smooth skin with each thrust. Nora's body undulated, rising to meet Will and taking in the full length of her each time.

Nora's breaths became more punctuated, each ending on a sound somewhere between a moan and a sigh. Her gorgeous mouth, the sight of her hands fisting in the sheets, almost undid Will. She leaned forward, bracing a hand on either side of Nora's head. Nora opened her eyes and they locked gazes.

"I needed to kiss you," Will said.

One of Nora's hands came up to Will's neck. She gently pulled Will's mouth down to hers. The taste of Nora's mouth, the press of their bodies, sent ripples through Will. The change of angle created a delicious friction against Will's clit. Even without a vibrator tucked into the harness, it wouldn't take much longer for her to come.

The shift must have had the same effect on Nora. Her sighs were definitely moans now. And she was muttering Will's name, interspersed with ohs and yeses. The sounds were so fucking sexy, Will couldn't take it.

Will increased the pace. She wanted—needed—to hear Nora come undone, to scream her name. Over and over, she pushed into Nora, filled her. Will swore she could feel Nora clench around her, pull her in deeper and tighter. She felt Nora begin to tremble beneath her. Nora's words became a chorus of yes. It grew louder and louder until Nora called Will's name. As she did, her body went stiff.

It was the sound that did Will in. She thrust into Nora a couple more times, then gave herself over to the quaking orgasm. A groan escaped her lips, along with something that sounded like a whimper. She rode it, imagining their bodies fused in a shared ecstasy.

In what felt like seconds, but was probably a few minutes, Nora's breathing evened out. Will eased herself just far enough away to slip off the harness. She slid back toward Nora, easing an arm under her. In sleep, she curled into Will without hesitation. Will allowed herself to read all sorts of meaning into the unconscious gesture. Things between them were shifting. Nora's brain might not be fully caught up, but her body was on board. Will hoped her heart was, as well.

Will stood in the kitchen, preparing the coffee pot for two. The sky was light, but the sun had yet to appear between the trees. It was a rare day that she beat Nora out of bed. Not that they'd spent that many nights together, but still. Will relished the quiet, as well as the prospect of bringing Nora coffee in bed, perhaps climbing back in with her. Nora's body would be soft and warm, pliant from a good night's sleep.

Even if things between them continued to go well, there wouldn't be many mornings like this. As soon as the high season rolled around, Nora would be up before dawn every day, preparing breakfast and focusing most of her attention on her guests. Will didn't mind. In truth, she relished the idea of them working side by side before Will went off for a day aboard the Dolphin Fleet. She'd come home just as happy hour rolled around. She'd shower and put on clean clothes, then as the guests headed out for dinner or a show or an evening stroll, they would sit in the garden with a glass of wine. Nora would talk about her day and then they'd make dinner together. They'd read books in the library or, if no one was around, put on a movie in the sitting room.

It was so easy to imagine, even easier to want. She hadn't let herself at first. The thrill of their physical chemistry, the fear of jinxing it—those forces had kept her mind squarely in the moment. But now she let herself dream.

Last night had felt like they were a couple. A real, honest to God, no longer a secret, couple. She was hesitant to press, but wanted desperately to know if Nora felt the same way. It mattered so much. It felt like the time to get things on solid footing, before the constant presence of guests and the summer staff. It might only be March, but it felt like time was running out.

Feeling less buoyant, but resolved, Will poured coffee and returned to Nora's room. She found her still asleep. Will set the mugs on the table by the bed, then stripped off the shirt and flannel pants she'd thrown on. Under the covers, she inched toward Nora, slid a hand over her hip.

Nora rolled toward her, moaned softly. Just like the night before, the gesture—unguarded and likely unconscious—gave Will hope. Will nuzzled her neck. Nora shifted to give her better access. Will took advantage, placing a line of kisses from her shoulder to her ear, then along her jaw to her chin.

"I could wake up every morning for the rest of my life like this." Will whispered the words, fairly certain Nora would neither hear nor respond to them. She took Nora's contented sigh as all the answer she needed, at least for now.

She ran her hand up Nora's side, cupped her breast. When Nora's eyes fluttered open, Will caught her gaze for a moment, then leaned in to kiss her. It started lazily enough, but she could feel Nora wake against her. Both her body and her mouth came alive, turning the gentle warmth of sleepy affection into something hotter and more insistent.

Will broke the kiss so she could lavish attention on other parts of Nora's body. Before she could go far, Nora framed Will's face with her hands. "What are you doing to me?"

Will offered what she hoped was a playful smile. "If you have to ask, I'm afraid I might not be doing it right."

Nora smiled, but her gaze, her eyes, remained serious. "That's not what I meant."

"I'm enjoying you." Will didn't know if that would satisfy her, but she continued. "I'm delighting in you, worshiping you. Hopefully, I'm pleasing you, too."

There was a softness, a vulnerability, on Nora's face that threatened to take Will's breath away. "You make it seem like you'll never get enough."

Given that her feelings frightened even her a little, Will knew better than to let them all come flooding out. She trailed a finger down Nora's cheek. "I'm not sure I ever will."

"I don't...I'm not exactly sure what to do with that."

She might be pressing her luck, but Will decided to go there. Even if it was in baby steps. "You don't have to do anything with it. At least not right now. Just know how much I adore spending time with you."

Nora glanced away, but Will kept her gaze firm. Eventually, Nora looked into her eyes again. "Okay."

"And I mean all of it—working, relaxing, talking, sleeping."
Will raised a brow. "Being in bed and not sleeping."

"We seem to do that last one really well."

"Exceptionally well. And since I finally woke up before you,
I intend to take full advantage."

Will kissed her again. She hoped, even if Nora didn't yet
feel comfortable with the words, she'd let Will show her in other
ways. Will poured all of the passion, all of the hope she'd allowed
herself to feel, into that kiss. As the kiss grew into more, Will
poured herself into that as well.

Perhaps it was wishful thinking on her part, but Will
believed that Nora gave it back to her in return. Never had they
made love so slowly, or with such care. When Nora came, it
felt like surrender. And while Will had no desire to conquer her,
the beauty of it left her breathless. Even her own orgasm felt
different, leaving her shaky, but feeling indescribably whole.

CHAPTER NINETEEN

Wat the fuck?"

Nora jerked her head in the direction of the voice. Even before she saw Graham standing in the doorway, Nora knew it was her. She instinctively pulled at the sheets to cover herself. Not that it mattered. She glanced at the clock. It was the middle of the afternoon and she was in bed with Will, naked. There was no other way to interpret what was happening. "Graham."

Without answering, Graham turned on her heel and disappeared. Nora heard her footsteps in the hall. But by the time she pulled on a robe and followed, Graham was gone.

She stood in the front hall, staring at the door. As though staring might make Graham reappear. Or might undo what had just transpired.

She heard footsteps behind her, felt Will's hand on her shoulder. She shook her head. This could not be happening.

"Is she gone?"

At the sound of Will's voice, Nora whipped around to face her. "Yes, she's gone. I have to get dressed. I have to find her."

"Calm down. I'm sure she was weirded out, but it's not that big a deal."

Nora looked at Will with a mixture of disbelief and anger. "It most certainly is a big deal. I can't believe I let this happen."

She tried to brush past Will, but Will blocked her path. She looked confused and exasperated. "What do you want me to do?"

Nora pushed past her, this time with more force. "You've done enough. You should go."

Nora went to her room, leaving Will standing alone. Will remained there, trying to process what was happening. Yes, Graham walking in on them was less than ideal. But Nora made it seem catastrophic. Catastrophic and all Will's fault. And what about Graham? Will expected surprise, awkwardness maybe. But Graham walked out without even waiting for a conversation.

Almost as quickly as she'd disappeared, Nora emerged from her room fully dressed. "Where are you going?" Will asked.

"I don't know. But Graham couldn't have gone far on foot. I assume she didn't drive here, at least."

"Why don't we call her? Even if she's upset, I can't imagine she wouldn't pick up."

Nora fixed her with an icy stare. "You don't know anything."

And then, just like Graham, she was gone.

Will hugged her arms around herself. The sudden chill that rippled through her had nothing to do with the temperature. What was she supposed to do now? Standing in Nora's foyer probably wasn't it. She headed back to the bedroom, tugged on the rest of her clothes, and pulled her phone out of her pants pocket. Nora would certainly be trying to get Graham on the phone. Not wanting to make the situation any more overwhelming than it already was, Will settled on a text. She started and erased several before settling on one she felt okay with.

I'm sorry that was crazy weird. Your aunt is freaking out. Please call her. And me.

Whether or not Graham replied, Will decided she needed to get out. Nora's reaction sat heavy in her chest. Even if Will could understand her worry about Graham, the cold and dismissive way Nora had spoken to her left her feeling panicky. And small. She'd not felt that small since her last fight with Kai.

She'd returned her phone to her pocket, but took it out again. She turned the ringer all the way up, then started to text Nora. She agonized even more over what to say to her. In the end, she couldn't find a way to articulate even a fraction of what she was feeling. She decided to keep it simple.

Please touch base when you hear from Graham. I'll do the same.

She added an "xo," then deleted it. Added it and deleted it a second time, then hit send. She grabbed her wallet and keys, then let herself out. She stood on the porch for several minutes, obsessing over whether she should lock the door or leave it open. Surely, Nora had her keys. And it wasn't like Will would need to get back in until she'd heard from Nora. She flipped the lock and pulled the door closed behind her, trying to dispel the foreboding that came with the gesture.

Unsure of how much she should try to intervene, Will walked to Commercial Street. She'd keep an eye out for both Graham and Nora. And then what? Go home. There wasn't much else she could do.

Feeling both restless and useless, she walked the length of Commercial, past the Boatslip and into the residential part of the West End. Not that she expected to happen upon them, but turning around still felt like admitting defeat. By the time she got back to the center of town, the last thing Will felt like doing was returning to her apartment. But the sun was beginning to set. It was cold and she only had a light jacket. And she wasn't doing anyone any good.

She climbed the hill alongside of the monument quickly, making her legs burn. From the driveway, she could see lights already on in her apartment. She walked in to find Kaylee and Cheyenne on the couch, drinking beer and watching a Red Sox spring training game.

"Hey, lover boy. We didn't expect to see you tonight," Kaylee said.

"Yeah. Trouble in paradise?"

For the first time since she'd moved in, Will detested the fact that she had roommates. "Not feeling all that great. Just going to try and sleep it off."

Cheyenne's face took on a sympathetic look. "That sucks. You need anything?"

Will offered a weak smile. "No, I'm going to crash in my room."

"We'll turn down the game."

Will waved a hand. "No, don't do that. I'll be fine."

Without waiting for a response, Will headed to her room. She turned on the overhead light, then flinched at how bright it seemed. She swapped it out for the lamp on her nightstand, then flopped on the bed. She kicked off her boots and pulled out her phone. No response from Nora or Graham. Great.

She checked the clock. Barely seven. Emerson should be done with dinner. She dialed her number and tried to decide how to explain what had transpired in the last few hours.

"Hey, stranger." Emerson's voice was upbeat and familiar.

Before she could stop herself, Will started to cry. "Hey."

"What's wrong?"

Will made a sound somewhere between a laugh and a cough. "How do you know something is wrong?"

"Because I know you. What is it? What happened?"

Will took a deep breath. "Graham just walked in on Nora and me."

"Walked in on you—"

"In bed. Not having sex, but in bed. Naked."

"Ah. Okay. What did she say?"

"'What the fuck?'"

"Hey, I'm just asking."

Will shook her head, even though Emerson couldn't see her. "No, that's what she said. All she said. Then she left."

"Oh."

"And Nora flipped out and went chasing after her."

"Oh, man. Do you think she's really pissed?"

Will sighed. "Graham or Nora?"

"I was talking about Graham. Why would Nora be pissed?"

"I don't know, but she freaked out. I told her to calm down and she pretty much said I didn't know anything. Then she told me to leave."

"Whoa."

"Yeah. I've texted both of them, but neither of them has replied. And now I'm home and hiding in my room and I have no idea what to do."

There was a pause on the line. "Do you want me to come over?"

That she offered meant the world to Will. It also made her feel like a fuck-up. Once again. "No. It's late. And a school night."

"I haven't turned into a total early bird. I want to help. What can I do?"

How many times had Emerson asked her that? How many times had she let Emerson calm her down, or lift her spirits, or bail her out of trouble? She'd finally thought that things were balancing out, that she had her shit together enough that she wouldn't be in need of rescue. As much as she wanted Emerson to say whatever she would say that would invariably make her feel better, Will suddenly regretted calling her. "Nothing. I think I needed to say it out loud. I'm sorry I bothered you."

"You didn't. You never bother me. Ever."

"Thanks. This will work itself out, I'm sure. Thanks for listening."

"Will, I've hardly listened at all. Do you want to talk in person? You can come here, too. Liam is doing homework and Darcy is helping me upgrade my website. You're not interrupting anything."

But that was just it. She was interrupting. Emerson was having a perfectly nice, normal evening at home with her family and Will was busting in with all her drama. Yet again. "I'm good. Really. Thanks, though."

"Are you sure?"

Emerson sounded incredulous, but Will was pretty sure she wouldn't push it. Will cleared her throat and channeled as much positivity as she could muster into her voice. "Totally sure. Have a good night. I'll check in tomorrow."

"Okay. Call anytime. I mean it."

"I will. Love you."

"You, too."

Will ended the call and stared at her phone. Although she wanted to talk to Nora to hear her voice, trying to talk to her before the Graham situation was under control would be a lost cause. She dialed Graham's number. It rang and rang. Will tried to formulate what she wanted to leave as a voice mail.

"What do you want?" Graham's voice, more wounded than angry, caught Will off guard.

"I want to talk, and to apologize."

"For sleeping with my aunt or for lying to me about it?"

Shit. She really should have thought out what she wanted to say before calling. "I didn't lie."

"Oh, I'm so sorry. Let me rephrase. Are you sorry for having an affair with Aunt Nora or for keeping it a secret despite the hundred or so times we've talked and texted in the last two months?"

"I…"

"Yeah, that's what I thought. I guess that explains why you weren't interested in me."

"Graham." For the first time since it happened, Will flashed back to the awkward kiss after the New Year's party. She'd taken Graham's explanation—and quick dismissal—at face value. Clearly, a colossal misjudgment on her part.

"You could have at least told me, instead of letting me make a complete fool of myself."

"I didn't mean to keep it from you. Nora thought—"

"What? That I wouldn't take it well? No shit."

"Graham, I'm really sorry. I never wanted you to get hurt."

The extended silence made Will think that maybe Graham had hung up on her. "Well, you could have fooled me."

Graham did hang up, then. Will looked at the screen of her phone. Call ended. Will stood and started to pace. Talking to Nora couldn't go any worse than that. Will dialed her number and waited. This time, it did go to voice mail. While she waited for Nora's greeting to end, she scrambled for the right words. "Hi. It's me. I don't know if you found Graham, but I just talked to her. She's angry, but she at least took my call. I'm at my place. I don't know what to do right now, but I'm sorry. Please call me."

Will ended the call. Now, on top of feeling useless, she could add pathetic. Great.

She sat on the bed again, flopped back, but left her legs dangling over the edge. She stayed like that until her back began to ache. She pulled her legs up, rolled onto her side. She looked at her phone for the millionth time. She sent Nora a couple of pleading texts. She stared at the wall. She checked her phone again. She heard her roommates go to bed. She turned off her lamp and waited for it to be morning.

CHAPTER TWENTY

Nora walked for what felt like hours. She tried the pier, the Squealing Pig, the benches in front of the library as well as the ones in front of town hall. There were a thousand places Graham could have gone or she could still be walking. If she didn't want to be found, Nora had little hope.

Where are you?

Nora looked at her phone. The last half dozen texts had been from Will. Finally, one from Graham. She stopped walking just long enough to type a reply. *I'm looking for you.*

Waiting for Graham's answer was torture.

I'm home. Your place.

Relief washed over her. *I'll be right there. Please don't go anywhere.*

The walk back didn't take more than fifteen minutes, but it felt like an eternity. She arrived panicked again and out of breath and found Graham sitting on the front stoop. "Graham."

"The front door is locked."

Will must have gone. That fact made her heart hurt, even if she knew it was for the best. She'd taken her keys—she always took her keys—so she unlocked the door and let them in. "Thank you for coming back."

Graham didn't make eye contact. "I didn't really have anywhere else to go."

Nora took a deep breath. That was partially true, but Nora knew she had at least one credit card. If Graham had been adamant, she could have checked herself into a hotel. "I'm still glad you came back."

Graham shrugged. "I left my stuff. I didn't even have my wallet."

Okay, so maybe she really didn't have a choice. Still. Nora didn't intend to waste the opportunity to apologize, to explain. "I'm sorry."

Graham turned on her, eyes puffy and red. "Sorry you're fucking Will or sorry I caught you?"

Despite the crushing guilt in Nora's chest, she was still Graham's aunt and bristled at the accusation. "There's no need for that language."

"I'm only articulating what you're doing. Oh, wait. Or is she fucking you? That's probably her style."

"Graham."

"Don't 'Graham' me, Aunt Nora. I can't believe you would do this to me."

And just like that, all the casual conversations, all the little observations of the fall returned. Nora remembered why she'd been hesitant to give Will a chance. She'd been convinced Will was trying to make a move on Graham. As that fear had been dispelled, she'd lost sight of the flip side—that Graham had an interest in Will. "I had no intention of hurting you. I hope you can believe that."

Graham shook her head. "You didn't even like her. I'm the one who convinced you to hire her, to give her a chance."

"And you were right."

Graham laughed, but there was no humor in it. "I can't fucking believe it. Seriously."

Nora's heart ached. How could she have been so stupid? "It just happened. We spent so much time together. What can I do?"

"Right now? Nothing."

"You'll stay, though? You can have your old room. Will is gone and she isn't coming back."

Graham picked up her bag and, without another word, disappeared into the room she'd occupied for so many months. Nora sat on the stairs and scrubbed a hand over her face. How could she have made such a terrible mistake?

❖

Will jerked awake to the sound of a text notification. She must have fallen asleep at some point because the sun shone bright against the blinds of her room. She fumbled in the covers for a moment until she found her phone.

Graham is here. She doesn't want to see you. I don't either.

The anxiety of the night before became a chill that settled in her chest and worked its way out. It wasn't just that Nora didn't want to see her, although that stung plenty. No, it was the dismissive tone. More than anger or frustration, it told Will loud and clear that she didn't matter.

The need to hole up vanished. In its place, a desperation to get out, get as far away from her current situation as she possibly could.

She didn't have a lot of options. Her funds were getting low, so any sort of paid accommodation was out of the question. Immediately, she thought of Leigh. Their friendship was one of the few that hadn't imploded during the reign of Kai. Even though they weren't super close, they'd crashed at each other's places plenty over the years—when they'd lived in the same city and when they hadn't.

An hour and a flurry of texts later, she'd learned that Leigh was traveling for work, but would love nothing more than to have Will check on her place and stay a while. She then had an exchange with Emerson, filling her in on her plans and promising she'd only be gone a week.

It took her less time to pack than it had taken her to decide to leave. She finished cramming clothes into her duffel bag and looked around. A small part of her was tempted to clear out completely. It wouldn't be hard. Except for the thrift store furniture she'd bought with her roommates to make the apartment homier, she didn't own much. She could box up the books and mementos, fit everything in her car.

She shook her head. She was done with running. Regardless of what happened with Nora or with Graham, Provincetown was her home now. Clearing out for a little while was a breather, a reset button. Not only did she believe that, she'd promised Emerson it was true. Sure, that promise might be all that stopped her right now, but she'd take it. She went out to the living room and scribbled a note for her roommates, assuring them she'd be back in a few days. She threw her things in the back of her car and got on the road.

Will spent the twenty minutes it took to get to Wellfleet wrestling with whether to stop and see Emerson. As much as she didn't want to disappear without seeing her, stopping to say goodbye had a weird formality to it. Or finality, maybe. Either way, she didn't want it to be a thing. And she'd promised she would be back soon. That's what mattered.

It took about eight hours to get to D.C. She was equal parts disappointed and relieved that Leigh was in Europe for work. As much as she missed her, she appreciated not having to explain herself, at least not right away.

She knocked on the next door neighbor's door as Leigh had instructed. Wayne, a retired accountant in his seventies, was chatty, but Will was able to keep the conversation superficial. After procuring the key and promising to let him know if she needed anything, Will let herself into Leigh's condo and breathed a sigh of relief.

She unpacked the groceries she'd picked up to tide her over for a couple of days, then wandered around the beautiful space. She'd visited once before, but not since Leigh had redone the kitchen and bathrooms. It was a bit modern for her personal tastes, but Will couldn't fault the design or the precision of the work.

Upstairs, she found a giant jetted tub in the master bathroom. She'd never been one for baths, but this tub warranted an exception. She ran the water as hot as she could stand it and pulled off her clothes.

Half an hour later, she dragged herself from the water, relaxed but exhausted. After pulling on boxers and T-shirt, she checked her phone. She had a text from Emerson, checking to make sure she'd arrived. The casual tone of it didn't seem forced, nor did the assertion that Will knew how to get in touch if she needed anything.

Something about that brief exchange brought Will close to tears. It wasn't the first time Emerson had offered support. Like before, she'd done it lightly, without pressure or judgment. When she was with Kai, she'd resented that support. Even with a gentle delivery, it implied something was wrong. At the time, Will had refused to accept that. Thinking about her reactions—flip, dismissive, even exasperated—gave her a profound sense of regret.

She knew better than to try to say as much in a text. Poor Emerson would think she was having a full-on meltdown. She'd save it for now. But once she was home, she'd find a way to show Emerson how much the subtle interventions meant to her. In the meantime, she kept her reply light, going so far as to call her trip a mini vacation before her job on the Dolphin Fleet started again.

Will climbed into Leigh's gorgeous queen sized bed. It wasn't so big it should feel lonely, but it did. She'd gotten more used to sleeping with Nora than sleeping alone. Will shook her head. She would not wallow. Wallowing would do absolutely no good.

Will was telling herself the same thing four hours later when she'd yet to fall asleep. She finally drifted off as the sun rose. When she woke however many hours later, she had no idea where she was or how much time had passed. She snagged her phone from the nightstand and breathed a sigh of relief. Just after ten. Even if she wasn't well-rested, she'd likely not upended her entire sleep pattern.

She changed into running clothes and headed for the trail not too far from Leigh's place. She kept an easy pace, enjoying the spring air and the feeling of blood moving through her muscles. When a beep interrupted Pitbull's latest take on who wants whom, she slowed to a walk. The text was from Graham.

We need to talk.

Will didn't disagree, but she couldn't bring herself to reply. The statement gave no indication of how mad Graham was, or who she was mad at. It was chicken shit of her to avoid dealing with it, but Will told herself she could have a day to regroup. Given how badly her attempt to talk to Nora had gone, she expected things with Graham to be just as ugly.

Will resumed running. She thought of Graham as a sister. It was like how she felt about Emerson, only Will got to feel protective of her. She hadn't had that with Emerson in ages. And Graham looked up to her, like she had her act together. Will really didn't want to lose that.

Why hadn't she just told her? Will increased her pace. Because Nora explicitly asked her not to. Will had thought it strange, but Nora was so focused on not telling anyone at first, Will lumped it all together. She shook her head. She was so excited about Nora giving her a chance, she was perfectly happy to go along with pretty much anything Nora wanted. Okay, maybe not happy, but willing.

It hadn't seemed like a problem at the time. She figured Nora just needed some extra time, that once she got used to the idea of them together, things would sort themselves out. Like with the engagement party.

Will berated herself. Despite all her promises to be her own person, she'd let herself get pressured into something she knew was a bad idea. She'd ruined things not only with Nora, but probably with Graham as well. She hadn't learned anything.

Will stopped running and realized she had no idea where she was. Fortunately, her phone had plenty of charge and she was able to pull up her GPS app. Unfortunately, she'd gotten herself close to five miles from Leigh's place. She contemplated a Lyft, but even the short distance would cut into the cash she had. Deciding she'd rather eat the rest of the week, she routed herself back on foot.

When she was about a mile away, the sky opened and, in a matter of seconds, she was soaked through. Fitting, really, given how the last couple of days had gone. She tucked her phone in her pocket to stay dry and hoped she remembered the route well enough to get the rest of the way back. She considered running it, but there wasn't any point.

Back at Leigh's she peeled off her squishy shoes and the socks plastered to her feet. She did the same with her clothes. Even her underwear were soaked. She left the soggy pile near the door and headed to the bathroom, opting for a quick shower instead of another soak.

Between the exercise and the dry clothes, she felt almost human. She was also starved. She opened the fridge, wishing she'd bought more groceries. She settled on a yogurt and sat at the island. As much as the run had cleared her head in the moment, now that she was sitting still, all the questions and doubts and fears and self-loathing came roaring back to life.

She'd been so stupid to think she could have it all. Or that what she had with Nora meant something. Or perhaps more accurately, meant something to more than just her.

CHAPTER TWENTY-ONE

*P**lease talk to me.*

Will looked at the message. It was the third such request from Graham. She'd ignored the first two. Even if part of her believed Graham deserved to rail against her, she couldn't open herself up to that. If anything, Graham and Nora needed some time to sort out what had happened. Almost as much as she regretted hurting Nora, Will hated herself for creating such a chasm between family. Hopefully, with time, it would heal. Time and her not sticking her nose in and making matters worse.

Please. I'm not mad anymore. I'm worried about you.

Will sighed. She'd convinced herself that not making contact was the better thing to do. Kinder. But it didn't seem like Graham was going to give up anytime soon. Will didn't want to cause her any more worry, or angst, than she already had. She typed out a response.

I'm okay. I'm just sorry for everything.

The three little dots told her Graham was composing a reply. What had they done before the little dots?

I'm sorry, too. I had no right to blow up on you. Can we talk?

The idea of seeing Graham made Will a little nauseous. Of course, it was less frightening than the thought of seeing Nora. Or of not seeing her, really. At this point, Will couldn't imagine either. She'd managed to get by on not thinking at all. And ice cream. She'd eaten probably three gallons of it in the last few days, and not much else.

Yeah. Okay.

More dots.

I wish we could have met up before I came back to school, but FaceTime?

Will chuckled. *I'm in D.C. House sitting for an old friend.*

Graham's reply was something along the lines of the universe wanting them to make up. Will grudgingly agreed and they made plans to meet that evening.

Will walked into the restaurant. The hostess station was abandoned, so she scanned the tables and found Graham sitting at a high-top in the bar area. She walked over to join her, forcing herself to make eye contact and offering a sheepish smile. "Hey."

Graham hopped off the stool and flung her arms around Will. "I'm so glad to see you."

Will tried to shake off her surprise and returned the hug. "Really?"

"I'm so sorry I flipped out on you. I was totally out of line."

Will let Graham's words sink in. She'd expected to do the apologizing. "I'm...it's fine. You didn't do anything wrong."

Graham rolled her eyes and climbed back onto her stool. "Of course I did. Let's order a drink and we can sort it all out."

As if on cue, a waitress appeared. Graham ordered a beer and Will followed suit. When the waitress disappeared, they sat for a moment in awkward silence. Will opened her mouth to say something just as Graham did and they talked over one another for a second. "You go," Will said.

Graham nodded and began to speak, but the waitress returned with their drinks. She set the pint glasses on the table and looked at Will. "Y'all ordering some food or you good with the beers?"

"I think we're okay for now." She glanced at Graham, who nodded.

"Okay. I'll check on y'all in a little bit."

When the waitress had gone again, Graham took a long sip of her beer. She set it down and took a deep breath. "So, as I was saying, I'm sorry."

Will did the same. "Me, too."

"It's none of my business who Aunt Nora sleeps with. Or you, for that matter."

Will sighed. "Still, I'm sure it was pretty shitty to walk in on us like that."

Graham shook her head. "It was shocking. I'll give you that much. I had no idea. Literally, none."

"We shouldn't have kept it a secret." Will couldn't bring herself to point fingers at Nora for that decision, even if it might help her with Graham in the moment.

"I think, because I talk to you both practically every day, it felt like more than a casual omission."

"That's totally fair."

Graham shrugged. "I don't like being mad, though, especially at my favorite people."

Graham's quickness to forgive made Will feel even worse about putting her in that position in the first place. "Is there anything I can do to make it better?"

"For me?"

Will offered a rueful smile. "Yes, you."

Graham sighed. Like, really sighed. "No. I feel like I owe you an explanation, too, though."

Will looked at her quizzically. "What do you mean?"

"I didn't freak out only because I was caught off guard."

Graham's comment about getting why she wasn't interested echoed in Will's mind. "Yeah."

Graham looked away. "I've clearly been harboring a crush on you." She glanced at Will, cringed, then looked away again.

Will, who'd just taken a sip of beer, choked on it. Even now, when it all made sense, it felt implausible. "Really?"

Graham rolled her eyes, then shook her head. "Yes, really."

"I am so sorry." Will put extra emphasis on the 'so.'

"I mean, I knew you didn't reciprocate those feelings. You said as much on New Year's. It's not like you led me on or anything. I thought I was over it." She shrugged in a way that seemed self-deprecating. "Obviously not."

Will ran her fingers through her hair. She probably should have seen it coming. Her attention had been so squarely on Nora, even before the party. In hindsight, it was idiotic not to have at least talked to Graham about the kiss the next day. "You know I find you utterly wonderful."

Graham rolled her eyes even more dramatically. "You don't have to say that."

"It's true. You're beautiful, too, but you already know that." The look on Graham's face told Will maybe she didn't already know that. "I mean it."

Graham cleared her throat and looked away again. "Well, thanks for that. But that's not why we're here."

Will reached across the table and squeezed her hand. "You're really special, you know. You're going to make a very lucky woman extremely happy one day."

Graham smiled, and maybe blushed a little. "Thanks. Now, can we finish making up?"

Will nodded. "Absolutely. Tell me what you need, how I can make it better."

"I'm the one who's supposed to make it better. You ran away because I flipped out. I need to find a way to make it up to you, fix it."

If only it was that simple. Based on her last conversation—if you could call it a conversation—with Nora, they had much bigger problems than Graham catching them in the act. Will didn't see any way of making it right, much less finding a way to make it work. Since following that train of thought would likely reduce her to a pile of tears, again, she focused her attention on Graham. "If you're not mad at me, then we're good. You didn't do anything wrong. Besides, I'm pretty sure I could never stay mad at you."

Graham nodded. "Okay, good. We're good. But what about Nora?"

Not sure she was ready to go there, especially with Graham, Will noted that the waitress was heading their way. "Are you hungry? How about we get a bite to eat?"

"Sure. We aren't done with this conversation, but sure."

After a quick perusal of the menu, they put in an order. While they waited for the food to arrive, Graham folded her arms and leaned forward. "So is it just an affair or are you in love?"

Damn. The girl wasted no time. "You cut right to the chase, don't you?"

Graham shrugged. "I care about you both. Let's just say I have a vested interest. So?"

So. Will didn't know what to say. There was no doubt as far as her heart was concerned, but she felt strange proclaiming her feelings for Nora to Graham when she'd never shared them with Nora directly. "I don't know."

Now that they weren't talking about her, Graham's gaze was unwavering. "Don't know how you feel or don't know how she feels in return?"

Will made a face. She didn't want to lie to Graham, but the situation felt hopeless. "Both."

"Okay. That's a starting point at least."

Will shook her head. "I don't think it matters."

"What do you mean? Of course it matters."

"Nora made it clear she was done with me. That's why I left town. I felt bad about you, but things with Nora did not go well. I'm pretty sure I'm the last person she wants to see, much less be with." Their food arrived and Will busied herself with putting ketchup on her fries and taking a bite of her turkey club.

Graham stole one of her fries, then took a bite of her Caesar salad. She chewed thoughtfully. After swallowing, she pointed her fork at Will. "Did she ever tell you about Jordyn?"

The name wasn't even vaguely familiar. "No."

Graham shook her head and tsked. "Of course she didn't."

"Who's Jordyn?"

"Only the woman that stole her money, broke her heart, and almost cost her the inn."

"Wait. Yeah. Sort of." Will remembered the conversation she and Nora had over lunch. It had felt at the time like Nora was confiding in her, but clearly she'd downplayed how dire the situation had been.

"It hit her really hard. She hasn't been in a relationship since."

"I didn't know that." Will was no stranger to baggage. Her heart felt heavier at the thought of Nora being completely closed off.

"You know, I didn't ask if the two of you were in love. I asked if you were."

Will took her time chewing, in part to buy time and in part because she'd not eaten a real meal in days. "Like I said, I don't think it matters."

"You do love her."

Love. It was a word Will didn't shy away from, but not one she threw around lightly. She'd not used it with Nora, or even her private thoughts about what they shared. Still. With the weight of the last two weeks pressing on her heart, she knew there wasn't another word to describe it. Lying wouldn't do a damn thing to change it. "I do."

"You have to tell her. You have to work it out."

"It's not that simple."

Graham pounded her fist on the table. "I refuse to be the reason you aren't together."

Will's heart broke a little at the sight of her, eyes pleading and heart so clearly holding onto the notion that if you want something badly enough, you can make it happen. "You aren't. I promise."

"I don't believe you. I'm guessing things were going great until I showed up and blew everything to pieces."

Will thought about that assertion. Things had been going great, at least on some level. Even if they hadn't talked specifically about feelings, Will refused to believe there weren't any. She and Nora weren't where she wanted to be, but it felt like they'd been getting closer. "Tell me more about Jordyn."

Graham eyed her suspiciously. "Don't change the subject."

"I'm not. If there's any chance of working this out, I need to know about her."

Graham sighed and angled her head. "It's not really my story to tell."

Will respected that Graham didn't want to break confidences, but she needed something. More than what Nora had given her. "Don't tell me all the details, just the overview. What anyone even a little bit close to her would know."

Graham seemed to consider her options. After a long moment, she pushed the rest of her salad aside. "It was a long time ago. Ten years, maybe? I was still in high school, so even I don't know all of it. Aunt Nora had bought the inn and I came to spend the summer with her and help out."

Will nodded, settling in for however much of the story she was going to get.

"Jordyn answered an ad she'd put out for housekeeping help. This was before Tisha came along. She was young, probably early twenties, and a musician. Nora hired her and she moved into the maid's quarters at the back of the house. The room that's Nora's now. Nora and I shared the adjoining rooms."

On more than one occasion, Will had traded work for a roof over her head. It might not be the ideal arrangement, but it could serve a purpose.

"I adored her. She was fun and had so much energy. She'd clean all morning and then play her guitar in the garden in the afternoon. She'd have gigs at night. I was too young to go to most of them, but she had talent. Charisma, too."

"And she and Nora started dating?" Will had a hard time picturing it. Aspiring musician seemed so against type for her.

"Neither of them said as much, but they started spending lots of time together. I saw Jordyn leave Nora's room early one morning, so it was pretty obvious."

"What happened?"

Graham shrugged. "I went home at the end of the summer. We were supposed to go and visit her for Thanksgiving, but my parents said she decided to book guests for the week instead. I heard them talking about giving her a loan. When I went to stay with her for a few days over Christmas, Jordyn was gone. Aunt Nora didn't tell me what happened, but I knew it was something bad. She had this sadness around her, but anger, too. I asked my mom about it when I got home."

"What did she tell you?"

"That one of Aunt Nora's employees had stolen from her and it had almost cost her the inn. I couldn't tell if she knew Nora and Jordyn were together. I don't think it would have made a difference in terms of them loaning her money, but I never said anything."

Will took a deep breath. That certainly explained a lot about Nora's reticence to get involved with her. Or to be open about it. "That's a pretty big secret for you to have to carry around."

Graham shrugged. "She always felt more like my sister than an aunt. And it's not like my parents pumped me for information."

"Still." Will shook her head. "And did you and Nora ever talk about it?"

Graham thought for a moment. "Not specifically, you know? As I've gotten older, she's cautioned me against being too open, too trusting."

Will chuckled, thinking about her own conversations with Nora. "She's very protective of you."

Graham rolled her eyes. "Tell me about it. I really think that's part of what's going on now."

"How so?"

"Part of why she was so upset is because I was so upset. She hated the idea that her actions had resulted in me being unhappy."

Will lifted a shoulder. "They sort of did."

"Yeah, but not really. Once the shock wore off, I calmed down. Now I think you'd be great together."

Again, if only it were that simple. "I appreciate the vote of confidence, but I don't think that's the only problem."

"What else is there?" Graham's tone showed her exasperation. "If you love her, fight for her."

The thought had occurred to her, more than once. But again and again, Will circled back to the question of whether or not she could make Nora happy. The selfish part of her asserted that she could. The rest of her—the much larger part—wasn't so sure. Because, really, what did she have to offer? Not much. Would it be fair to convince Nora to be with her if it was a lopsided relationship?

Knowing these new details about Nora's past didn't help, either. She'd been hurt, badly. She deserved a woman who could be her hero, a knight in shining armor who protected and championed her. Even if Will wasn't unscrupulous, she was none of those things.

"I can see those wheels turning. What are you thinking?"

Will flinched, forgetting she was in the middle of a conversation. "Sorry?"

"I asked what you were thinking."

"Oh." Will didn't want to burden Graham any more than she wanted to do so to Nora. "I'm just not sure it's that kind of relationship."

"God. You're about as stubborn as she is."

Will smiled. That, she'd believe. "Enough about me and all my drama. How's school?"

Graham sighed, but didn't press the conversation any further. "It's almost done. I have one final and I'm defending my thesis in two weeks."

"That's so great. I'm so happy for you. And if it's not weird to say, proud of you, too."

"Thanks. You know, part of why I came for a visit was that I finished my thesis a week ahead of time."

Will shook her head. "You came for a celebration and, well, ugh. I'm really sorry."

Graham pointed a finger at her. "No more apologies. That's over and done."

"Okay."

"So." Graham ran her finger through the condensation on her beer glass. "Are you going back?"

It was a fair question. She had taken off without a word to anyone but Emerson. And she'd be lying if she said she hadn't considered starting from scratch somewhere new. But she'd learned the hard way that running didn't solve her problems. They always seemed to find her. And she liked her life in P-town—her job, being close to Emerson, and this newfangled thing of being Liam's aunt. Even if things with Nora were over and done, her life, her future, were there. "I am."

"That's a relief, especially since the other reason I came to town was an interview. I just accepted a permanent position with the Dolphin Fleet."

"Graham, that's so awesome. Congratulations."

Graham smiled. "Thanks. I knew last fall it's what I wanted, but I didn't know if they'd have an opening. I might have to tend bar on the side to make rent, but it's my dream job."

"And you deserve it." The waitress brought the check and Will insisted on paying. "It's really the least I can do."

In the parking lot, Graham gave her another hug. "You'll come to my graduation, right?"

Knowing that would likely involve seeing Nora made Will's stomach clench. "Wouldn't miss it."

CHAPTER TWENTY-TWO

How long exactly are you planning to mope?" Martha eyed Nora over the rim of her martini glass.

Nora scowled. "I'm not moping."

"Could've fooled me."

"I was stupid. I let myself make some impulsive, bad decisions. I'm now paying the price for those bad decisions. It's not the end of the world."

"That's such a matter-of-fact way to talk about a broken heart."

Nora sipped her own drink, enjoying the way the brininess played off the herbal notes in the gin. No one made a dirty martini better than Martha. "Who said anything about a broken heart?"

Martha merely raised a brow. Nora resisted the urge to set down her drink and scrub her hands over her face. The last couple of weeks had been rough. Even still, she hadn't thought of it in terms of heartbreak. Stupidity, sure. Self-loathing, regret, and a general umbrella of should have known better. She could even admit—if only to herself—she'd developed feelings for Will. But that was a long way from a broken heart.

Martha finished her drink and popped an olive in her mouth. "Well, your mouth is saying one thing, but the rest of you is screaming another."

Nora shook her head. "I've been brokenhearted. Like, sitting on the floor of the shower and sobbing, don't eat for days brokenhearted. This is an aberration."

"Don't get me wrong. I'm glad you aren't falling apart. But you don't need to be in a heap to have a broken heart."

Nora thought back to the days—weeks—after Jordyn left. The pain and betrayal were overlaid with a profound sense of shame. She'd not seriously contemplated disappearing, but more than once, she'd thought not existing might be preferable to figuring out a way to pick up the pieces. When the fog finally began to lift, she promised herself she'd never open herself up to that kind of hurt, or that kind of risk, ever again.

And she hadn't. Even as she and Will got closer, she'd held the softest, deepest parts of herself back. She'd actually started to think she had everything under control—a closeness to Will, sexual chemistry that didn't leave her completely vulnerable and raw. And Will either hadn't minded or hadn't noticed. And then all hell broke loose, threatening her relationship with Graham and making her feel like a complete fool.

It was that, what her fling with Will could have cost her, that had put her in such a low place now. Not a broken heart. Of course, it didn't help that Will had gone completely MIA. According to Graham, she and Will had spoken, made up even. And by her accounts, Will should be back in town for work by now. That part, the not even trying to come to a truce, added insult to injury.

"Look, spring is finally starting to show itself. I've got lots of reservations. Tisha is back and everything is smooth sailing. I've got nothing to mope about."

As if summoned by the sound of her name, Tisha poked her head out the front door. Even though she hadn't been part of the conversation, Nora half expected her to launch in, too. She'd been back only a couple of days, but Nora got the feeling she sensed something was up and was merely biding her time to say so. "Nora, you got a woman on the phone who wants to book a bridal shower."

Nora stood, grateful for the interruption. "I have to take this."

Martha waved a hand at her. "I have to go anyway. I'm picking Heidi up in an hour."

"Leave the glasses. I'll get them when I'm done."

Martha stood, came over, and gave Nora a hug. "If you want to not fall apart over drinks again soon, you call me."

Nora smiled. "Will do."

She spent the next half hour on the phone, planning a bridal shower for twenty for early June. Since she had only two of her rooms still open for the weekend, she gave the maid of honor some suggestions of other accommodations close by. When she hung up, Tisha stood nearby with her hands on her hips. "You gonna tell me what's going on?"

"Low key bridal shower in June. Afternoon tea, in the garden if the weather cooperates."

"That's not what I'm talking about and you know it."

Nora sighed. Tisha wouldn't nag, but she'd work in subtle digs until Nora talked. It was easiest to save them both the trouble now. "I dated someone over the winter and it ended. Nothing major, but Martha is a worry wart."

Tisha narrowed her eyes. "Did you end it or did she?"

"I did." Technically, that was true. Although Will seemed perfectly happy to walk away without a second thought.

"And you're glad it's over."

"Not glad, but it's for the best."

"Okay, then. As long as you're okay." Tisha nodded slowly. "I'm glad you got some."

Nora laughed in spite of herself. "Thanks. Now, don't you have some work to do?"

Tisha spread her arms wide. "It is all done. A well-oiled machine."

"Are you heading out for the day?"

"Yeah. The snacks are ready to go and all the morning's laundry is done."

Nora smiled. "I'm glad you're back."

Tisha flashed a wide grin. "Me, too. My sister, she was driving me crazy."

Tisha left and Nora looked at the clock. She had two check-ins due to arrive any minute. And one couple was already out doing some shopping. It might not be the cozy quiet she enjoyed when Will was around, but this was how she liked things—busy, efficient, and steady.

❖

Will walked into her apartment. She'd only been gone a week, but the space had that almost foreign feeling that comes with a much longer absence. Kaylee and Cheyenne were gone, probably at work. Will appreciated the chance to re-acclimate and settle in solitude.

She carried her bags to her bedroom, putting clean clothes back in her dresser and closet. Toiletries and books went back to their homes. When she was done, Will stood in the small living room and looked around. It felt like home. There was something to be said for that. When she'd come to P-town originally, she didn't know if she would find that again, or at least not as quickly as she had.

Will contemplated calling Nora. She also considered showing up at the inn. They should talk, although Will had no idea what she'd say. Mostly, she wanted to hear Nora's voice. See her face. But Nora likely had guests, and she wouldn't want a scene. And she hadn't given Will any indication that she wanted to see her.

Will wandered into the kitchen and perused the contents of the cabinets and refrigerator. The eating habits of her roommates had diminished significantly in her absence. Kaylee must be working nights again. There were a lot of boxes of macaroni and cheese. Will chuckled. She'd remedy that. And a trip to the grocery store would make her feel like she'd accomplished something.

She pulled out her phone to make a quick list and found a text from Graham, checking to see if she'd arrived. Will smiled, grateful they'd been able to clear the air and put their friendship back in order. Even if she couldn't have Nora, it helped to know she hadn't lost Graham, too. She typed a reply, then sent a similar text to Emerson. Emerson replied right away, asking to get together. Perfect.

Happy to have two items on her agenda for the afternoon, Will headed out. She met Emerson on MacMillan Pier. They got sandwiches from the little deli and walked down the pier a ways. They sat on the edge, dangling their feet over the beach below.

"I'm glad you're back," Emerson said.

Will took a deep breath. "Me, too."

"Did you find what you were looking for?"

The choice of words gave Will pause. Had she? "I guess so, considering I was mostly looking to get away for a little while."

Emerson nodded. "Good."

Unspoken questions about Nora and Graham hung in the air. Part of her was glad that Emerson didn't pry, but she knew Emerson worried and wanted to know. "I saw Graham."

"Yeah?"

"My friend's place was only about an hour from where she is, so we met for beers. We ended up having dinner, too. I think we're good."

"I'm glad."

Will recalled their conversation and chuckled. "Turns out she had a bit of a crush on me."

"Ah."

"Yeah. I had absolutely no idea." She didn't disclose the kiss or the fact that maybe she shouldn't have been so clueless.

Emerson laughed. "You've always tended to be oblivious to having admirers."

"Is that true?"

"Uh, yeah. Definitely in high school, but even beyond that. We'd be out and people would try to catch your eye or keep your attention. You pretty much never picked up on it."

"Am I that self-absorbed?"

Emerson shook her head. "Not at all. If anything, it's because you're humble. It doesn't occur to you that people find you attractive."

"I guess. It's so weird. Anyway, turns out Graham's thing really was a crush and not a whole I think I'm in love with you sort of thing. She freaked out mostly because she was so shocked. Well, that and she felt like two people she cared about and trusted were keeping a giant secret from her."

"That would do it."

Will sighed. "Yeah. She actually just accepted a full-time job with the Dolphin Fleet. She's going to be moving here permanently after graduation."

"Oh, that's great. So…"

Emerson trailed off and Will knew what she was dying to ask. "I haven't talked to Nora."

Emerson crumpled her sandwich wrapper and looked out at the water. "Do you want to?"

"Yes."

"Are you going to?"

"I don't know."

Emerson turned to her, raised a brow. "Why not?"

Will took the last bite of her sandwich and chewed it slowly. She tried to distill the cacophony of questions and doubts in her mind to a couple of key points. "I don't know if she wants to see me. I don't know what to say. The last time I saw her, she made it clear everything about us had been a mistake."

Emerson sat quietly. Will imagined she was looking for a kind way to say that maybe it was all for the best. "I don't think it's fair to hold someone to things they said in a moment of crisis."

Not what Will expected, by a long shot. "You don't think that's when a person's true feeling come to the surface?"

"I know it's not."

Will folded her arms. "Care to elaborate?"

"When Liam got hurt last summer, Darcy and I had a huge fight. Darcy accused me of overstepping and I said some horrible things in return. I still regret it."

"What did you say?" The question came out and Will realized she was asking Emerson to relive it. "Sorry. You don't have to elaborate."

"I told her she was treating me like an irresponsible baby-sitter, who also happened to be a fuck buddy."

"Ouch."

"Exactly. In the moment, it's exactly what I felt. But it was over the line. I think, if anything, I've learned that when it involves a third party—like Liam, or in your case Graham—sometimes the focus is so much on what's going on with them that you can't really tend to the relationship itself."

Will sighed. It made sense, but a little voice in her mind told her that she and Nora didn't have that kind of relationship. Yes, she was in love. And it felt like Nora might be starting to reciprocate those feelings. Yet, Nora seemed perfectly content to brush off her hands and move on and not look back. "That assumes there is enough of a relationship in the first place."

"I saw the two of you together. I can't pretend to know what she's thinking now, but I'm certain the feelings weren't one-sided."

Will thought back to those magical weeks. Not only had she been happy, she'd allowed herself to believe she and Nora had a future. With the memories came the feelings that went along. "She hasn't called or texted me. Not once. It's been over a week."

"You could call her." Emerson's tone was mildly impatient.

Will thought back to her last text from Nora. "She made her feelings clear. I have to respect her wishes."

"She said that stuff when she was freaking out." Emerson sighed. "Does she even know you're back?"

"I don't know."

"Don't you think you should tell her?"

"Yes, but…" Even with Emerson, who she trusted more than anyone in the world, Will hesitated to own just how much of a coward she was. "Waiting keeps the possibility alive. There's no resolution, but there's no rejection either. I'm just not ready to have the door shut in my face. Permanently."

Emerson slung an arm around her shoulders. "I can see that."

"I'm a total chicken shit. I know. You don't have to tell me."

"I wasn't going to. If anything, I'd tell you that you have a tendency to sell yourself short."

"I appreciate the attempt to prop up my ego, but—"

"No buts and no propping. Like I said before, you've always been humble. But Kai really did a number on you. She convinced you that you should be grateful for whatever crumbs of love or affection people toss your way."

"God, you make me sound pathetic."

"Bruised, not pathetic. Those kind of head games take their toll."

For every time that Kai told her she was lucky to have anyone love her, she also showered Will with compliments. And Kai's jealousy had always seemed designed to make her feel special. Only now did Will realize how much it left her second guessing herself. And the fact that Nora went from cold to hot back to cold didn't help. "Yeah."

"You're afraid to talk to Nora because you're afraid she doesn't want to be with you."

Will rubbed her forehead. "I think we've already established that I'm a coward."

"Do you feel like your behavior was unforgivable?"

"No, it's not that. I'm not sure she really wanted to be with me in the first place. Like, in a real relationship."

"Because?"

"Because we went in with a lot of ground rules. Her rules. And because she's beautiful and smart and amazing and I'm…"

"Not worthy of that?"

In that moment, Will's angst faded. Regardless of what happened with Nora, she was so grateful that she'd come to P-town. She'd spent several years convincing herself that the distance between her and Emerson was a natural part of growing up. That wasn't true at all. In leaving Kai, she'd not only escaped a crappy relationship, she'd reclaimed her sister. And her life. "I love you."

"I love you, too. You're changing the subject."

"I mean it, though. I'm so sorry that I let us grow apart."

Emerson looked her square in the eyes. "We both did that. And then we came to our senses."

Will nodded. "Yes. I'm very glad of that. And that I came here. It feels like home. I didn't realize how much I missed that feeling."

Emerson's gaze went to the harbor. "P-town has that effect on people. Having it and you in one place is the best of all worlds."

"And a soon-to-be wife and son who adore you."

Emerson grinned. "That, too. And speaking of, I didn't forget what we were talking about. You deserve that, too. Whether it's with Nora or someone else, you have so much to give. Don't ever doubt that."

Even if she didn't always believe it, Will appreciated hearing it. "Thanks. I'm not sure what I'm going to do yet, but thanks either way."

Emerson punched her in the arm. "I hope it all works out so I can tease you about your inadvertent love triangle."

Will cringed. "Really?"

Emerson shrugged. "Too soon?"

"Yeah. By, oh I don't know, a billion years." Just the phrase 'love triangle' gave her a stomachache.

"Sorry."

Maybe if she and Nora lived happily ever after, it would be funny. Maybe. "Whether I reach out to Nora or not, I'm going to see her next week at Graham's graduation. I promised Graham I would be there."

Emerson nodded slowly. "Well, there's that. I'll just leave you with a little piece of advice a very wise person gave me not that long ago."

Will raised a brow. "Are you about to tell me I should grovel?"

"No, because unlike me, you didn't make a total ass of yourself."

Right. She needed to remember that. "Okay, what then?"

"Are you in love with her?"

There was no point in denying it. "Completely."

"Then value that enough to fight for it. Don't sell yourself short. You can't expect Nora to take you seriously if you don't."

"Huh." Will took a deep breath. "Did I give you that advice?"

"Not this time."

"Where'd it come from, then?"

Emerson smiled and shrugged. "Liam."

"Smart kid."

"You don't know the half of it."

CHAPTER TWENTY-THREE

I'm just saying it would make sense for the two of you to ride together." This was the third phone call in as many days and Graham's message hadn't changed.

Nora stopped pacing the length of the kitchen long enough to pinch the bridge of her nose. "I appreciate you trying to patch things up, Graham, but I don't think it's a good idea."

"But if you shared the driving, it would be better for the environment."

"I'm not against carpools. This situation is more complicated than that."

"Maybe being in a car together for eight hours is exactly what you need to clear the air."

"There's nothing to clear."

"Okay, you're always obstinate, but now you're just lying."

How could she explain to Graham that this wasn't a simple fight she and Will needed to make up from? She'd first have to find a way to explain that she and Will weren't in an actual relationship to begin with. At least, not a real one.

That's what Nora continued to tell herself as the days passed. As much as it might have felt like they'd crossed the line into something like a relationship, Nora refused to accept that she'd allowed herself to get involved, yet again, with a person who would walk away at the drop of a hat. This might not have the financial devastation that followed Jordyn's disappearance, but it had the potential to pack the same level of humiliation. She refused to let that happen. If she could hold onto the idea that they'd simply had an affair—even if it was ill-advised—she could deal with Will walking out without so much as a backward glance. Or coming back to town without even bothering to let her know.

Even if Will never really left her thoughts. Even if Will's eagerness to be helpful, or the way she listened when Nora talked, felt nothing at all like Jordyn. Even if the physical chemistry left what she'd had with Jordyn in the dust.

"Look, we indulged a mutual attraction. It probably wasn't the best idea, but it is what it is. We were both consenting adults. I don't have any hard feelings and I hope Will doesn't either." Okay, maybe not no hard feelings, but the overall sentiment was accurate.

"I talked to her. I saw her. I can say with confidence she feels terrible."

Not terrible enough to call or come over. "The way everything went down was awkward at best. I feel badly about that, too, but it's not your problem. I'm sorry you had to deal with it in the first place."

"Will you please stop apologizing?" Graham's voice took on an edge of irritation. "I overreacted. I'm sorry for that. I can't stand the thought that I'm the reason the two of you aren't together."

Nora's own increasing irritation vanished. Graham was such a special young woman. And her intentions were so good. "Honey, you aren't the reason. What will it take for me to convince you of that?"

Graham didn't miss a beat. "You could get back together."

"We weren't together in the first place." It may have felt for a moment or two that they were close, but that had clearly been an illusion. "I hate to burst any romantic bubble you may have, but it's true."

She could hear Graham sigh. "Okay. I guess I'll have to settle for you being civil toward one another at my graduation dinner."

"Graham." Surely she couldn't expect Will to sit through dinner with not only Nora, but with Colleen and Peter.

"She's driving all the way from Provincetown to celebrate with me. Us. You wouldn't have me exclude her, would you?"

Nora realized she'd been very effectively backed into a corner. "Fine."

"Thank you."

"Your mother doesn't know anything about this. I'm asking you to keep it that way."

"Of course. What you do in your personal life is none of her business."

Nora resisted pointing out the irony of Graham's assertion. She just needed to keep her head down and get through the next week. After Graham's graduation, Graham would return to Provincetown, but have a place of her own. Even if she and Will remained friends, the chances Nora would have to see Will on any kind of regular basis would be slim to none. And then maybe, just maybe, things would settle down and get back to normal. "I appreciate that. I'll see you soon."

"I can't wait." Graham's usual bubbly tone was back. Nora breathed a sigh of relief.

"Me either." Nora shook her head. She mostly meant that.

"Love you."

"Love you, too. Bye."

"Bye."

Nora set down her phone and looked around. She shouldn't be surprised that Graham and Will had talked, or that they had made up enough that Graham wanted Will at her graduation. She'd just been trying so hard not to think about Will at all. She hadn't been successful at that, but still.

"Who died?" Tisha stood in the doorway, frowning.

"What? No one."

"Then why do you have that look on your face?"

She had no intention of admitting the nature of her thoughts. "Just distracted. I was talking to Graham about her graduation."

Tisha looked suspicious. "You're still going, aren't you?"

"Of course. We were just ironing out the details. We'll go to lunch after the ceremony, but I should be able to get on the road by late afternoon, so I'm only planning to be gone for one night. So that leaves you with two happy hours and one check out. Are you sure you can handle that?" They'd already discussed it, but Nora knew raising the question would be an adequate distraction.

"I've got my niece coming in to help me. We'll be fine. Why are you changing the subject?"

Okay, so maybe not an adequate distraction. Tisha knew Nora better than almost anyone. "We're talking about Graham's graduation, are we not?"

Tisha narrowed her eyes. "Something is up with you. Been up since I got back. You don't have to tell me what it is if you don't want to, but don't act like it's nothing. I'm not blind."

Nora felt a twinge of regret. "I'm in a bit of a funk. I'd rather not talk about it. Please don't think it has anything to do with you."

"Don't act all wounded, now. I'm just calling it as I see it."

Nora gave her an exasperated look, but smiled. "Did you come all the way back from Jamaica just to give me a hard time?"

Tisha quirked a brow. "Seems someone's got to do it."

"Or not."

"Wait." Tisha pointed a finger at her. "Is this something to do with whoever you were dating while I was gone?"

Nora hated to lie. Especially with Graham coming back to work, she just knew something was bound to come out somehow. "The person I dated knows Graham. She'll be at Graham's graduation."

Tisha's eyes got huge. "Is it that handsome thing she brought home with her that night we did that party? The clam bake?"

Normally, Nora appreciated that Tisha never forgot a detail, or a face. In a business made on repeat customers, it often made the difference between a satisfied guest and a truly happy one. This was not one of those times. "How do you even remember her? It was six months ago and you barely met her in passing."

"I remember a handsome face, especially one that I caught staring at you every chance she got."

"You're exaggerating."

"I'm not. And clearly I was on to something." She nodded slowly. "She was good, I bet. How long did it last?"

Nora was so done having this conversation. She rolled her eyes. "Not long enough for her to speak two words to me since it ended."

"Okay, okay. We don't have to hash through it all."

"I'd appreciate that."

Tisha shook her head slowly. "But a friend of Graham's. That sounds messy."

"Too bad you weren't here in January with all your brilliant advice."

"Bah. I would have told you to go for it."

Nora laughed because it was true. "I'm sure you would have. Now, if you'll excuse me, I'm going to go make some lists."

Nora headed to the kitchen to the rich sound of Tisha's laugh. "Is that what the kids are calling it these days?"

CHAPTER TWENTY-FOUR

Will looked in the mirror and straightened her tie. She thought back to the last two times she'd done so— New Year's and Emerson and Darcy's engagement party. It was hard to wrap her head around how much had changed in less than six months. She turned away from her reflection and sighed.

When was the last time she'd been this nervous? It was hard to conjure a moment that had filled her with such anticipation. Even the day she decided to leave Kai brought with it relief, a sense of calm. Then, at least, she'd known what was happening, had some control over the situation.

This? This was a whole different ball game. Other than knowing she'd physically see Nora, she had no idea what the day would hold. Yet, even that uncertainty couldn't overwhelm the aching need to see her, hear her voice. Will felt like an addict who'd spent the last few weeks in withdrawal.

She shook her head. The metaphor of addiction should give her pause.

She went to the kitchen and found Leigh reading the *Wall Street Journal* with a cup of coffee. "You look like such a grownup right now."

Leigh looked up and smiled. "I could say the same about you."

Will lifted a shoulder. "Better late than never, right? Thank you for letting me crash at your place again."

Leigh waved a hand. "Of course. I'm glad I got to see you this time. Are you sure you won't stay another night?"

"I'd love to, but I hate to take more than a couple of days off work. Besides, if the day turns really awkward, I'll have the excuse of needing to get on the road." She'd filled Leigh in on the highlights of her mess of a personal life.

"I hear you. Just know you can change your mind."

"Thanks." Will crossed the room and gave her a hug. "For now and before."

"Anytime."

"And you're going to come crash with me sometime this summer?"

Leigh grinned. "Promise."

Will grabbed her bag and let herself out. She plugged the address of the campus into her phone and headed out. It took only a half hour to get there, but another forty-five minutes to park and catch the shuttle from the far-flung parking lot.

She contemplated getting lost in the crowd, sitting off on her own. It wasn't that she didn't want to see Nora. It was the idea of seeing her with her sister and brother-in-law. Will was pretty sure that would take uncomfortable to a whole new level. She didn't wish that on herself or Nora. But before she could sidle up to a large family speaking Korean, her phone buzzed with a text from Graham.

The fam is to the left of the stage, three sections back. They're saving you a seat.

So much for being unobtrusive.

Will weaved her way through the crowds, looking for Nora. She spotted her standing in the middle of a row, looking around. She assumed—hoped—Nora was looking for her. She lifted her arm to wave.

As she did, Nora turned in her direction. They locked gazes and it felt to Will like the whole universe paused. The cacophony of conversations going on around her faded into a low din. The rush of blood in her ears made her dizzy. She consciously reminded herself to breathe. Was that a hint of a smile on Nora's face or was she imagining it? Will couldn't read her at all. She wondered if her own face reflected the mishmash of emotions—hope, fear, longing, love—crashing around in her chest.

Will realized she didn't even know if Nora wanted to be looking for her or had been guilted into doing so by Graham. Regardless, it was too late to back out now. Someone bumped into her and Will realized she'd been blocking part of the aisle. She walked quickly to where Nora was, sidestepped her way down the row until she stood next to Nora. Will fought the urge to touch her, or to lean in and smell her perfume.

"Will, it's good to see you. This is my sister, Colleen, and her husband, Peter." Nora's expression was pleasant, but cool, reminding Will of the night they first met.

Will took turns shaking their hands. "It's a pleasure to meet you."

"Graham has told us so much about you," Peter said.

Great. There were at least a thousand ways of interpreting that statement. And at least half of them left something to be desired. "She's such a great person, and so good at what she does. You must be proud."

Both Colleen and Peter beamed. Colleen said, "It's hard not to be. It was so nice of you to make the trip for her graduation. I know it means a lot to her."

Will smiled. "Wouldn't miss it."

She was saved from further conversation by the start of "Pomp and Circumstance." She stood with the rest of the crowd and watched the procession of faculty in their ornate, mismatched robes. Students followed. She had no chance of seeing Graham, but it was still fun to watch. She hadn't been to a college graduation since Emerson's. Then, she'd been with her parents. She'd been so proud of Emerson, but it was laced with knowing she'd disappointed them by not finishing her own degree. She'd stopped worrying about that achievement, but the sudden pang of missing her parents caught her off guard. She gripped the back of the chair in front of her and willed herself to stay focused and in the moment.

"Are you okay?" Nora's voice pulled her back to reality.

Will forced a smile. "Yep."

Nora glanced down at Will's hands. Will's gaze followed and she realized her knuckles were white from holding onto the chair so tightly. She let go and put her hands in her pockets. "I'm fine. Really."

Just as when she'd arrived, Nora didn't press or try to make conversation. Will had no way of knowing if Nora had nothing to say or if she felt inhibited by the presence of her sister. She wondered if they'd have a moment alone at some point during the day. She didn't know what she'd do with it, but she wanted it nonetheless.

When the procession ended, Will took her seat next to Nora. The closeness of the chairs brought the side of Nora's leg, as well as her arm, into contact. Through the thin fabric of Nora's dress, Will could feel the warmth of her body. It created an instant wanting that made her ache. Any attempt she'd made to convince herself she wasn't in love with Nora evaporated.

Throughout the ceremony, Will stole glances at Nora. Twice, she caught Nora looking at her. Even without smiles or knowing stares, Will let herself believe it had to mean something.

Fortunately, Graham's school was large enough that they did not call individual names. The ceremony ended in just over an hour and families began the arduous task of attempting to locate one another. Will followed Graham's family to their pre-arranged meeting place.

They found Graham with a group of her friends. Will smiled and shook hands with a dozen people she'd likely never meet again, then fell into the role of photographer. She snapped endless permutations of Graham with her parents and Nora, some of her friends. After what felt like an eternity, Colleen insisted on getting a few with Will in the frame.

Will put her arm around Graham's shoulders. "Congratulations."

Graham beamed. "I'm so glad you're here."

"Me, too."

They smiled for the camera, then Graham motioned Nora over to join them. Graham slung an arm around each of them and pulled them in close. "See how nice this is?"

Will stole a glance at Nora, who was looking right at her. Will shrugged and offered a tentative smile. Nora returned the smile, but shook her head.

"Now you two." Graham slipped away and gestured for Will and Nora to get closer. "My Provincetown family."

Nora stepped toward her. Will couldn't resist putting an arm around her waist. She felt so good, so right. All the memories of their quiet mornings together, days working on projects, nights cuddled on the sofa came flooding back. Even more than the sex—and God, did she miss the sex—Will missed the simple intimacy they'd managed to create. She hated the idea that might be gone forever.

"Who's hungry?" Peter's question interrupted Will's thoughts. Probably for the best, at least for the time being.

❖

Nora opted not to take the shuttle and made the trek to her car on foot. The walk gave her the chance to clear her mind. It had gone fuzzy the moment she saw Will and had yet to refocus. Having Will sit so close, then posing for pictures together, hadn't helped.

Part of her wanted to be irritated with Graham for putting her in this situation in the first place. She knew better, though. Seeing Will wouldn't be hard if her feelings weren't such a tangled mess. The reality was that she was as hung up on Will now as she'd ever been. And Will clearly didn't feel the same.

Nora tapped the address of the restaurant into her phone, poking at the screen angrily until the directions appeared. She closed her eyes and counted to ten. It would be fine. They'd eat, keeping the attention on Graham. And then she'd get in her car and have eight blessed hours of peace and quiet to get herself together. And then she'd be home and too busy to think about anything but work until Labor Day.

When she got to the restaurant, Nora stopped in the restroom to freshen her makeup. By the time she found the table, everyone had been seated, leaving a place for her between Colleen and Will. She took a deep breath and steeled herself.

Fortunately, Graham was bubbly with excitement. Between graduation and her imminent start date as a real member of the Dolphin Fleet, she didn't need much prompting to keep the conversation going. Nora joined in the toast to Graham's accomplishments, then managed to enjoy a beautifully done crab pasta. And not once did she find herself staring at Will's hand, resting on the table and close enough for her to touch. Okay, maybe once.

She swore she could feel Will's body radiating heat, smell her cologne. Nora caught herself closing her eyes when Will spoke, just to savor the sound of her voice. Fortunately, no one else seemed to notice. She wondered if Will felt even a hint of the yearning she did.

Over panna cotta, she asked Graham about her start date and when she planned to arrive.

"Did I tell you I found a place? It's a room in a three-bedroom unit not too far from the inn."

Nora shook her head. "I do wish you'd reconsider staying with me."

"I imposed longer than I felt comfortable. I'll be super close and we can get together all the time."

"I know, but—"

"I don't want to cramp your style." Before Nora could open her mouth to protest, Graham winked at her. "And I don't want you cramping mine."

Nora hadn't given too much thought to Graham's style, except when she was worried about Will being a part of it. She studied the niece she'd continued to think of as a young woman in need of protecting. In truth, Graham had proven she had a good head on her shoulders. Nora chuckled. Given the mess she'd gotten herself into, perhaps she was the one in need of a protective eye. "Point taken."

After a mild argument over the check, Peter pressed his credit card onto the waitress. "Thank you so much for the meal, and for including me in such a special day," Will said.

Graham gave Will a knowing look, although Nora didn't know exactly what meaning it held. "You're practically part of the family."

Nora twisted her napkin under the table. "I hate to eat and run, but I feel like I should hit the road."

"We'll walk out with you." Graham stood and the rest of the table followed suit. Outside, Graham linked an arm through Nora's and then through Will's. "Are you sure you have to drive back tonight?"

"I do. Tisha got her niece to help her cover today, but I promised I'd be home. We've got a full house tonight and most of the rest of the week."

"I'm sure you're close to full steam," Will said.

Nora smiled. "Pretty close. It's not peak until June, but we won't slow down until September."

Graham eased her arms free and made a point of walking over to where her parents stood. Will shrugged. "Not subtle, that one."

Nora laughed. "No, she's not."

"I guess I'll see you around town?"

Nora couldn't tell if Will was being dismissive or angling for something more. "I'm sure we'll cross paths. Have a safe trip back."

Will nodded. "You, too."

Nora hesitated. She couldn't help but feel as though she hovered on the precipice of something. She didn't know what, and she certainly wasn't about to act on it. Especially in front of her family. She settled on a smile. The least she could do was try to convey there were no hard feelings. "Bye."

Will searched her face, then leaned in and kissed her lightly on the cheek. "Bye."

As quickly as the kiss began, it ended. Will stepped back and Graham enveloped Nora in a hug. "I just need to pack up my place here. I should be there in a few days."

Nora focused on Graham. "And you'll let me take you to a celebratory dinner for landing your first real job."

"I definitely won't say no to that."

She hugged Colleen and Peter next. "You pick a week you can come out this summer and I'll hold a room for you."

"If you don't hassle us about letting us pay, we might make it two," Colleen said.

"You drive a hard bargain. We'll see." Nora offered a final wave and climbed into her car. She was anxious to get home, but had a sense of foreboding. As much as she enjoyed driving, the task suddenly felt daunting rather than promising. She must be tired. And truth be told, she had a feeling the next eight hours would involve thinking about Will more than clearing her head.

As with any task she didn't relish, Nora resolved herself to tackle it head on. She squared her shoulders and started the engine. Perhaps some show tunes instead of NPR or an audiobook. She queued up a station and hit the road.

She'd just pulled out of the restaurant parking lot when she caught movement in her peripheral vision. Although it felt like slow motion, she could do nothing to stop the SUV coming at the side of her car. Nor could she get out of the way.

A thousand thoughts raced through her mind, ranging from her poor car, to the guests waiting for her at home, to just how far she was from home. She heard the impact before she felt it, but then she felt nothing. As her mind faded to black, she wondered if Will was already gone.

Chapter Twenty-five

Will climbed into her car and sat for a moment. If she gave Nora a couple minutes head start, she wouldn't have the chance of ending up right behind her. Wondering if Nora was looking at her in the rear view mirror. Wanting her to and feeling awkward about it the whole time.

When she thought enough time had passed, Will pulled out of her spot, just in time to see Nora turning out of the restaurant parking lot. Even though they were going the same way— practically to the same place—something about her disappearing from view made Will profoundly sad. If seeing Nora again had reinforced her feelings, it also left her with absolutely no idea what to do about them. Nora had been almost painfully pleasant, and completely detached. It would have been almost easier had Nora ignored her.

The sound of crunching metal and breaking glass sent a stab of ice into Will's chest. It couldn't be. There had to be a hundred cars in earshot, the odds of it being Nora were tiny. But something in the pit of Will's stomach insisted otherwise. She threw her own car back into park and, after a mad tangle with her seat belt, leapt from the driver's seat. She could see Graham already running in the direction of the noise.

Will saw the SUV first. Hulking and black, it blocked her view of whatever it had hit. A few more steps and Nora's dark green hatchback came into view. Or, what was left of it. The SUV had T-boned Nora's car, crushing the passenger's side completely. Will choked down the bile in her throat and kept running. Her legs felt like lead pushing through water.

After what felt like an eternity, she reached Nora's car. Graham was there, too, yelling Nora's name. Will's own voice had vanished. She opened her mouth, but no sound came out. Graham yanked open Nora's door. Powder from the airbags swirled in a cloud around Nora's head, which bent forward at an awkward angle.

"Don't move her." Will heard her own voice more than she was aware of speaking the words. "She might have a neck injury."

Graham's body froze and she turned her face to Will. Fear shone in her eyes. "She's unconscious."

Will's lifeguard training, which had included basic emergency response, kicked in. "Call 911. Let me make sure she's breathing."

Graham stumbled back and Will stepped forward. She leaned into the car and pressed fingers to Nora's neck. The thud of Nora's pulse helped to calm her own. "Nora. It's Will. Can you hear me?"

Nora's eyes fluttered and she moved her head slightly. She mumbled something Will couldn't decipher.

"Don't move. You've been in an accident. Help is on the way." Will swallowed, willing her voice to remain calm. "You're going to be okay."

Nora's left hand fumbled and Will took it. The warmth and gentle pressure as Nora squeezed it brought tears of relief to her eyes. "Don't go," Nora said.

Will held on until the ambulance arrived. It couldn't have been more than a couple of minutes. She reluctantly let go so they could do their job. After checking her vitals and extricating Nora from the vehicle, they situated her on a stretcher with a brace around her neck. As they wheeled her to the waiting ambulance, Will realized that Nora's sister and brother-in-law had made their way over. Graham stood between them with a look of horror etched on her face.

"It's a precaution." Will spoke to Graham and her parents, but wanted to reassure herself as much as them. "It's better to be overly careful if there's a chance of neck injury."

Will returned her attention to Nora and the paramedics. Nora's eyes were closed again, but she had a wince on her face that told Will she was conscious. That was a good sign. She took her hand once more and squeezed. "They're going to take you to the hospital. We'll all be there in just a few minutes."

"Don't go." There was more force behind the words this time, making Will feel about a million times better.

"You can ride with her if you want," one of the paramedics said.

Will looked to Graham and her family. Although both Colleen and Peter looked confused, Graham nodded. "Go. We'll be right behind you."

Will climbed into the ambulance and, at the paramedic's instruction, took a seat on the narrow bench across from Nora. She reached over and took Nora's hand. Nora's eyes opened fully this time. Although she couldn't turn her head, her eyes angled in Will's direction. Will shifted so she would be in her line of sight. They locked gazes. Will might have imagined it, but she'd have sworn a ghost of a smile passed over Nora's lips. "You're here."

"I am. And I'm not going anywhere."

"I hurt everywhere."

"I know. You're going to be all right, though. Everything is going to be all right."

Nora closed her eyes again. Will closed her own for a second. The back of the ambulance offered a surprisingly bumpy ride. Having never ridden in one in her life, it struck her as odd. She filed the detail away.

If Nora was awake and able to speak, she likely didn't have life-threatening injuries. Although there was still the worry about internal bleeding. The little she knew about that came from hospital shows. In those cases, people who seemed fine wound up dead moments later—not where she wanted her brain to go right now. No, Nora had to be okay. Despite the unyielding tension in her chest, Will allowed herself to believe it.

On top of that, Nora seemed glad she was there. Wanted her there. That meant almost as much. Okay, maybe not almost, but it was huge. Maybe there was a glimmer of hope for them after all.

When they arrived at the hospital, Nora was wheeled off for X-rays and other tests. Will stood with a nurse, attempting to answer questions about Nora's health history. She realized quickly how little she knew. Before she could wallow in it, Graham, Colleen, and Peter arrived. Colleen took over answering questions while Graham fished Nora's insurance card from the purse she'd thought to grab from Nora's car.

Once the admitting nurse let them go, Graham grabbed Will by the arm. "Was she conscious in the ambulance? Did she say anything?"

Graham, Colleen, and Peter all looked at her expectantly. "She was, and she knew who I was. She also said she was in pain, which is probably a good thing. It means there probably isn't any nerve damage."

"That's good," Graham said.

"Very good," Colleen added.

Graham shook her head. "You were so calm in the moment. I thought Emerson had the medical training."

Will smiled. "I was a lifeguard. Not that it gave me anything official, but I learned a lot about keeping my cool."

"Well, you did that in spades." Graham put an arm around her. "I'm glad you were there."

Will still didn't know what, if anything, Graham's parents knew about her relationship with Nora. "It all worked out okay."

"I did tell them," Graham whispered in her ear. "On the ride over. It's cool."

The statement raised more questions than it answered, but Will merely nodded. "Okay."

Graham looked over Will's shoulder. "I think we might be in the way here."

Will realized they were standing in the middle of the registration area, forcing people to go around them to get to the desk or the waiting area. "Right."

They moved to the waiting room and sat in a pair of ugly plastic chairs connected at the seat by a thick metal bar. "Are you mad that I told them?"

Will shook her head. "Not at all. It's just…" She struggled for a simple answer. "I'm not sure Nora would want them to know. And I'm even less sure there is an 'us' to talk about."

Graham reached over and patted her leg. "It's going to be fine. My mom didn't seem at all surprised. On top of that, she seemed happy. I think she worries about her sister being lonely."

"Yeah, but—"

"No but. You make Aunt Nora happy. And unless you've been lying to me, she makes you happy, too. If both of you could stop being so stubborn, I'm pretty sure you could live happily ever after."

If only it was as easy as all that. Will sighed. "We'll see."

"Colleen Connor?" A doctor looked around the room expectantly.

Will and Graham hurried over to where Graham's parents stood. Will tried to focus, but her mind swirled with the implications of Colleen and Peter knowing about her relationship, of them not having a problem with it. She made out "broken wrist," "bruised ribs," and "overnight for observation." The doctor vanished almost as quickly as she came and Will kicked herself for not catching all of the details. "Now what?"

Graham smiled at her. "Now we wait until she's been moved to a room."

Will nodded. A room. That meant Nora didn't need the ICU. Just that knowledge sent a wave of relief through her.

"Why don't we take a walk?"

As much as she feared missing any news, she didn't want to spend the next however long hovering and pacing. "Sounds good."

They exited the sliding glass doors and took a right, taking the sidewalk that led to the parking garage. Graham guided them around the perimeter of the hospital, chatting about her new place and her excitement over working together again. Will didn't know if it was Graham's intention, but the enthusiastic chatter provided a perfect distraction. The next thing she knew, Graham's phone rang and they were heading back in to go up to Nora's room.

By the time they got there, Colleen and Peter were there, but Nora was not.

Colleen said, "They took her for an MRI. Basic concussion protocol."

"Of course." Will didn't know if it was or not, but she nodded. Nodding gave her a sense of control somehow.

"She'll be back up shortly. I think we're going to go get a cup of coffee."

Graham nodded as well. "That's a good idea. Take a little walk, too. It was good to get some air."

Will continued to nod.

"Do either of you want anything?"

Will appreciated the offer, although she wondered if it came from manners or an attempt to include her. "I'm okay, but thanks."

"I'll take a hot tea," Graham said.

"You got it." Peter kissed Graham on the temple and he and Colleen left.

Will and Graham were left alone in Nora's empty room. Will gave into the urge to pace, an urge she'd barely held in check while Graham's parents were present. Her mind went in a dozen different directions, leaving her with a twitchy nervous energy. "I think I should go back."

Graham, who'd begun flipping through a magazine looked up at her. "What?"

"To P-town. To Failte. I think I should go."

"Right now?"

The pieces began falling into place. "She was so anxious to get back tonight because she has guests."

Graham frowned. "You're right. Tisha is there, though. It's not like the place is unstaffed."

Will nodded slowly. That was good. Still. Every selfish bone in her body screamed for her to stay, to sit by Nora's bed and not take her eyes off her. Hold her hand and keep her promise not to go anywhere. But her heart told her to think about what would matter most to Nora. Knowing there was an extra pair of hands at home would give her peace of mind. It would allow her to focus on healing and not hurrying back to work.

Will swallowed. At this point, she had no idea how long healing would take. She hated the idea of being hundreds of miles away. It wouldn't be that long. They'd ruled out internal bleeding and were doing the MRI as a precaution. Given Nora's coherence right after the accident, it was unlikely there was anything worse than a mild concussion.

"If she has a full house—and I'm guessing she does—it's more work that Tisha can handle on her own. I want her to know everything is taken care of."

Graham sighed. "I'm sure it would mean a lot to her, but it's late. Shouldn't you at least get some sleep first?" She quirked a brow. "I don't think I could handle two car accidents in twenty-four hours."

Will chuckled. Sleep was the absolute last thing on her mind. Even without the adrenaline of the last few hours, seeing Nora had both her body and mind going full speed. She'd need to sleep at some point, but it wouldn't be for a while. "I'm so awake right now, it's not even funny. I promise I'll pull over if I start to fade. And I'll text you every couple of hours either way."

Graham looked resigned, but also relieved. "It's a very romantic gesture, you know."

Will glanced at the empty bed. "That's not why I'm doing it."

"I know. That's what makes it so romantic."

Would Nora think so? And if she did, would it be welcome? "At the moment, it feels like the right thing. And that's what matters."

"You better watch it, or I'm going to develop a crush on you all over again."

Will looked at Graham with alarm.

"Relax. I'm kidding. Go. Please be careful and please stay in touch."

"I promise." Making a decision, having a plan, gave Will a greater sense of calm than she'd had in the last few days. She looked around the room before realizing she didn't have anything with her. Then she realized she didn't have her car, either. "Shit."

"Your car is still at the restaurant."

Will nodded. "I'll get a Lyft."

Graham stood and walked over to her purse. "Take my car."

"I couldn't—"

"Of course you can. Leave me your keys and I'll drive yours back. My parents have to get their car from the restaurant, too. As long as that doesn't freak you out. I imagine I'll be just a day or two behind you."

It was exactly the kind of thing she and Emerson would do. The trust and the closeness Graham's offer implied made Will's heart full. A few weeks ago, she'd thought she'd lost the two people she was closest to besides her sister. And now there was a chance she'd get both of them back.

"You're freaked out. I can tell by the look on your face. As soon as my parents come back, I can take you to get your car."

"No, I'm not freaked out. I was just...I was thinking how glad I am you and I made up. You're a really good friend."

Graham's smile was lopsided and a little shy. "Me, too."

"Could you call Tisha? We should let her know what's going on and I'm not sure she knows who I am."

"On it."

It relieved Will to know she'd be expected. "Thanks. And you'll call or text with any updates?"

"Promise. Please be careful. I'll see you soon."

"You too." Will pulled Graham into a hug to hide the fact that, again, she was on the verge of tears.

Graham told Will where to find her car and Will didn't waste any time leaving. Partly because she was anxious to get on the road and partly because she didn't want to be around to explain things to Graham's parents. It might be cowardly of her, but she didn't think it was her place to tell them what she and Nora did or didn't mean to each other.

Graham's car carried so much of her personality—from the upbeat beach tunes on the radio to the miniature humpback whale hanging from her rearview mirror. Will found it oddly comforting as she punched in directions to her GPS at least as far as the highway. As she pulled out of the hospital garage, she wondered again if she was doing the right thing.

She knew that she was. Regardless of whether it won Nora back or not, it would help Nora focus more on her recovery than on getting back to work. She'd probably still be plenty focused on that, but having Will at Failte might prevent her from doing anything rash. Because whether Nora liked it or not, Will had learned quite a bit about how things at Failte ran. Even if Tisha didn't know her from Adam, she'd surely not refuse a competent pair of hands.

When she crossed into Connecticut, Will stopped for food and caffeine. She wished fleetingly for Emerson's haphazard approach to sleep and schedules as she stretched her legs. She checked her GPS and decided she had a couple hours of wiggle room if she needed to stop for a power nap. That thought helped her press on, windows down and radio cranked loud.

CHAPTER TWENTY-SIX

Nora's lids felt heavy and her head throbbed. Quick on the heels of this realization came the smell. She sniffed the air. The combination of antiseptic and plastic and food that had been cooked too long was at once familiar and foreign. The smell told her something was wrong.

Nora struggled to open her eyes. In the dim light, she could make out a television mounted to the wall, her legs under unfamiliar blankets. In the corner of the room, someone slept in a chair. Nora squinted at the figure. It was Graham.

The pieces came together—Graham's graduation, seeing Will, dinner at the restaurant overlooking the water. After hugging goodbyes, she got in her car to begin the trek home. Someone hit her car. The image of the SUV turning, pulling out even though she was already in the lane. With nowhere to go.

And now she was in the hospital.

Nora wiggled her toes, then her fingers. She looked at each extremity to ensure it remained intact. It was then she noticed the bulky cast on her right arm. Well, hell.

She lifted her arm and winced, both from pain and the weight of the cast. "Damn it."

"Huh?" Graham bolted up in the chair. "What?"

"Sorry. I didn't mean to wake you."

Graham hurried over to the bed. "Don't apologize. I'm so glad you're awake."

Graham looked ragged. She still wore her dress from dinner, but it was wrinkled. Mascara was smudged under her eyes. How long had she been there? "What day is it?"

Graham smiled, easing some of the alarm that had taken hold. "Sunday still."

Oh. That was a relief. "I was in a car accident, right? How bad?"

Graham took her hand. "Bad enough to total your car. But other than some bruised ribs, a concussion, and a broken arm, you're okay."

Another relief. And she'd been in the car alone, so that was good. The image of Will came into her mind. Will holding her hand, telling her everything was going to be okay. Had that been in an ambulance? Did it really happen or was her mind playing tricks on her? Nora looked past Graham. No one else was in the room with them.

As if sensing the questions in her mind, Graham said, "Mom and Dad went to get some coffee. They'll be back soon. Will was here, too."

More thoughts than Nora could hold onto swirled around her mind. The loudest and most pressing was where Will had gone. Whether she was coming back. But even in her compromised state, she knew she didn't want to broadcast that to the world. She forced her brain and her gaze to focus on Graham, who looked like she'd been through hell. "I've gone and stolen all of the attention from your day."

Graham gave her an exasperated look. "Stop it. You came. That made the day perfect."

Graham's comment brought the details of the rest of the day crashing back. The ceremony, seeing Will. The dinner that was at once wonderful and easy and awkward and hard. The uncomfortable hug that still managed to fill her with longing. She'd been both sad and relieved to climb in her car to head home.

Home. She had guests. God, how could she have forgotten? "Tisha. I need to call her. She's expecting me. I told her I'd be back in time for breakfast and checkout."

Graham smiled. "Already taken care of. I left her a message telling her you're okay and that you're in good hands. That's actually where Will is. She headed back so she could lend a hand."

Nora comprehended the words, but she struggled to wrap her head around their meaning. Much less the implications. For the first time since waking, her heart began to race and panic danced around the edges of her brain. "Wait. What?"

"Will was here. She actually rode with you to the hospital in the ambulance."

So she hadn't imagined it.

"Once we got word that you were going to be okay, she decided to go back to P-town. She said she could do more good there than here. She took off in my car a couple of hours ago. I called Tisha to fill her in and let her know help was on the way."

Nora couldn't decide what made her more nervous—the significance of Will's actions or the thought of Tisha's reaction when Will showed up and jumped into morning chores without so much as a by your leave. She took a deep breath. She could handle Tisha. She'd grouse about someone swooping in and messing with her system, but she'd ultimately appreciate the help.

Will was another story. Seeing her had stirred up all sorts of feelings, but she had no way of knowing if Will shared any of them. Even knowing Will stepped in to play hero raised more questions than it answered.

"She's still in love with you."

Nora started. She'd forgotten Graham was standing right there. Her brain was even fuzzier than she thought. Is this what having a concussion felt like? "I know you want that to be true."

"I know it's true. You didn't see her face when we realized you'd been in an accident, or when the paramedics said she could ride with you. And when she decided to go, it was obvious that leaving you was killing her. But she knew that's what you'd be most worried about and she wanted to put your mind at ease."

Could it be true? Nothing in Will's behavior over the last month gave Nora any inkling that she was in love. Even the graduation and dinner seemed more like a chore to her than a pleasure. Will's clear discomfort at having to see and talk to her only reinforced that. Nora tried to focus her eyes on Graham's face. She seemed older suddenly and it felt like, perhaps in this moment at least, their roles were reversed. Realizing Graham was an adult, her equal, didn't bother Nora. If anything, it made it easier to talk to her. "I don't understand. She was so aloof with me."

"She was terrified of you."

That made no sense. "She's the one who left."

"After you told her to."

Okay, that much was true. But if Will truly cared for her, she would have come back. Or called. Something. The fact that Will had returned to town and not made any attempt to contact her still stung. Even as she knew she was guilty of the exact same thing. "But she vanished completely."

"Because she took what you said at face value and was convinced she'd ruined our relationship."

"You and I worked it out. You made up with her, too. Still, nothing."

Graham sighed. She crossed the room and took Nora's hand. "She decided you were better off without her."

Despite Will's maturity on just about every other front, that notion struck Nora as juvenile. She said as much to Graham.

"How much do you know about Will's past?" Graham asked.

Nora shrugged, then winced. "Quite a bit, actually."

"Then I'm surprised you would say that. For as strong as she is, her heart is pretty fragile."

"I—" Her reply was cut off by the arrival of an orderly with her dinner tray. He set it down on the wheeled table and moved it close. The smell turned her stomach, but she wasn't enough of a snob to say so. "Thank you."

"You are most welcome. Take care."

He disappeared and almost immediately a nurse came in. "I see your dinner is here. Good. The doctor wants to start you on oral pain meds tonight to make sure they agree with you before you are discharged tomorrow."

"I have to stay the night?" Nora realized how petulant she sounded and bit her tongue.

"Just for observation. Assuming all goes well, the doctor who does morning rounds should clear you to leave."

She supposed it could be worse. "Okay. Thank you."

The nurse set a tiny paper cup on the tray and poured her a glass of water. "I have to watch you take it."

"Right." She took the pill and a long sip of water.

The nurse gestured to the tray. "I'm sure that's not the most appealing thing you've ever seen, but trust me when I say you'll want to chase that with some food."

"I will. Thanks." The nurse left and Nora lifted the cover from the plate. A pile of sad-looking broccoli stood out against a monochromatic palette of chicken and mashed potatoes. Nora sighed.

"Do you want me to go in search of a vending machine? I think if any occasion warrants a candy bar for dinner, this qualifies."

Nora laughed, appreciating Graham's attempt at lightening the mood. Until the movement sent a stab of pain through her ribs. "Christ, that hurts."

Graham cringed. "Sorry."

"No, no. I'm fine. Just more sore than I care to admit." And apparently whinier, too. "This is fine. I've certainly had worse."

"That's the spirit."

Nora reached for the fork, only to be reminded that her right hand was in a cast. She picked it up with her left and awkwardly maneuvered a bite of potatoes into her mouth. They tasted as bad as they looked. But that didn't give her an excuse to be sullen. She stabbed a piece of lifeless broccoli and ate it. "It's fine."

"Do you want me to cut your chicken?"

Since that would be less mortifying than picking up the whole thing at once like a caveman, she acquiesced. While Graham worked, Nora studied her face. So pretty. And full of life and optimism. She'd been so intent on looking out for Graham, she'd been blind to how well Graham looked out for her. "About Will—"

Before she could continue, the door opened again and Colleen and Peter breezed in. "You're awake. And eating. That's excellent."

The level of enthusiasm told her just how worried her sister had been. On principle, she forked another bite of potatoes. "And medicated with a promise of going home tomorrow."

Colleen looked to Graham for verification. Graham nodded. "So says the nurse."

"Oh, I'm so glad."

"I feel badly that you've been stuck at a hospital all day because of me. You should really go home and get some rest."

Without missing a beat, Graham nodded. "It doesn't make sense for all of us to hover the rest of the night. You two go home and I'll stay. I can sleep anywhere."

They spent a few minutes arguing about it, but Graham eventually won out. Nora started to thank her, but her eyes felt inexplicably heavy. Those pain pills were something potent. She fell asleep and dreamed about Graham and Will and being home.

Chapter Twenty-seven

Will succumbed to a nap just shy of the Bourne Bridge, but kept it to an hour. She arrived at the inn a little before four in the morning, which gave her plenty of time to make breakfast. She slipped Nora's key into the lock and let herself in the back door. Other than the small light over the sink, the kitchen remained dark and quiet.

She'd beat Tisha here or Tisha had decided she could handle it. Either way, Will was relieved to have the space to herself. In addition to feeling intimidated by Nora's manager, something about being in Nora's space alone felt intimate. Like she'd woken up first and Nora might simply be in bed, naked and asleep. Will wanted to wallow in that feeling.

She checked her phone for the millionth time. She'd gotten a confirmation that Nora was okay, in her room, and likely to be discharged in the morning. That was around eleven and she hadn't heard anything since. She shook her head. She was being impatient. It was four o'clock in the morning and Graham had probably fallen asleep. And Nora was likely resting, too. That's what they were supposed to be doing.

Telling herself that did little to ease the tightness in her chest. Nor did reminding herself that Nora's injuries weren't life threatening. No amount of reassuring could undo the image of Nora, jostled around in the back of the ambulance or unconscious and pale under the harsh fluorescent lights of the ER admission area. Will shook her head again, as if doing so might chase away the mixture of worry and fear. She had work to do and needed to focus.

Will had no idea what Nora planned to serve her guests. And since going out for groceries wasn't an option, she should start by figuring out what she had on hand. Bread and eggs seemed safe, so she prepped a French toast casserole that wouldn't need constant attention. Sausages would be a nice complement, along with sliced fruit. Between that and the usual spread of breads and bagels for toast, she figured everyone would make do.

It was just after five, though, and she was out of things to do. She rifled in the freezer and found a couple of pie crusts. Perfect. It only took about twenty minutes to prep a pair of quiches. That should give everyone more than enough options. Maybe too many. But no one would complain about that.

At six, Will flipped on the coffee. She was probably running ahead of schedule, but she needed a cup for herself as much as anything. She pulled out all the things for the coffee bar—half and half, almond milk, and the little bowl of sugar. Grateful she'd watched Nora do it so many times, she arranged cups and refilled the basket of tea bags. Back in the kitchen, Will poured herself a cup of coffee. She was in such a hurry to caffeinate, she scalded her tongue. She swore under her breath, but heeded the warning to be more careful. She filled the carafe slowly, carrying it out to the dining room before setting the second pot to brew.

The first of the guests wandered downstairs a little after seven. Will greeted them, introducing herself as a friend filling in for the morning. They were first timers and hadn't met Nora when they checked in the day before, so they took her explanation at face value. The second couple proved trickier. They'd stayed before and Nora had told them she'd see them.

Will didn't feel like it was her place to air Nora's business, but she didn't want them to get the wrong impression. She settled on, "She went to Maryland for her niece's graduation and was held up unexpectedly." It seemed to work.

Will excused herself to the kitchen, where she pulled out the quiches and slid her French toast bake into the oven. When it had ten minutes left, she put the sausages in a skillet to brown. She carried the basket of bread out to the buffet and set it next to the toaster, then the platter of fruit she'd sliced. Butter, jam, warm maple syrup. By the time she was done, eight people hovered in the dining room. It might not be exactly how Nora would do it, but it wasn't half bad.

"Please," she gestured to the food, "help yourselves."

Shauna, half of a Manhattan power couple, smiled. "Plates?"

"Agh." Of course she would forget the plates. "Sorry about that. I'll be right back."

Will hurried into the kitchen, opening cabinets at random until she remembered the plates lived in the buffet in the dining room. She returned to the dining room, avoiding eye contact with Shauna or any of the other guests. She opened the side door and took out ten plates. Unfortunately, she'd not left any room on top for them, so she set them on the table. Without being prompted, she yanked open the top drawer. Forks and knives and napkins sat ready to go. She breathed a sigh of relief and put them next to the plates.

She stepped back and took a deep breath, praying she hadn't forgotten anything else. "Thank you so much for your patience. If I'm forgetting anything else, please let me know."

Clint, the meteorologist, snagged the top plate. "It all looks delicious."

Will nodded and smiled at the murmurs of agreement. She watched as people filled their plates, refilled their coffee, and returned to their conversations. Relieved, she allowed herself to slump slightly against the door frame. All at once, the adrenaline that kept her going vanished. In its place, exhaustion. She blinked a few times to clear her vision. She needed to keep it together for just a little bit longer.

Confident there was more than enough food, Will retreated to the kitchen. She immediately went for her phone. Finally, a text from Graham.

Nora is awake and ready to be home. Just waiting around for a doctor to do discharge.

Will read the message five times. Only when a tear plopped onto her screen did she realize she was crying. Will swiped at her eyes and laughed at herself for being such a mush.

Aside from forgetting plates, breakfast went off without a hitch. I may have made too much food. :)

Will hoped that would give Graham, and maybe Nora, a chuckle.

When the back door to the kitchen swung open, Will spun around. Although it made no sense, she half expected to find Nora standing there. Instead, it was Tisha, who crossed her arms and looked at Will with suspicion.

"What are you doing here?" The tone, combined with Tisha's thick Jamaican accent, managed to be both judgmental and dismissive.

"Nora was in a car accident."

"When? Where? Where is she now?" The immediate shift in her voice helped Will relax.

"Right after Graham's graduation. She's going to be okay, but she's in the hospital. She's still down in Maryland."

"And she asked you to come here?" The suspicion was back full force.

"Yes. No. Well, sort of. Graham and I discussed it. Graham stayed to be there when Nora woke up and I came here to cover things." Will didn't add that she and Nora had barely returned to speaking terms. "We knew she had guests and you were expecting her. Graham was going to call you."

"Nora sent me a message that she was on her way home. I thought everything was fine. My niece broke her phone, so I gave her mine to go out last night."

"It must have happened right after that. And I—Graham and I—didn't want to leave you in a lurch. So here I am."

Will's phone pinged. She glanced down at the screen.

Doc here now. I'll text with an ETA.

Will looked at Tisha. "It sounds like she's being discharged now. That means she and Graham should be here by this evening."

So glad. PLEASE be safe on the road.

After sending the reply, Will tucked her phone in her pocket. Tisha remained standing there, staring at her. Will swallowed. "I, um, I made breakfast. I'm sure it wasn't as good as Nora's, but it seemed to go over okay. I'm going to clean up from that and then I can do anything else that needs doing."

Tisha nodded slowly. She seemed to be assessing instead of judging, which Will took as a good sign. "It was good of you to do that."

Will couldn't be sure, but she had a feeling that was about as big a compliment as Tisha bestowed, at least on people not part of her inner circle. "I just...I didn't want her to have to worry about it."

"You know her well, it seems."

Two compliments in one day. Fearing she might be on the verge of crying again, Will cleared her throat. "I know how she feels about this place, at least, and her guests. So, what else is there to do? I'm happy to take orders."

Tisha narrowed her eyes. "When did you sleep?"

"I took a nap on the road."

"You look like shit."

Will couldn't say why, but the insult made her feel infinitely better. It seemed to imply a detente, or at least an acceptance of her presence. "Thanks."

"You should get some rest now. I can take it from here."

Will wanted to brush off the help, insist that she was fine. Honestly, though, every muscle in her body hurt, including some she didn't even know she had. The idea of a shower and a few hours of sleep before Nora got home were enough to make her weep with gratitude. "Are you sure?"

"I'm sure. And then you can help me figure out what to do to get ready for when she gets home."

And just like that, they were allies. "Thank you. I don't need long. Is anyone in the room Graham used? I can go home, but—"

"It's free. You'll have to use Nora's bathroom, though. Do you know where that is?"

Will, full-on punchy at this point, laughed and then tried to cover it with a cough.

Again, Tisha narrowed her eyes. To her credit, though, her only reply was, "I'm going to take that as a yes."

Will went through Nora's room to get to the bathroom. The space smelled like her—lavender and sunshine and something Will never had been able to identify. Will looked at the bed and, as she would have expected, memories came crashing over her. Although they'd spent their first night together upstairs, all the other nights and all the other mornings were in this room. She could see Nora standing at the dresser putting on makeup, in front of the closet contemplating an outfit. She could see Nora in the bed, peaceful in sleep or looking at her with eyes that made Will's insides melt.

She lost track of how long she stood there, finding a certain comfort in just being in Nora's space. A door closing elsewhere in the house jerked her back to reality. Will went into the bathroom and stripped, stepping into the shower and cranking the water as hot as she could stand it. She emerged wrapped in a towel, then looked down at the sad pile of clothes she'd worn for more than twenty-four hours.

She'd forgotten to bring in her bag. The realization hit her at the same time she remembered that her bag, with clean underwear at least, sat on the back seat of her car. Which was in Maryland. Or, perhaps by now, somewhere in between.

She contemplated a quick dash down the hall to the laundry room, but the idea of being caught made her fear she'd lose all the credibility she'd just earned. Will sighed. She'd worn worse. Once Nora was home and settled, she'd go home and change. She didn't consider the possibility of not coming back. Or what she would do if Nora didn't want her around. She shoved aside the notion. Nora would need help whether she wanted it or not. Will intended to give that help. They'd sort out the rest eventually. They had to.

She went to the door and stuck her head out into the hallway. Seeing no one, she decided to make a dash for Graham's room in just the towel. She was almost there when Tisha appeared, as though summoned from Will's desire not to be seen.

"Do you have clean clothes?"

Damn it. "I don't. I ended up switching cars with Graham. I'll just put these back on."

"Let me wash them for you."

"You don't have—"

"It wasn't a question. They'll be clean and dry before you wake up."

Will handed over the pile, suddenly sheepish. "Thank you."

"Now go. Sleep. Do you want me to wake you?"

Will was starting to see why Nora valued her so much. The woman got shit done. "I've got my phone. I'll set an alarm."

"Okay, then. Get to it."

Will escaped into the bedroom and closed the door. She felt weird about sleeping in Graham's bed naked, but she didn't see how she had much choice. Telling herself it wasn't Graham's bed specifically helped. She draped the towel on the doorknob and crawled under the duvet, letting out a moan of pleasure. She couldn't remember the last time she'd been so exhausted.

When her alarm went off a few hours later, Will sat upright and looked around. It took her a moment to remember where and what day it was. Her clothes sat in a neat pile on the chair. Tisha must have come in while she was asleep. Will glanced down at her bare breasts and said a silent prayer that she'd been securely under the covers.

She pulled on the clothes, minus the tie, pretty sure that Tisha had gone so far as to iron them. Feeling more like herself, she spent a minute deciding between making the bed and stripping it. In the end, she settled on stripping. She didn't know when it would be needed again and didn't want to presume she'd be welcome.

Will found Tisha in the kitchen, putting the finishing touches on the snacks for happy hour. "Can I give you a hand?"

Tisha waved her off. "I'm just about done. Did you get an update on when they'll be here?"

Will looked at her phone. "Nothing in the last couple of hours. Based on when they left, I'm thinking around seven."

"Okay. I'll do happy hour and clean everything up. Hopefully everyone will scoot off to dinner and it'll be quiet."

She couldn't tell if Tisha might be trying to get rid of her. Before she could get shooed away, Will said, "I'd like to stay until they arrive, so I'm really okay with being put to work."

"You seem to know how things run around here. Did you work here over the winter?"

Even without the uncertainty of her future with Nora, Will decided it wasn't her place to tell Tisha what had transpired. "Nora hired me for a couple of projects, but I picked up things here and there and helped her a few times when she was busy."

Tisha nodded. "I know she doesn't have enough work to keep someone on all winter, but it's lot for one person."

Will smiled. "I don't know how she does it."

"She works too much is how."

"Agreed." Will thought for a moment. If she could make an ally out of Tisha, it might help her prospects in the long term. "I'm hoping she'll let me continue helping while she recovers. I'm sure if it's just the two of you, she'll push herself more than she should."

Will watched as the seed she planted took root. "It sounds like you know her better than most. I could handle the extra work, but you're right. She won't have it."

"I have another job, but I'm free early morning and most evenings. If you want to put in a good word for me, I'll do whatever needs to be done."

"Well, you handled breakfast on your own, so you're clearly capable. I'll see what I can do."

The offer was far more than she'd bargained for after meeting Tisha for only the second time a few hours before. "Great. What can I do in the meantime? Oh, besides laundry. I stripped the bed I slept in, so I'll get that set of sheets going."

"How about I do sheets and you do the people?"

"The people?"

"The guests. Nora stays out in the dining room and sitting room during happy hour to make sure there's enough wine and food. And she chats people up. I did it yesterday and I'd just as soon not have to do it again."

Will smiled. She knew an introvert when she saw one. "I'm on it. And thanks to you, I'm even dressed for it. Thank you, by the way, for washing them. The ironing was above and beyond."

Another wave of hand. "If it gets me out of socializing with strangers, it was more than worth it."

"I guess that makes us even." Which made her glad. She liked being even. And although she wouldn't complain about housework, she'd much rather play host. She glanced at the clock on the wall, then the tray of cheese and fruit. "Is this ready to go?"

"Yes, and I'll have the fig and gorgonzola tarts out of the oven in just a minute."

Will picked up the tray. "I'll be back."

She carried the food out to the dining room and set it on the sideboard in the sitting room under the window. She pulled wineglasses from the cabinet below, along with the small plates Nora used for happy hour, napkins, and two bottles of red. She returned to the kitchen for white wine, then rooted around in the cabinet for a chiller and the corkscrew. She opened the wine and arranged everything just as Tisha emerged with the tarts and a shallow basket of water crackers.

Tisha set them in the places Will had left and surveyed the spread. She nodded. "Looks good to me."

"Thanks. I'll stay out here and socialize. Hopefully Nora and Graham will be home soon."

"I'll go do some prep for tomorrow morning. We can sort out who's going to do what later, but that'll make it easier."

"Sounds good." Will really wanted to say that she appreciated it, but doing so made her feel an ownership of the whole thing and she didn't want to come off as any more presumptuous than she already had.

The front door opened and a couple walked in. They each carried an armful of shopping bags and were laughing about something one of them must have said before they entered. Tisha looked at Will and raised a brow. "That's my cue."

Will chuckled at how quickly she hightailed it back to the kitchen. Then she turned her attention to the guests and prepared to make them feel completely at home.

CHAPTER TWENTY-EIGHT

Nora watched the scenery change as Graham drove them along Route 6. Her mind swirled with the events of the last few days, up to and including the fact that Will was currently running things at the inn. It baffled her, overwhelmed her. More than anything, it confused the hell out of her.

The one benefit to having so much on her mind was that she forgot how physically uncomfortable she was. Although, at this point, that might be preferable. For the tenth or so time since they got on the road, Nora did an inventory of her body.

Her head ached, but as long as she didn't move quickly, the shooting pain had subsided. The same was true of her arm. The dull throb was tiring, but not unbearable. The rest of her was okay. She felt jostled and bruised—which, technically, she was— but not anything she couldn't handle.

Of course, all she'd attempted to do so far was sit quietly. The idea of getting back to work loomed over her. As badly as she wanted to throw herself back into it, she didn't know if it would be physically possible, at least for a few days. She could ask Tisha to put in some overtime and, even though Graham was due to start work, Nora knew she'd help some. And there was Will. Nora shook her head at the thought.

"What is it? What's wrong?" Graham's eyes darted between Nora and the road, a look of concern on her face. "Do you need another pain pill?"

"No, no. I'm fine."

Graham didn't look convinced. "You don't have to be the tough broad around me, you know."

"Tough broad? What is a twenty-three-year-old doing using that phrase?"

"Don't try to change the subject. I'm trying to tell you it's okay to fall apart a little."

Part of her wanted to fall apart. She'd just lost use of her primary hand for six weeks. Even with Tisha back, there's no way they'd be able to stay on top of everything. The idea of imposing on Graham upset her almost as much as having to cancel reservations. "I don't fall apart. It's not my style."

Graham let out an exasperated sigh. "I know it's not your style. That's the point. I thought…I thought we'd gotten close."

"Of course we're close. Why would you doubt that?"

"Because if we can't be vulnerable around each other, what's the point?"

Nora studied her niece. She couldn't tell if Graham was truly upset or working an angle. Either way, she had a point. Being unflappable wasn't all it was cracked up to be. "You're right."

Graham reached over and squeezed her leg. "About being in pain or falling apart?"

"The latter. I'm worried about the next few weeks."

"I get it. But you have me. I'm sure I can postpone my start date or do a flex schedule for a month or two."

Nora shook her head. "Absolutely not. You are about to start your professional life. I will not interfere with that."

"I'm not chucking my career. You make it seem like a much bigger deal than it is. Between Will and me, I'm sure we'll be able to cover everything."

"About Will." Nora had no idea what about Will, but something. She didn't want to drag Graham into it, but she also couldn't have Graham going on like she and Will were an item or, worse, a team.

"You're not seriously still mad at her?"

"No." Nora was a lot of things, but mad wasn't one of them. "She loves you."

Graham had said as much at the hospital, but Nora thought it might be wishful thinking on Graham's part. Not to mention hers. "It's complicated."

Graham shook her head. "It was momentarily complicated by my meltdown. Please don't throw away the chance to be happy because of that."

"I didn't. It's not..." Nora didn't know what she was thinking, much less what to say.

"I wish you could have seen her face after the accident. I was freaking out, but it had nothing on the panic in her eyes. And after, at the hospital, it was so obvious that she didn't want to leave. But when we realized you had guests expecting you, she didn't hesitate. Not for a second."

It was at least the third time Graham had said as much. Nora was still struggling to reconcile that fact with everything she'd come to believe about Will. Even if Will had better motives than Jordyn, she'd made it clear sticking it out wasn't her thing. Trying to reason it out brought Nora's headache back with a vengeance. She closed her eyes and pressed fingers to her temples. "Maybe I am ready for another pain pill."

"The bottle is in your purse at your feet. I can pull over if you want me to get it."

Nora waved a hand. "I'm not a total invalid."

She opened the bottle and shook out two pills, washing them down with the water Graham had been encouraging her to drink the entire ride. She closed her eyes again and leaned her head back against the headrest. If she could just get home, settle back into her own space, she'd be able to sort everything out.

When the car stopped moving, Nora opened her eyes. She hadn't intended to fall asleep, but she must have. She felt groggy and out of sorts. Maybe she should have held off on the pills. She unbuckled her seat belt and reached for the door handle. Her movements were slowed, like being under water. She struggled to keep her vision clear. Before she could get out of the car, Graham rounded the hood and took her hand. Nora's instinct was to wave her off, but she was unsteady. Attempting to maintain her pride wasn't worth the chance of falling down in a heap in the middle of the parking lot.

They'd taken about two steps when the front door of the inn flew open. Will and Tisha ran out, looking as though they might fall over each other in their rush to get to her.

Tisha spoke first. "Thank God you're alive. This one," she hooked a thumb at Will, "scares me half to death in the kitchen this morning, then tells me you're in the hospital. I've been worried sick."

"Didn't you get my message?" Graham asked.

"No." Will and Tisha spoke in unison.

"Nothing major." Nora kept her voice light. Hopefully, she could convey more confidence than she felt. "I'm sorry you worried for nothing."

Tisha looked her up and down. "I worried for plenty. You look like death warmed over."

Nora cringed at the description, mostly because she knew it was true. "It looks worse than it is."

"And you're a liar. Let's get you inside." She went to Nora's other side and put a hand on her back.

Despite Will's rush to meet them, she hadn't said anything. Nora studied her, trying to figure out what was going on in her head. Not knowing, combined with Graham's commentary in the car, left Nora uneasy. Still, she couldn't ignore what Will had done. "Thank you for coming back here and taking care of things. I don't know how to repay you."

Will, who'd seemed to be equal parts relieved and terrified, now looked like she was on the verge of tears. She shook her head. "You don't...there's nothing to repay."

Tisha waved a hand impatiently. "Whatever it is, you two can sort it out later. Let's get you inside."

Will looked over at Graham. "Are there things in the car to unload?"

Graham nodded. "All of Aunt Nora's stuff is in the back seat."

Will skirted around them, keeping at least ten feet between herself and Nora. Although Nora still had no idea why Will had done what she'd done, it seemed like all she wanted now was to get away as fast as she could.

As much as Nora wanted to be in the sitting room, the pain medication left her groggy. And she didn't want guests to happen upon her sprawled on one of the sofas. She allowed Tisha and Graham to lead her to her room. She slipped off her shoes and eased onto the bed. Even staying on top of the covers, settling onto the pillows felt heavenly. It took all of her will power not to drift off. "I really am okay. I just need another day to recoup."

Tisha raised a brow. "You are the most stubborn woman I have ever met."

Nora was about to protest when Will appeared in the doorway with her bag. "Just set it by the closet. Thank you for bringing it in."

"You're welcome." Will put the bag down. She retreated to the doorway, but didn't leave entirely.

They'd need to talk, but at the moment, Nora could barely muster the energy to keep her eyes open. "I just need to sleep off the medicine and I'll be myself again." She lifted the cast feebly. "Well, mostly."

"I think rest is an excellent idea," Graham said. "Holler if you need anything and one of us will come running."

They hustled out of the room. Nora glanced around, half expecting something in her surroundings to have changed. Everything was just as she'd left it, though. She realized she'd only been gone three days. It felt like so much longer. Was it the accident that made it feel that way? Or seeing Will?

Will. What was she going to do about that? Before she could come up with any answers, sleep took her.

❖

Will, Graham, and Tisha filed out of Nora's room. With all the guests out for the moment, Will led them into the sitting room. They stood in a circle and Tisha crossed her arms over her chest. "How is she really?"

Graham took a deep breath. "Okay. The concussion is mild. Other than no contact sports for a couple of months, she doesn't have any restrictions."

Tisha cocked her head to the side. "And beach volleyball season is just getting started. She'll be so disappointed."

Graham snorted out a laugh. Will took that as a sign that it was safe to chuckle herself. The idea of Nora, even at her most free, diving around in the sand was almost too much. "And her arm?"

"A full break, but a clean one. They were able to set it without surgery, so six weeks in a cast should do the trick."

Tisha shook her head. "Six weeks without her right hand? She's going to go absolutely crazy."

Graham smiled at that. "I know. She's pretty banged up at the moment. Even though she won't admit it, I'm hoping she lets it keep her in bed a couple of days. Then we can deal with the rest."

Will didn't know what the next few days or weeks would hold, but she'd find a way to be useful one way or another. "My shifts this week are all on the 11:00 and 3:00 tours, so I can come for a couple of hours in the morning to help with breakfast and cleaning rooms. I'll see if I can keep that schedule for at least a few weeks."

Graham nodded. "I'm meeting with Chris tomorrow and will see if I can schedule earlier to be around in the evenings."

"If no one is in your room, I can stay over in case she or the guests need anything during the night." Will spoke the thought as it occurred to her, then immediately regretted it.

Both Graham and Tisha turned their gazes to Will. "Let's talk about that, shall we?" Graham said with a mischievous twinkle in her eye.

"Um." She might have confided her desire to be close if only Graham had been in the room. But despite their newfound understanding, Will still didn't feel like she could disclose the full situation to Tisha. "It makes sense. You have a new place to settle into and roommates to get to know."

Graham shook her head. "I'm not arguing. I'm just curious about whether you're going to admit the real reason."

"Agreed." Tisha moved her hands to her hips. "I'm thinking you're in love with Nora, yeah? Is she in love with you, too?"

It was a loaded question if ever there was one. Even if Will was inclined to confide in Tisha, she honestly didn't know what to say. For better or worse, Graham chimed in. "Yes."

Tisha looked from Graham to Will and then back to Graham. "But?"

Graham put her hands on her own hips. "What makes you think there's a but?"

Tisha looked at her blandly and Will found herself relieved that, even though the conversation was about her, she sat on the periphery. "Because you answered instead of that one." She hooked a finger at Will.

"It's complicated," Graham said.

Will couldn't suppress a snort of laughter. She did her best to cover it up with a cough.

"Considering I find her in the kitchen and Nora's told me whatever was going on in the winter is over, I got that far myself."

Will tried to process the fact that Tisha knew about what had happened between her and Nora. Graham sighed. "There was a misunderstanding that was all my fault and—"

"It wasn't your fault." Will redirected her attention to Graham. "You didn't do anything wrong."

Graham rolled her eyes. "There was a misunderstanding that had to do with me and I've been trying to fix it."

Tisha nodded slowly. "Nora kept it from you."

"Uh, yeah. And I reacted badly because of my own stuff. Anyway I'm over it and I wish they'd just go back to how things were."

Tisha turned her gaze toward Will. "And how were things, exactly?"

Will wrestled with how much to share. Despite her initial hesitation, Tisha and Graham knew Nora better than anyone save, perhaps, her sister. Confiding in them might not win her Nora back, but she wasn't above asking for their help. And if Tisha were dead set against it, better to know than be undermined when she wasn't looking. "We were seeing each other, spending a lot of time together." Will couldn't bring herself to say "sleeping together," but figured it was implied.

Tisha's face gave nothing away. "How long?"

"It started in February."

"February?" Graham's tone pitched high, but she quickly recovered. "What happened?"

So they were doing this. Will took a deep breath. "There was a huge storm and Nora's water heater blew. I stayed to help minimize the damage and the snow got so high Nora invited me to stay rather than try to fight my way home. We had dinner, talked. It just sort of happened." That was all true. Even though she'd hoped for it, she hadn't plotted or tried to manipulate the situation.

"I'm not really surprised," Graham said.

Will wished she and Graham were back on entirely solid footing, because the desire to laugh out loud at that assertion was strong. "Really?"

Graham gave her an exasperated look. "I mean, in retrospect. You two definitely had chemistry. But it would take something like a snow storm for Aunt Nora to let her guard down."

Tisha hummed her agreement. "And when did your misunderstanding happen?"

Again, Graham answered before Will could. "Early April. I came for the weekend as a surprise. Only the real surprise was on me."

Will winced at the description. But she knew better than to apologize again. "I figured I was the last thing Nora needed to deal with, so I bailed."

"And then she," Tisha wagged a finger at Graham, "meddled."

"I tried to fix what I messed up."

Will shook her head. "And I realized I messed up, too. I don't know if Nora will take me back, but I want to make it up to her." As she said the words, Will realized just how much she meant them. "I want to be here."

Graham smiled. "And you should be."

"Let me go check the reservation book." Tisha disappeared in the direction of the kitchen.

Will turned her attention to Graham. "Thank you for lending me your car. I'm glad I was here."

"Considering Tisha didn't get my message, I am, too. And I know it means a lot to Aunt Nora."

Will swallowed. "I hope you don't think I'm trying to take advantage of the situation."

Graham rolled her eyes. "You are the only person I know who would sacrifice all her free time as a gesture for the woman she loves and then worry about being seen as selfish."

Will frowned. "You know what I mean."

"I do. And I'd never wish an accident on anyone, but since that's what happened, I think it's a perfect chance for you to stick around."

Will scrubbed a hand over her face. "But is that what Nora wants?"

"She might not be quite ready to admit it, but I believe in my heart that it is." Graham leaned in and bumped her shoulder into Will's. "That doesn't mean she might not be cranky in the meantime."

Will laughed. She could handle cranky. If she believed she was truly helping, and that there was even a sliver of hope for her and Nora, she could handle anything. "I promise I won't be scared off again."

Graham grinned. "Good."

CHAPTER TWENTY-NINE

Nora brushed a piece of hair from her eyes and let out a huff. She glanced at the clock. It had taken her twenty minutes to strip and make one bed. And she was exhausted. She glared at the cast, already beginning to look dingy. This was going to be a long four weeks.

She scooped up the linens and headed for the hall. Three rooms to go. She found Will hovering near the door.

"Hi." Will offered her a bright smile.

"Hi." Despite Nora's protests, Will continued to appear morning and night. And when there was a room open, she stayed the night as well. She was pretty sure that, if Will wasn't at her actual job, she was at the inn.

"Tisha said you were turning over rooms so she could wash dishes. I thought you might like a hand."

"Will, you really don't—"

Will lifted a hand. "How many times have we discussed this? I want to be here. I would enjoy being here more if you stopped harassing me about it."

Nora narrowed her eyes. Her instinct was to argue anyway. She loathed the idea of being so helpless. Or of Will showing up day after day out of some sense of obligation, or misplaced loyalty. "I just wish I could understand why."

Will closed her eyes for a moment. When she opened them, she looked directly into Nora's. "I don't know if we can ever go back to how things were. But I've decided that I want to try."

Nora smiled slightly, but shook her head. "You can never go back."

She expected Will to accept that answer, but instead she lifted her chin. "Not back, then. Forward. Being with you is the happiest I've ever been. I think I made you happy, too. Despite initially running away with my tail between my legs, I've come to my senses. I'm not going to be so easily scared away again, and I'm not going to disappear."

Nora opened her mouth to speak, but no words came out.

Will flashed a grin. "Why don't you take those downstairs and let me take over from here? You can put up your feet for a minute or start getting ready for happy hour."

Without waiting for a response, Will brushed past her and disappeared into one of the rooms. Nora stood there, trying to figure out how she felt about being steamrolled. It was kind of nice. Nice, Nora realized, because it wasn't really steamrolling. It was more like she and Will were evenly matched. Not something she had a lot of experience with. And not that she had any intention of putting her feet up, but when was the last time someone in her life even told her she should?

Jordyn had gotten her to loosen up. At the time, she'd relished playing at being carefree. In hindsight, it had all been a ploy to get her to let down her guard. Which was why she took such pains to keep it up now. But being with Will was different. Sure, Will tried to get her to relax sometimes, but the motivation never seemed to be reckless abandon. If anything, Will seemed to thrive on responsibility.

Nora started downstairs, then abruptly stopped. Being with Will. Had she really just thought that phrase? And not even as a question, but more of a passing thing. What was she supposed to do with that?

"Why are you still standing there? You're supposed to be resting."

The sound of Will's voice snapped her back to reality. She turned around to find Will standing in the hall with an armful of sheets. "I thought I'd wait for a second set so I can put them on to wash."

Will looked at her curiously, but didn't question her. She handed her the pile. "Okay. Take these. I'll be down with the rest soon. Now, seriously, go relax."

Nora carried the linens downstairs and to the laundry room. She shoved them into the machine, added detergent, set the cycle. She stood there for a moment, watching the machine fill with water and begin to spin. It was kind of hypnotic, actually. She lingered, allowing the repetitive sound and motion to empty her mind of thoughts.

"What are you doing?"

Nora jumped. She whirled around and found Tisha standing in the doorway, looking at her like she'd lost her mind. Nora straightened her posture and lifted her chin. "Laundry."

Tisha peered around her. "That cycle started twelve minutes ago."

Had she really been standing there for twelve minutes? "I guess my mind wandered."

"Clearly."

"Will insisted on taking care of the rest of the rooms, so I can take over the happy hour setup."

Tisha angled her head. "Or you could take it easy for a few minutes."

Nora let out a noise that sounded more like a growl than a sigh. "Why is everyone so adamant that I take it easy? I'm fine."

Tisha regarded her blandly. "You're barely two weeks out of a serious accident. Your body needs to recover."

"Aside from this," Nora waved her cast with annoyance, "I am recovered. What I'm not okay with is everyone treating me like a child."

"Then maybe you should stop acting like one."

"What is that supposed to mean?"

"It means you're short-tempered, stubborn, and teetering on the verge of a tantrum when you don't get your way."

The insult stung. A lot. "I am not."

Tisha raised a brow. "Are, too?"

How could she have walked into that so easily? Nora took a deep breath. Her own agitation didn't justify lashing out at the people trying to help her. "I'm sorry. I don't mean to be difficult. I hate having to rely so much on other people."

"Other people or just Will?"

❖

Will carried the remaining linens down the stairs. She headed to the laundry room to drop them off, but stopped when she heard voices. Nora was still there and Tisha was with her. Will hesitated, not wanting to break into their conversation, but not sure where else to go. And then she heard her name. And it was Tisha who'd said it. Will held onto the pile of sheets, but tiptoed closer. She slid to the left to stay out of view and angled her head, as though that would help her hear better.

"Part of me still can't believe I'm saying so, but the girl's got sticking power. And she's not afraid of work," Tisha said.

Nora sniffed. "Did you hear that? You yourself just called her a girl."

"I didn't mean it like that."

Nora made a sound that conveyed frustration. "Let's just say that she's all those things. All those things and more. What would she want with me? I'm locked into this place and almost old enough to be her mother."

"So you admit it. You do want her."

Will's mouth hung open. Guilt over eavesdropping warred with her desperation to know Nora's response. Added to that was her disbelief that Tisha was making a case on her behalf. Will leaned forward, craving and fearing what Nora might say.

"Hey, Will." Graham's voice came from behind her.

Will dropped the linens and spun around. "Hi, Graham."

Will turned back in the direction of the laundry room. Tisha emerged, briefly caught Will's eye, then disappeared into the kitchen. Nora followed quickly behind. She did not make eye contact with Will, looking past her to Graham. "What a lovely surprise. What brings you by?"

Will watched as Graham's gaze moved back and forth between them. She definitely picked up on the weird energy. "Um, I just got out of work. I thought I'd check in and see if I could help with anything." She glanced at the pile of sheets. "But it looks like you have everything under control."

Nora said, "Why don't you stay for a drink? Happy hour will be starting soon."

"Only if I can help out."

Will watched as Nora shook her head. "Tisha informs me that's under control as well. Will you stay anyway?"

Graham grinned. "I suppose I could be talked into it. We should sit on the porch. It's gorgeous out."

"That sounds like a great idea." Will bent to retrieve the pile she'd dropped. "You two go sit and I'll bring something out for you."

"Absolutely not." Nora's tone made Will flinch. "You two go sit. I'll bring out a tray."

Graham rolled her eyes. "Jesus, you two. Let's all go to the kitchen together, then we can all go sit on the porch."

Nora laughed, sending a wave of relief through Will. Nora looked at Graham and said, "When you sound like your mother, I know things are out of hand."

They filed into the kitchen. Tisha was there, acting as though she'd had no part in the previous conversation. "Everything is ready and I took the liberty of making extra since Graham is here."

"You didn't have to do everything." Nora's tone was more conciliatory than accusing this time. "Thank you."

Tisha shrugged. "I'm outstanding in the kitchen. You just don't let me do it very often."

"I…"

Nora trailed off and Tisha broke into a boisterous laugh. "I'm just being mean to you now, woman. I'll never say I'm glad you broke your arm, but I like things turned on their head. It's good for you."

Will wondered if Tisha was including her in the category of things turned on their heads. In a million years, she wouldn't have expected to find an ally, much less a champion, in Tisha. Perhaps she was right—there was something to be said for shaking up the status quo.

Tisha hefted a tray of drinks and a plate full of canapés and the four of them filed back through the house and out the front door. Will took a spot on the swing with Graham while Nora and Tisha settled into the Adirondack chairs.

"This is nice," Nora said.

Will chuckled to herself. She had the feeling it was a reluctant admission on Nora's part. Still, she couldn't imagine Nora making a similar statement just a week prior. As far as Will was concerned, they were making progress, and she wasn't about to complain. "Agreed."

They sat like that for a while, quietly sipping cocktails and enjoying the afternoon sunshine and light breeze. It allowed Will to close her eyes for a moment and daydream. It was so easy to imagine a lifetime of afternoons just like this. She would need to keep working so that she contributed as much as possible, but she could also help out at the inn. And in the brief lull between the comings and goings and feeding of guests, they could sit together and just be. The calm certainty of it was something that had eluded Will much of her life. She might not have been able to put a finger on it until recently, but now she could think of nothing she wanted more.

The sound of footsteps on the path pulled Will from her reverie. She didn't recognize the couple, but they weren't carrying bags, so they must be returning. Both Nora and Tisha got to their feet. "You look like you could use a cocktail," Nora said.

Both men laughed. One of them said, "I could always use a cocktail."

Nora turned to Graham and Will and pointed a finger at them. "Stay."

Will glanced at Graham, who rolled her eyes, but laughed. Will smiled. "No argument here. I think I've pressed my luck enough today."

Tisha and Nora went inside with the couple. When Will and Graham were alone on the porch, Graham turned to her. "So, any progress?"

Will shrugged. "I think so? I seem to have won over Tisha. That's got to count for something."

"It's huge." Graham shook her head. "I still wish you could just go back to how things were."

Will patted her thigh. "I don't think that would have worked out anyway."

"What makes you say that?"

"I think we were playing at being in a relationship rather than actually being in one." Even more, they'd been playing by Nora's rules. Will sighed. "Does that make sense?"

"Not really."

"We were kind of holed up here. We didn't go out together. We were never a couple. I met a few of her friends, but they mostly just thought I was working here."

"Really?"

Only in saying it out loud did Will realize how much what she and Nora had wasn't a relationship. "Emerson and Darcy knew what was happening because I told them, but Nora never went with me to their house or anything."

The one night that stood out as different was the engagement party. Will finally felt like they were a real couple. Then Graham had surprised them. Will didn't have the heart to say that part.

"Wow."

That was it. That was the hurdle they needed to cross. Or finish crossing. Or maybe re-cross. And as much as Will wanted to play it cool and bide her time, Nora needed to understand that's what she wanted—needed—if they had any hope of being together. "Yeah."

"So, what are you going to do?"

"I need to convince Nora to take a chance on me."

"I know she talks a good talk, but I see the way she looks at you. The fact that you've stuck around—"

Will finished the sentence. "Drives her absolutely nuts?"

"Yes, but only because needing help of any kind drives her nuts. Honestly, I think it's been good for her. And you've made it clear you won't be easily deterred."

"Even when she tries to shoo me away with a broom."

Graham snickered. "I never said she'd make it easy."

"But anything worth having rarely is."

"Well said, my friend. Well said."

CHAPTER THIRTY

Will let herself in through the kitchen door and found Nora bent over the oven, a tray of scones in her good hand. Although her first reaction was to worry about Nora overdoing it, the sight of it made her smile. "Those smell delicious."

Nora smiled. She'd stopped giving Will a hard time every time she showed up, so that was something. "I made a double batch. You're welcome to one."

"Since I'm not a paying guest, I'll do my best to wait until after breakfast has been served."

"Nonsense. You show up every day and work for hours. You don't let me pay you. The least I can give you is a scone."

Will shrugged. "If you insist."

"I do." Nora placed a scone on a saucer, added a large dollop of clotted cream, and handed it to her. "Coffee is ready, too."

This wasn't the playful banter she missed, but it was better than silence. Or the stilted conversations they'd had in the first couple of days after Graham's graduation. Not that she believed in signs, but she'd been looking for a reason to talk with Nora about their future. Or, maybe more accurately, a moment. "Thank you. What can I do to help?"

Nora slid the remaining scones into a large, shallow basket. "Those quiches are ready to go out."

Will spent the next few minutes helping Nora set up the buffet. Then, while Nora chatted up her guests over breakfast, Will cleaned up the kitchen. She'd just about finished when Tisha came in the back door. "You beat me again."

Will knew the statement was a compliment. "I'm off today, so I thought I'd come early and make myself useful."

Tisha nodded her approval. "Where's Nora?"

Will gestured toward the dining room. "Hostessing."

Tisha went over to the reservation book on the desk. "Two checkouts today, with new people due this afternoon."

"I can help you flip rooms as soon as they're empty."

Tisha waved a hand. "I don't need help. Can you keep Nora occupied while I work? Woman is dead set on doing everything."

Will smiled. "I think I can manage that."

Nora breezed back into the room and eyed them both with suspicion. "What are you two plotting now?"

"This one has gone and cleaned the whole kitchen already. I'm trying to convince her to go sit out in the garden, enjoy the sunshine a bit."

Nora nodded. "I think that's a lovely idea."

Will caught Tisha's meaningful stare. She looked at Nora innocently. "Only if you join me. I was hoping to talk with you, anyway."

Nora looked around the kitchen. "Well, I guess there's nothing to do in here."

Will opened the back door, swept her arm, and bowed. "After you."

Nora went ahead of her and Will stole a final glance at Tisha, who winked at her. Will swallowed the nervous laughter that rose in her throat. She wondered if Tisha had any inkling she was about to profess her undying love.

Nora led the way to her favorite spot in the garden. As much as she resented not having her full strength and stamina, she had to admit this slower pace had a certain charm. Of course, the slower pace was only possible because Will had spent the last few weeks pulling the weight of a full third staff member. Not to mention the extra help Graham had been offering, too.

Nora sat and studied Will, who looked nervous all of a sudden. Will joined her on the bench and she couldn't help but think they were about to have a serious talk. Maybe Will was finally tired of hanging around. Really, she'd persevered longer than Nora thought she would. She told herself it would be a relief to no longer go through the motions of protesting how much Will doted on her. But telling herself that didn't stop a knot from settling in her stomach.

"Thank you for agreeing to talk with me."

Nora folded her hands in her lap. "I talk with you every day."

Will offered a small smile that Nora couldn't decipher. "You know what I mean."

"We don't have to do this, you know. You've gone above and beyond anything I could have asked for or expected. You don't need my permission—or blessing, or whatever—to get on with your life."

Will's head jerked around and she locked eyes with Nora. "Is that what you think I'm doing? Walking away?"

"I just figured—"

"Is that what you want?"

Nora tried to get a handle on the direction of their conversation. "We're not here to talk about what I want."

Will shook her head. "Oh, but we are."

"I don't understand."

"I want to talk about what you want and what I want." Will sighed. "And whether there's any hope of those two things being in alignment."

Nora had been expecting something else entirely, so she didn't know what to say. "How about you start?"

Will nodded, her expression grave. "I don't want things to be like they are now."

"I know you've been working essentially two jobs. I hope you know I never wanted to impose on you like that and I never wanted you to feel obligated to step in."

"It's not about the work. I don't mind that." Will turned on the bench so that she was facing Nora. "I don't want to go back to how things were before Graham walked in on us, either."

So she was done. Although it didn't surprise her, Nora didn't expect hearing it to hurt so badly. "I don't want to hold you here, hold you back."

"I want a real relationship. A partnership."

Realizing how much she'd held Will back sent a stab of pain right to her heart. "And what we had, all the time you're spending here, is getting in the way of that."

"No." Will seemed to search her face, but Nora couldn't figure out what she was searching for. After what felt like an eternity, she continued. "Nora, I want those things with you."

"What are you saying?"

"I'm saying I was drawn to you from the moment we met. And what we had this winter was wonderful, magical even. But it wasn't real."

It was possible that her brain had stopped functioning, but it felt like Will was contradicting herself. Before Nora could stop herself, she said, "It felt real to me."

"You're right. I'm sorry, I didn't mean to say it wasn't real. I meant to say it wasn't a real relationship. It was only part. Just like what we have now is only part. A different part. I want it all."

The words made sense, but the meaning stubbornly refused to come together in Nora's mind. It seemed, almost, like Will was saying she wanted to get married. But she hadn't used that word. And none of that fit into the narrative she'd constructed. "I don't mean to be dense, but you're going to have to explain."

Will took a deep breath. "I love you."

Nora blinked. She opened her mouth, but no words came out. She'd not bargained for falling in love with Will, or having those feelings returned. Even now, the idea of it terrified her.

Could she give her heart again? Did she have room in hers for another person? Whether she wanted it or not, this was what she had. She could deny it, refuse it, but doing so wouldn't change the reality of it.

Will continued, "I'm in love with you. Maybe I should have led with that. I've been head over heels for you from almost the moment we first met. And when we started sleeping together, I thought it was enough. Or, maybe, I thought the rest would come naturally. But obviously things didn't work out like that."

"I—"

Will lifted a hand. "Now that I'm going, please let me finish."

Nora nodded.

"After what happened with Graham, I convinced myself that you were done with me. It wasn't hard because I didn't think I brought much to the table to begin with."

"You have to know that's not true."

"I didn't. I was feeling plenty sorry for myself when Graham knocked some sense into me. I didn't allow myself to feel hopeful, but then you got hurt. I couldn't stay away. I thought maybe if I showed you I was worth having around, I might convince you to give me another chance. But I realized that wasn't enough. I want more than being useful, more than being someone you don't mind having around."

"You deserve more than that."

Will nodded. "I do. But you do, too. You're beautiful, successful. You deserve someone who is your equal in every way, who not only appreciates you, but complements you. Someone who can give you everything you deserve."

Nora shook her head. She'd spent plenty of time thinking about what it meant to be equal with someone. Only, in her book, it was someone who respected her, someone who would feel content with the life she'd worked so hard to build. Someone who wanted to continue to build it with her.

As if reading her thoughts, Will said, "And more than that, you deserve a woman who is brave enough to shout her love from the rooftops, a woman who will delight in being your partner, but who will also sweep you off your feet and worship you for the amazing creature you are."

"I'm so much older than you."

"I thought we'd established I find you gorgeous, exquisite."

The fear, the nagging voices, refused to release their grip. "It's more than that. I'm set in my ways. I'm past the age of having children. I'm—"

"Perfect. For me, at least, you are absolutely perfect."

For the first time, hope and something that felt an awful lot like joy, bubbled up. They expanded, taking up the space where the doubts had lived. "I think you can do better than me."

Will smiled. "And I think you could do far better than me. Does that make us even?"

Did it? Could it really be as simple as that? "That's one way of looking at it."

Will took both her hands. "Look, life doesn't come with guarantees. I think we've both learned that lesson the hard way. But I can guarantee that I'm all in. I want this more than I've wanted anything and I'm willing to work for it, as long and as hard as it takes."

"I..." Nora trailed off. What could she possibly say in response to that? After everything she'd done to push her away, Will was offering her the world.

"You don't have to give me an answer right now. Clearly, I've been mulling this over for a while. I want you to take your time and, whatever you decide, I want it to be what's truly in your heart."

"I don't need time."

"No?"

The look in Will's eyes—equal parts hope and fear—melted Nora's heart even further. If this gorgeous, big-hearted woman could bare her soul, then by God, she could, too. "I was drawn to you the moment we met, too."

"You were?"

"Most definitely. It felt absurd, though, so I shoved it aside. And then I was convinced you were after Graham."

Will shook her head and sighed. "I'm still trying to figure out what I did to give everyone that impression."

"You two spent a lot of time together. You're much closer in age than you and I are. And even when she denied it, I had a feeling she had a thing for you."

Will nodded, looking deflated. "I guess that makes sense."

"Anyway, the last thing I ever expected was for the two of us to get involved. And then we did."

"And you thought it was a terrible idea."

Nora smiled. "I did. I'm sorry I gave you such a hard time. Or if it felt like I was ashamed of you. It was never that. If anything, I was ashamed of myself."

"I still don't understand why."

"There's a lot of judgment when someone my age takes up with a much younger woman. Especially if that woman does work for you."

"I never thought of it that way."

"You wouldn't. You always assume the best of people, which is one of the things I love most about you. I used to be the same way and then I got burned."

"Jordyn."

Nora looked away for a moment. "Yes. Even though not a lot of people know about that, the voice in my head kept screaming that only a complete fool would go down the same disastrous path twice."

"I get it. If someone who seemed remotely like Kai appeared in my life now, I'd run the other way as fast as I could."

Will's eyes held such a deep sadness, it was all Nora could do not to gather her up and try to kiss away the pain. She might still get to, but she needed to get the rest of this out. "But the last few weeks have taught me a critical lesson. You're nothing like Jordyn."

Will raised a brow.

"It was unfair of me to lump you in together because you have some similar features."

"And you thought I was an irresponsible drifter."

Having Will articulate it stung, but Nora didn't deny it. At this point, she owed Will the truth. "I did, but mostly because that's what I wanted to see. I think you've proved me wrong ten times over."

"I know it didn't help that I disappeared for a while. I did it because I thought it would make your life easier."

"But you came back. And when I needed someone the most, you were there."

"I wanted to be. I'm so glad you let me."

"I need you to know I'm not in love with you because you've been slaving away here every day." Will grew very still. Nora thought she might have stopped breathing. She rushed on. "I'm in love with you because of who you are, of who I am when we're together."

Watching the emotions play across Will's face—disbelief, understanding, joy—filled Nora's heart with a mixture of emotions. She had plenty of her own joy, along with some regret over how reticent she'd been. Not that it mattered now. Will smiled at her, her eyes bright with emotion. She didn't speak, but simply nodded.

More than a little overwhelmed by the intensity of the moment, Nora took a deep breath. "Now what?"

Will lifted a shoulder, still smiling. "We live happily ever after?"

Nora let out a small laugh, but she placed a hand on Will's leg. "I'm serious."

Will nodded. "Well, we keep doing what we're doing. I love how much time I'm spending with you."

"But I'll be done with this wretched cast soon and back up to full speed. I don't want you to keep working two jobs, but I don't know if I can hire you full-time."

Will shook her head. "Not at all. I like my job. And as much as I love you, I learned the hard way that living only for another person is not healthy for anyone."

"Well said. So maybe..." Nora had never been a forward person, at least when it came to relationships. But something about Will made her brave, made her whole. "Maybe you spend less time here working and more time having quiet dinners in the garden, or drinks on the porch, or nights in my bed."

Will's smile was slow and sexy. "I can't think of anything I'd rather do."

Chapter Thirty-one

Nora stood on the back porch and looked out at her garden. With the start of June, it had come alive with lush greenery and color. Her perennials were coming along nicely and she—with Will's help—had put in all the annual flowers the weekend prior. They'd need a month or so to really be at peak, but already it was beginning to feel like summer.

A large wooden table dominated the lawn, with benches along each side to seat a dozen people. Smaller tables filled the rest of the space, each decked out with a red and white checked tablecloth. Mason jars overflowed with flowers. It was the first outdoor party of the season and she couldn't be happier.

"Do you know the first thing I ever thought about you? After noticing you were beautiful, that is." Will's arm slid around her waist.

Nora tipped her head so she could rest it on Will's shoulder. "What's that?"

"Damn, this woman knows how to throw a party."

She lifted her head and met Will's eyes. "Stop."

"No, really. The day we met, you were doing the rehearsal dinner for that older male couple."

Nora smiled at the memory—both of the party and of the first time she met Will. "That was a great party."

"I was so taken with you. I didn't want Graham to notice, but every time you came into view, all I wanted to do was stare."

She'd felt the same. She hadn't wanted to admit it of course, even to herself, but the attraction had been there. "It feels like ages ago."

"Agreed. We've come a long way." Will leaned in and kissed her. "Such a long way."

"All right, all right. Don't you two have some work to do?" Graham, who must have come in the back gate, planted her hands on her hips. Her tone was scolding, but her face playful.

Nora mimicked the stance. "You think because it's your party, you can start bossing everyone around?"

"Yes, yes I do." She bounded up the walk in her vintage sundress and put an arm around each of them. "I'm very high maintenance."

Will stood straighter. "Is everything to your liking, madam?"

She kissed them both on the cheek. "Everything is perfect."

The graduation party had been Will's idea. After Nora's cast came off, they found a weekend that wasn't completely booked and pitched the idea to Graham. Although modest, she'd not been able to contain her excitement. In addition to Colleen and Peter coming in for the weekend, they'd invited Will's sister and her family and the whole crew of the Dolphin Fleet. Nora couldn't think of a better way to celebrate Graham's achievement, or the promise of summer. "Good. You deserve it."

"Is it bad that graduation feels almost like a distant memory? I appreciate the gesture, but I'm mostly excited for a party."

Will smiled. That fateful day had only been a couple of months ago, but she felt the same. "Not bad at all. Especially since you're already a successfully established marine biologist."

Graham beamed at the statement. "I don't know about established, but I'm getting there. Really though, what is there still to do? How can I help?"

Nora shook her head. "Not a thing. Will set up everything out here, Tisha and I have the food ready. All you need to do is greet your guests and enjoy."

As she spoke, the first of those guests arrived. Graham went off to greet them and Will turned her attention to helping Nora finish things in the kitchen.

Over the next few hours, people came and went. Will introduced Emerson and Darcy to Nora's sister and her husband. Martha and Heidi came, too. Nora had finally told them the whole story and Will felt like they were on the path to becoming her friends as well. She chatted with them, and her coworkers from the Fleet.

As it had on so many other occasions, Will found her gaze and her attention drifting to Nora. Unlike many of those occasions, she didn't have to suppress the desire to stand close to her or rest a hand in the small of her back. Even more than the night of the engagement party, she felt like she and Nora were a couple. She realized now how much it was exactly what she'd always wanted.

Hours later, when the guests were all gone and the cleanup complete, Will coaxed Nora to join her in the garden for a glass of wine. "I think that was a success," Nora said.

"Complete success."

"I can't thank you enough for all your help today."

Will shook her head. "Don't thank me."

"Right. Sorry. Old habits die hard."

Will smiled. "I could also thank you for letting me be part of it."

"Nonsense. We did it together."

"Yeah." Will looked out at the garden, then back at the woman she loved. "Nora?"

Nora smiled. "What?"

"I like doing things together."

"Me, too."

When they'd last had a talk on this very same bench, Will had wanted nothing more than for Nora to give her a chance. The result exceeded her wildest expectations. "I like doing all things with you."

Nora lifted a brow, gave her a playfully suggestive look. "I do, too."

Will appreciated that sentiment, even if it wasn't what she was going for. "I'm not asking for any commitments or promises, but I want to put out there that I don't anticipate an end to that feeling. You—this—it's exactly what I want."

Nora didn't say anything right away and Will feared she may have overplayed her hand. But then Nora leaned in and kissed her in a way that left her breathless and filled with so much longing. When she finally broke the kiss, Will pulled back and opened her eyes. She found Nora looking at her with an intensity that made the kiss seem like nothing. Eventually, Nora smiled. "It's exactly what I want, too. Now, always."

The word put a lump in Will's throat. "Always."

About the Author

Aurora Rey grew up in a small town in south Louisiana, daydreaming about New England. She keeps a special place in her heart for the South, especially the food and the ways women are raised to be strong, even if they're taught not to show it. After a brief dalliance with biochemistry, she completed both a BA and an MA in English.

When she's not writing or at her day job in higher education, she loves to cook and putter around the house. She's slightly addicted to Pinterest, has big plans for the garden, and would love to get some goats.

She lives in Ithaca, New York, with her partner, two dogs, and whatever wild animals have taken up residence in the pond.

Books Available from Bold Strokes Books

A Country Girl's Heart by Dena Blake. When Kat Jackson gets a second chance at love, following her heart will prove the hardest decision of all. (978-1-63555-134-1)

Dangerous Waters by Radclyffe. Life, death, and war on the home front. Two women join forces against a powerful opponent, nature itself. (978-1-63555-233-1)

Fury's Death by Brey Willows. When all we hold sacred fails, who will be there to save us? (978-1-63555-063-4)

It's Not a Date by Heather Blackmore. Kade's desire to keep things with Jen on a professional level is in Jen's best interest. Yet what's in Kade's best interest…is Jen. (978-1-63555-149-5)

Killer Winter by Kay Bigelow. Just when she thought things could get no worse, homicide Lieutenant Leah Samuels learns the woman she loves has betrayed her in devastating ways. (978-1-63555-177-8)

Score by MJ Williamz. Will an addiction to pain pills destroy Ronda's chance with the woman she loves or will she come out on top and score a happily ever after? (978-1-62639-807-8)

Spring's Wake by Aurora Rey. When wanderer Willa Lange falls for Provincetown B&B owner Nora Calhoun, will past hurts and a fifteen-year age gap keep them from finding love? (978-1-63555-035-1)

The Lurid Sea by Tom Cardamone. Cursed to spend eternity on his knees, Nerites is having the time of his life. (978-1-62639-911-2)

The Northwoods by Jane Hoppen. When Evelyn Bauer, disguised as her dead husband, George, travels to a Northwoods logging camp to work, she and the camp cook Sarah Bell forge a friendship fraught with both tenderness and turmoil. (978-1-63555-143-3)

Truth or Dare by C. Spencer. For a group of six lesbian friends, life changes course after one long snow-filled weekend. (978-1-63555-148-8)

A Heart to Call Home by Jeannie Levig. When Jessie Weldon returns to her hometown after thirty years, can she and her childhood crush Dakota Scott heal the tragic past that links them? (978-1-63555-059-7)

Children of the Healer by Barbara Ann Wright. Life becomes desperate for ex-soldier Cordelia Ross when the indigenous aliens of her planet are drawn into a civil war and old enemies linger in the shadows. Book Three of the Godfall Series. (978-1-63555-031-3)

Hearts Like Hers by Melissa Brayden. Coffee shop owner Autumn Primm is ready to cut loose and live a little, but is the baggage that comes with out-of-towner Kate Carpenter too heavy for anything long term? (978-1-63555-014-6)

Love at Cooper's Creek by Missouri Vaun. Shaw Daily flees corporate life to find solace in the rural Blue Ridge Mountains, but escapism eludes her when her attentions are captured by small town beauty Kate Elkins. (978-1-62639-960-0)

Somewhere Over Lorain Road by Bud Gundy. Over forty years after murder allegations shattered the Esker family, can Don Esker find the true killer and clear his dying father's name? (978-1-63555-124-2)

Twice in a Lifetime by PJ Trebelhorn. Detective Callie Burke can't deny the growing attraction to her late friend's widow, Taylor Fletcher, who also happens to own the bar where Callie's sister works. (978-1-63555-033-7)

Undiscovered Affinity by Jane Hardee. Will a no strings attached affair be enough to break Olivia's control and convince Cardic that love does exist? (978-1-63555-061-0)

Between Sand and Stardust by Tina Michele. Are the lifelong bonds of love strong enough to conquer time, distance, and heartache when Haven Thorne and Willa Bennette are given another chance at forever? (978-1-62639-940-2)

Charming the Vicar by Jenny Frame. When magician and atheist Finn Kane seeks refuge in an English village after a spiritual crisis, can local vicar Bridget Claremont restore her faith in life and love? (978-1-63555-029-0)

Data Capture by Jesse J. Thoma. Lola Walker is undercover on the hunt for cybercriminals while trying not to notice the woman who might be perfectly wrong for her for all the right reasons. (978-1-62639-985-3)

Epicurean Delights by Renee Roman. Ariana Marks had no idea a leisure swim would lead to being rescued, in more ways than one, by the charismatic Hudson Frost. (978-1-63555-100-6)

Heart of the Devil by Ali Vali. We know most of Cain and Emma Casey's story, but *Heart of the Devil* will take you back to where it began one fateful night with a tray loaded with beer. (978-1-63555-045-0)

Known Threat by Kara A. McLeod. When Special Agent Ryan O'Connor reluctantly questions who protects the Secret Service, she learns courage truly is found in unlikely places. Agent O'Connor Series #3. (978-1-63555-132-7)

Seer and the Shield by D. Jackson Leigh. Time is running out for the Dragon Horse Army while two unlikely heroines struggle to put aside their attraction and find a way to stop a deadly cult. Dragon Horse War, Book 3. (978-1-63555-170-9)

Sinister Justice by Steve Pickens. When a vigilante targets citizens of Jake Finnigan's hometown, Jake and his partner Sam fall under suspicion themselves as they investigate the murders. (978-1-63555-094-8)

The Universe Between Us by Jane C. Esther. Ana Mitchell must make the hardest choice of her life: the promise of new love Jolie Dann on Earth, or a humanity-saving mission to colonize Mars. (978-1-63555-106-8)

Touch by Kris Bryant. Can one touch heal a heart? (978-1-63555-084-9)

Change in Time by Robyn Nyx. Working in the past is hell on your future. The Extractor Series: Book Two. (978-1-62639-880-1)

Love After Hours by Radclyffe. When Gina Antonelli agrees to renovate Carrie Longmire's new house, she doesn't welcome Carrie's overtures at friendship or her own unexpected attraction. A Rivers Community Novel. (978-1-63555-090-0)

Nantucket Rose by CF Frizzell. Maggie Jordan can't wait to convert an historic Nantucket home into a B&B, but doesn't expect to fall for mariner Ellis Chilton, who has more claim to the house than Maggie realizes. (978-1-63555-056-6)

Picture Perfect by Lisa Moreau. Falling in love wasn't supposed to be part of the stakes for Olive and Gabby, rival photographers in the competition of a lifetime. (978-1-62639-975-4)

Set the Stage by Karis Walsh. Actress Emilie Danvers takes the stage again in Ashland, Oregon, little realizing that landscaper Arden Philips is about to offer her a very personal romantic lead role. (978-1-63555-087-0)

Strike a Match by Fiona Riley. When their attempts at matchmaking fizzle out, firefighter Sasha and reluctant millionairess Abby find themselves turning to each other to strike a perfect match. (978-1-62639-999-0)

The Price of Cash by Ashley Bartlett. Cash Braddock is doing her best to keep her business afloat, stay out of jail, and avoid Detective Kallen. It's not working. (978-1-62639-708-8)

Under Her Wing by Ronica Black. At Angel's Wings Rescue, dogs are usually the ones saved, but when quiet Kassandra Haden meets outspoken owner Jayden Beaumont, the two stubborn women just might end up saving each other. (978-1-63555-077-1)

Underwater Vibes by Mickey Brent. When Hélène, a translator in Brussels, Belgium, meets Sylvie, a young Greek photographer and swim coach, unsettling feelings hijack Hélène's mind and body—even her poems. (978-1-63555-002-3)

A More Perfect Union by Carsen Taite. Major Zoey Granger and DC fixer Rook Daniels risk their reputations for a chance at true love while dealing with a scandal that threatens to rock the military. (978-1-62639-754-5)

Arrival by Gun Brooke. The spaceship *Pathfinder* reaches its passengers' new homeworld where danger lurks in the shadows while Pamas Seclan disembarks and finds unexpected love in young science genius Darmiya Do Voy. (978-1-62639-859-7)

Captain's Choice by VK Powell. Architect Kerstin Anthony's life is going to plan until Bennett Carlyle, the first girl she ever kissed, is assigned to her latest and most important project, a police district substation. (978-1-62639-997-6)

Falling Into Her by Erin Zak. Pam Phillips, widow at the age of forty, meets Kathryn Hawthorne, local Chicago celebrity, and it changes her life forever—in ways she hadn't even considered possible. (978-1-63555-092-4)

Hookin' Up by MJ Williamz. Will Leah get what she needs from casual hookups or will she see the love she desires right in front of her? (978-1-63555-051-1)

King of Thieves by Shea Godfrey. When art thief Casey Marinos meets bounty hunter Finnegan Starkweather, the crimes of the past just might set the stage for a payoff worth more than she ever dreamed possible. (978-1-63555-007-8)

Lucy's Chance by Jackie D. As a serial killer haunts the streets, Lucy tries to stitch up old wounds with her first love in the wake of a small town's rapid descent into chaos. (978-1-63555-027-6)

Right Here, Right Now by Georgia Beers. When Alicia Wright moves into the office next door to Lacey Chamberlain's accounting firm, Lacey is about to find out that sometimes the last person you want is exactly the person you need. (978-1-63555-154-9)

Strictly Need to Know by MB Austin. Covert operator Maji Rios will do whatever she must to complete her mission, but saving a gorgeous stranger from Russian mobsters was not in her plans. (978-1-63555-114-3)

Tailor-Made by Yolanda Wallace. Tailor Grace Henderson doesn't date clients, but when she meets gender-bending model Dakota Lane, she's tempted to throw all the rules out the window. (978-1-63555-081-8)

Time Will Tell by M. Ullrich. With the ability to time travel, Eva Caldwell will have to decide between having it all and erasing it all. (978-1-63555-088-7)

SPRING'S WAKE

What Reviewers Say About Aurora Rey's Work

Crescent City Confidential

"*Crescent City Confidential* is a sweet romance with a hint of thriller thrown in for good measure."—*The Lesbian Review*

"[*Crescent City Confidential*] ticks all the boxes I've started to expect from Aurora Rey. Firstly, *Crescent City Confidential* is written very well and the characters are extremely well developed, I felt like I was getting to know new friends and my excitement grew with every finished chapter."—*Les Rêveur*

Built to Last

"Rey's frothy contemporary romance brings two women together to restore an ancient farmhouse in Ithaca, N.Y. Tension mounts as Olivia's colleagues and her snobbish family collide with Joss's down-home demeanor. But the women totally click in bed, as well as when they're poring over paint chips, and readers will enjoy finding out whether love conquers all."—*Publishers Weekly*

"*Built to Last* by Aurora Rey is a contemporary lesbian romance novel and a very sweet summer read. I love, love, love the way Ms Rey writes bedroom scenes and I'm not talking about how she describes the furniture."—*The Lesbian Review*